"We can come back."

She didn't want to come back. Ever. She pushed up the steps, past him, and he waved her ahead.

Fe ascended to her mother's bedroom, the room she had not been permitted to enter without her mother. The room she had entered alone only once. Memories devoured the present.

The steps creaked. Every night. Phoebe followed her mother up for the bedtime ritual. When THEY *came back. The steps had creaked on the night Phoebe entered Momma's room alone.*

Fe stood at the top of the stairs, before the small crimson door, and shivered. It was too dark to actually see, but the color had imbedded in her memory from the many lonely nights she had come this far, only to retreat downstairs into light and quiet and safety. She did not turn the handle.

"We going in or what?" Philip wanted to know.

Her voice snapped through the dense air, "In a minute!"

He touched her shoulder and she jumped. "Take your time."

They're gone, she told herself. Mother took them with her. She promised she would. Sweat slid down Fe's backbone. The knob, cut glass, pressed into her wet palm. She turned it and pushed.

The door opened silently and blackness rushed to greet her.

—"When Shadows Come Back"

Coming in 2001 from DarkTales Publications...

The Asylum Volume 2: The Violent Ward
More tales of madness edited by Victor Heck

Dial Your Dreams
Stories by Robert Weinberg

Six–Inch Spikes
Stories by Edo van Belkom

Harlan
A novel by David Whitman

A Flock of Crows is Called a Murder
A novel by Jim Viscosi

Faust: Love of the Damned
A screenplay by David Quinn

The Shaman Cycle Series
Novels by Adam Niswander

and more...

www.darktales.com

Cold Comfort

by Nancy Kilpatrick

DarkTales Publications

Kansas City, Missouri • Chicago, Illinois
2001

Published in the United States by:

DarkTales Publications
P.O. Box 675
Grandview, Missouri, 64030

ISBN 1-930997-09-4

PRINTED IN THE UNITED STATES OF AMERICA (F)

Copyrights

"Woodworker" © 1995, first published in *Desire Burn* (Carroll & Graf).

"Alien Love" © 1997, first published as "Demon Love" in *Demon Sex* (Masquerade Books).

"What Matters" © 2001.

"Heartbeat" © 1995, first published in *100 Wicked Little Witch Stories* (Barnes & Noble Books), reprinted in *Whispered from the Grave* (Design Image).

"Megan's Spirit" © 1996, first published in *Seductive Spectres* (Masquerade Books).

"When Shadows Come Back" © 1991, winner of short story contest and published in *The Standing Stone #3* (Ebenrochk Enterprises).

"Snow Angel" © 1995, first published in *Northern Frights 3* (Mosaic Press).

"Brina" © 1997, first published in *Wetbones* (DarkEcho).

"The Children of Gael" © 1997 Nancy Kilpatrick and Benoit Bisson, first published in *Northern Frights 4*.

"Animal Rites" © 1992, first published in *Crossroads Vol 1, #2*.

"Base of a Triangle" © 1998, first published in *Horrors: 365 Scary Stories* (Barnes & Noble Books).

"Creature Comforts" © 1994, first published in *The Mammoth Book of Frankenstein* (Robinson Publishing, UK, Carroll & Graf US).

"Horrorscope" © 2001.

"An Eye for an Eye" © 1994, first published in *Cold Blood 5*, and *Best of Cold Blood* (Mosaic Press).

"Generation Why" © 1997, first published in *The Urbanite #9* (Urban Legend Press).

"...And Thou!" © 1997, first published in *Stigmata* (Heliocentric Net).

"Rural Legend" © 1998, first published in *Horrors: 365 Scary Stories* (Barnes & Noble Books).

"Youth Not Wasted" © 1994, first published in *Writer's Block Magazine #2*, and *Dark Ages #1*.

"The Power of One" © 1993, first published in *Sinistre* (Horror's Head Press), reprinted in *The Year's Best Horror Stories XXII* (DAW Books).

"Truth" © 1993, first published in *Deathrealm #20*.

"Inspiriter" © 1999, first published in *Northern Frights 5* (Mosaic Press).

"Punkins" © 1994, first published in *Northern Frights 2* (Mosaic Press).

"Vermiculture" © 2000, first published in *Northern Horror* (Canadian Fiction Magazine).

"The Middle of Nowhere" © 2001.

"Cold Comfort" © 2001.

"Whitelight" © 1993, first published in *Bizarre Bazaar* (Tal Publications).

"Projections" © 1995, first published in *Eldritch Tales #30*.

"Metal Fatigue" © 1994, first published in *Bizarre Sex & Other Crimes of Passion* (Tal Publications).

Praise for Nancy Kilpatrick...

"A captivating collection from an experienced and excellent wordsmith."

—Yvonne Navarro

"Give yourself time to explore each story to the fullest. This is haute cuisine, not barbecue!"

—Chelsea Quinn Yarbro

"Nancy Kilpatrick is never afraid to take risks, and her risks pay off."

—Poppy Z. Brite

"Nancy Kilpatrick has dug enough graves and shed enough blood (professionally and creatively speaking) to at last be recognized as one of our best dark dreamers. This outstanding collection is, thankfully, more incriminating evidence testifying to that fact.'

—Stanley Wiater
host of the Dark Dreamers television series.

"Nancy Kilpatrick's writing is both eloquent and erotic—her stories seduce the reader through the mutual attraction of dread and desire."

—Stephen Jones
editor of the Dark Terrors and Best New Horror series.

"Horror has never been so poetically exquisite before."
—Robert W. Walker

"Nancy Kilpatrick inhabits that shadow land of sensuality between terror and pleasure; she can be creepy, seductive, bleak, exquisite and terrifying—often all at once. She knows the intricacies of human minds and bodies at war with themselves, and her stories bring you into those battles in ways that make you think you've actually been there—because maybe you have."

—Thomas Roche
editor Noirotica series.

About the Artist

Alan M. Clark was born in Nashville, Tennessee in 1957. He graduated in 1979 from the San Francisco Art Institute with a bachelor of Fine Arts Degree. Clark has illustrated the writing of such authors as Ray Bradbury, Robert Bloch, Joe R. Lansdale, Stephen King, George Orwell, Manly Wade Wellman, Greg Bear, Spider and Jeanne Robinson, and Lewis Shiner, as well as his own.

His awards in the illustration field include, the 1994 World Fantasy Award for Best Artist, the 1992 and 1993 Chesley Awards for Best Interior illustration, the Chesley for Best Paperback Cover of 1994, and the Chesley for the Best Unpublished Color Work of 1994. He is the recipient of the Deathrealm Award, as well as the first International Horror Guild Critic's Award for Best Artist.

Clark created IFD publishing in January of 1999. To date the company has published four books; Bedtime Stories to Darken Your Dreams, Imagination Fully Dilated Volume II, Flaming Arrows, and Escaping Purgatory. He has said of the new company, "IFD Publishing is committed to the idea that art is never the product of a single mind but occurs instead when imaginations meet."

Currently, he and his wife Melody reside in Eugene Oregon. You can visit Alan's website at http://www.ifdpublishing.com.

Dedication

This is dedicated to Karl Edward Wagner, who is gone but will never be forgotten.

x

Table of Contents

Foreword

by Paula Guran

Nancy Kilpatrick is a survivor. If she were in one of those dreadful teen horror films, she'd be the one left alive at the end to tell the tale. Unlike the typical flick–chick—who is usually more breast than brain—Nancy could tell it well. *Really* well. Just like she's told the stories in this collection.

To be a storyteller in this day and age—especially in the realm of dark fiction—you have to be a survivor. You have to be prepared to place your stories in publications with infinitesimally small readerships or (these days) on the Web or limited edition anthologies or just about anywhere that will pay you. The amount paid is usually just as small. If you are good, if you are lucky, and if you have the persistence of survival—for every story accepted in a *Mammoth Book of Frankenstein* (an anthology that you can actually find in your local Borders or independent bookstore) or *Horrors: 365 Scary Stories* (which you could find *only* at Barnes and Noble) you'll probably place a dozen in those small press markets.

In the horror field, small press is done for love. If the money comes...well, that's so rare, let's just leave it at love. And don't expect the periodicals to last long enough to buy your work again in the future. No matter how good they are, magazines tend to succumb rather quickly for a number of reasons. In fact, most people have learned their lesson—there are very few magazines out there these days publishing fiction at all.

Don't get me wrong—Nancy Kilpatrick is an established pro, not some upstart just getting into the field. She has a bevy of real novels. She's an editor herself, with two big publisher anthologies to her co–credit. Her alter–ego, Amarantha Knight, has just about as successful a career in erotica as one can have as both an editor and a novelist. ("Erotica career" is an oxymoron, though, as it implies you make a living and have a future in it.) She's also done her part for the writing community serving in organizations and giving an always–helpful hand to newcomers. Nancy's been known to help out struggling new editors, too. (I know. I was one of them.) That's all part of the profession of writing.

Even with all that going for her—as well as talent, intelligence, and charm—she would not still be around writing today except for being... right, a survivor. Nancy's seen mass market horror reach a nadir. She didn't quit, she turned to small press to keep her novels alive. She's seen literal disaster strike a small press and her own books, and lived to publish again. She's seen vampires come and go, yet still brings fresh blood to the sub-genre. She's been screwed over, used, abused, censored, ignored, denied, and probably flattened a couple of times. She gets up, brushes the dust off the black dress, straightens the jewelry, deals with the bruises—I'm not sure what she does with the blood, we'd best not go there—and rises again. I'd be willing to bet she can survive anything but death and, considering her vampiric bent, maybe even that!

That's what it takes to be a writer—along with the ability and imagination—endurance.

This survival instinct finds its way into Nancy's stories, too, although surviving as one of her characters is not always a pleasant experience. Sometimes the characters may prefer cessation of existence rather than survival—but they survive. This is not to say that survival is a theme in her stories—this collection is particularly notable for the variety of its stories. But still—it creeps in. The stories here are divided into three sections: *Lovers* (love *is* survivable), *Killers* (you survive… or you don't), and *Lunatics* (one can survive madness and the mad can test the issue for others).

Lovers
Aileen in "Woodworker" finds an unusual way to live the "rest of her natural life…" in comfort and safety; An "Alien Lover" allows a lonely woman to find the "essence of life itself." A twist of the vampire mythos allows love to continue in "What Matters." Greg, in "Heartbeat," survives witchery—even though he may not want to. Megan survives a ghost in "Megan's Spirit." Phoebe survives the mundane in "When Shadows Come back." Coleen endures nature's wrath and fear itself in "Snow Angel." "Brina "involves a very protective supernatural godmother who makes sure her godchild happily survives (and her beau survives perhaps not so happily.) Promises—and curses—live on in "The Children of Gael"—they survive because some men destroy others in their need to live.

Killers
"Animal Rites" may be about species survival and "Base of a Triangle" about surviving on a different plane. The premise of "Creature Comforts" is the survival of Victor Frankenstein's creation. "Horrorscope" relates how life is person-eat-person, but it goes on. The narrator explains she has "fought to stay alive in the face of terrible despair" in "An Eye for an Eye." Rand is a survivor, of sorts, of media violence in "Generation Why." In "…And Thou!" survival is philosophical. The Elder Gods live on in "Rural Legend." "Youth Not Wasted" is con-

cerned with trying to survive the outrages of time.

Lunatics
Obsession endures in "The Power of One"; Gaye survives truth in the story of the same name; Paul, in "Inspiriter" attempts to survive the horror of his empty existence. Ancient beliefs live on in "Punkins." Dead matter is transmuted into fertile new life in "Vermiculture." "The Middle of Nowhere" might have to do with surviving grief. In "Cold Comfort" an individual survives winter in the city and an odd encounter only to lose himself. Anna is trying to survive her phobia in "Whitelight" and "Metal Fatigue" looks at the survivor of alien sex.

I have no doubt you will enjoy *Cold Comfort*. I think you'll also gain a new appreciation for the work of Nancy Kilpatrick. True, you may be somewhat altered by it, but... you'll survive.

Paula Guran
April 2001

Preface

The small press has been, traditionally, a teeth–cutting arena for young writers. Such markets have been easier to crack for getting that first sale. The scope and nature of the subject matter tackled by basement editors has frequently gone beyond where mainstream publishing was willing to tread. The standards for small press publications may not always be *tour de force* (but one can say the same for major houses!), still, at least everyone is enthusiastic and hopeful, not to mention encouraging. And for a young writer trying to get his or her name in print for the first time, small press makes the birth process of creative work fairly painless in a world where the odds are too often against survival.

In case you haven't noticed, multi–national conglomerates are eating up the publishing industry. The corporate–owned publisher's subsidiary is the distributor, which owns a share of a bookstore chain, which has an interest in the film and/or tv business. New writers working in a field with such a low market share as horror and dark fantasy are at a disadvantage. The Big Guys open up few spots on their lists, and a gaggle of established pro writers snag most of them. More and more, new writers cannot get read let alone find a contract with a major house in their mailbox. This is not gloomy talk, just reality. Oddly, all this reality bodes well for the small press.

Over the years, especially in my early days of publishing horror and dark fantasy, there were many small press editors I worked with that I did not meet, or even speak with by phone. Small press always has been a furtive business for the most part: guidelines that ranged from word–of–mouth to ten sheets of paper, but always contained the line "send us your best writing"; letters sent through the mails or the phosphors; contracts (if they existed at all) that were too long or too short or demanded too many rights or no rights at all. Payment often came in copies instead of cash. Or cents or fractions thereof per word, or even flat fees that sometimes made writing a check seem ridiculous— more than once I told an editor to keep the payment and just send me an extra copy of the publication. Days, weeks, months, years went by—one time seven years!—with no further word, but for the odd letter apologizing for beyond–our–control delays. The urge to pull a story would erupt from time to time, and then recede as more pressing concerns surfaced. And then, voila! A book/magazine/chapbook appeared in the mail, the cover with some lousy art, or some pretty good art, or no art at all, just lettering. Inside, a list of contributors, and there is your name among them! Half the time misspelled. Or missing from the list on the cover. Or you discover crucial words or text missing from the story itself. What followed, though, was inevitable: jumping up and down, phone calls to friends; celebratory dinners; fantasies of a big book deal; of appearing on television; mentally writing and rewriting fragments of wit to be used when your story becomes the First Horror Fiction Ever To Be Awarded the Nobel Prize for Literature!

Over the years there have been some amazing people who have cranked out publications at night after they finished their day job. Most managed against great financial and emotional and just–plain–living–a–life obstacles to get out publications that will long be remembered fondly: George Hatch produced gorgeous publications; Alayne Gelfand is still creating great vampire books; Stan Tal led the wave of erotic horror; William Raley tapped into urban dark fantasy, as does Mark McLaughlin still; both Lisa Jean Bothell, and Paula Guran continue to work tirelessly in all sorts of capacities, including publishing; Mark Rainey's *Deathrealm* was pivotal in this field; Pat Nielsen's *Crossroads* was truly a labor of love; Crispin Burnham through *Eldritch Tales* showcased a lot of talented writers; Don Hutchison turned the spotlight on Canada... I've mentioned a skeleton crew of the many many publishers and/or editors of small press books and periodicals who helped build a foundation on which today's small press stands.

No tribute to small press would be complete without mentioning Karl Edward Wagner. Karl, until the time of his death, wrote and edited horror for major houses, and the small press. In the horror and dark fantasy field he will always be remembered fondly for his series *The Year's Best Horror*, which spanned twenty–two volumes (published by DAW Books). Karl was tireless, and meticulous. He scanned everything in print, searching for material for his popular reprint tomes, and he was always receptive to new writers sending in their stories published in even the smallest circulation chapbooks. Karl helped a lot of writers in this field get a foothold in a major anthology, and I'm one of them!

The past is the past. What is most wonderful about today's small press is the fact that despite all the premonitions of doom and gloom surrounding the horror field, there are still men and women struggling hard to produce quality fiction books and magazines in a marketable package on a tight budget. The advent of desktop publishing, and print–on–demand has opened things up considerably. Small press is more than alive and well. It is flourishing. And it is needed, now more than ever. How else can new writers pay their dues and build a list of credits?

Small press is a wild and crazy adventure. It is grass roots at its best, run on a shoestring, fueled by passion. I am utterly delighted that I have had the opportunity to participate. *Cold Comfort* is my tribute. Over the years, I have placed quite a bit of short fiction with small press book and magazine publishers, including some of my first sales. This collection contains stories that small press editors liked and published, and consequently, for that reason, the works saw the light of day, and the dark of night. I wanted to place this collection with a small publisher, and I'm grateful to DarkTales for allowing me the chance to say "Thanks, small press! You raised me well!"

Nancy Kilpatrick
Montreal, 2001

Acknowledgements

This book would not be possible without the love and caring I have received from the following: Stephen Jones, Eric Kauppinen, Mike Kilpatrick, Sephera Giron, Mandy Slater, Caro Soles, Johanne Vigneault, Mari Anne Werier, and my dark companion Hugues Leblanc. And a warm and sincere thanks to the DarkTales guys for their faith and support in this work.

Nancy Kilpatrick
Montreal, 2001

Lovers

a Woodworker

Aileen hammered in the final nail. She raised an arm and used her rolled shirtsleeve to blot sweat from her forehead as she stepped back for a critical look.

The grain was straight, the lid level, dovetails snugly joined. Tomorrow night she would use coarse sandpaper, followed by a session with medium paper, then fine. She thought about using the sander Larry had bought her last Christmas but, God, she'd always hated machines, and the power supply here wasn't very good. And more important, the particles pressing the back of the paper as they rode the wood seemed sensuous. Got that from her Nana, who had preferred old–style woodworking. It was tradition, and, anyway, a bit late to think about changing her ways.

Aileen swept the floor of shavings. She used a ragged t–shirt to wipe clean the steel–edged plane, then the file and rasp, and hung each in its spot on the wall. Nana had bequeathed her these tools, just as she had passed down the love of working with fine woods by hand. A love that connected the female line.

Finally Aileen picked up the sharp half–inch chisel and honed the beveled edge against a whetstone. The birch handle had worn in one spot, where the thumbs of generations of women had gripped it. Nana had been given the chisel by her grandmother when she reached puberty. With it, she had also been handed two branches and no–nonsense instructions on slicing the end of one into a mortise and the end of the other branch into a corresponding tenon. She said it had taken the better part of a week to fit the parts together just so before she presented the joint to her grandmother. "She barely glanced at it and, lickety–split, handed me two new branches." The process was repeated over eighteen months. One joint a week at first, then two, then three until finally, one a day. Her Nana, frustrated, had almost given up but, somehow, she'd stuck it out. "By the end I was darned good with a chisel," Aileen recalled her saying, "and I could sure make the parts fit right."

Nana had taught her in the same way, so Aileen understood the frustration. She also knew how to join two halves perfectly so that for all intents and purposes they became inseparable.

One last look at her handiwork and reluctantly she headed up the dark stairs into a wall of heat, squinting at the light in the kitchen above.

"What's for dinner?" Larry, drying dishes at the kitchen counter, wanted to know. He snaked an arm around her waist as she tried to pass. Fingers found her left nipple through the soft fabric. Hot lips pressed against her sweaty neck. The heat made her cranky and the last thing she wanted was love.

"Meatloaf." She pulled away. "And scalloped potatoes, if you peel them for me. Otherwise fries."

"Fries'll do." He sat at the table and stretched out his denim–covered legs across the narrow room, forcing her to step over them to get to the refrigerator. It was more foreplay and she was in no mood for it.

She opened the top of the refrigerator, aware of how his gaze stroked her from across the room. The freezer light was dead. White mist from the frosty darkness wafted out and she fantasized about living alone in an igloo, in a place that was all ice and snow like the Arctic, where some of the year you'd be blessed with twenty–four hours of cool darkness. You wouldn't have to swelter under just a fan. Or fear heat stroke. You wouldn't have to worry about scorching sunlight burning you to a crisp. You could live your natural life in peace.

As usual, lately, Aileen wasn't hungry. For the last six months, since they'd been in this oppressive climate, it was as though she'd been steadily shrinking, as if the heat had been shriveling her. While Larry ate, she pushed nearly burnt potato sticks around her dinner plate and stared out the window at the pallid moon imprisoned by the muggy night sky. She hadn't wanted to move to Manila, where the weather made the days impossible and the nights nearly so. But Larry's job forced him to do field research. Forced them to leave North America and all that was familiar and be in this strange part of the world.

Outside rubber trees with stunned leaves hung paralyzed in the dense air. Still. Waiting. Deciding whether to live or die.

The next evening, when the scalding sun had set, Aileen headed down to the basement, and they were lucky to have a basement—most of the houses here didn't. Brick walls and an earth floor kept the room degrees cooler than the rest of the house. It made a difference and she preferred being here. If it weren't for Larry, she would be in the basement both night and day. She could work here, and that kept her sane.

She stretched out the sanding for an hour and a half, intoxicated by the sweet, wood–scented air. She mixed sawdust and white bond glue together and filled in accidental gouges. Then she mixed the stain.

Just like Nana, Aileen hated to stain a pale wood. Still, if she could blend the pigments right, the swirling grain would be accented rather than overwhelmed. Exotic hardwoods were her favorites, one of the few benefits of living in Southeast Asia. The compressed fibers flowed like sinewy muscles, the pores received like human skin. She ran a hand slowly over the smooth surface and felt a quiver run through her body, as if she were caressing a lover. The living wood was solid, hard to damage, enduring in this hostile climate.

As Aileen rubbed in the pungent oil stain, a drop of sweat dripped off the tip of her nose and landed on the wood, sinking into and melding with it. She thought about the heat and how it was getting worse. The last month had been bad. She'd stayed in bed during the day, when Larry was home, then would sneak down to the basement the minute he left. And she was up most of the night while he slept. It was a bit easier to breathe at night. Hiding in the basement. Hiding from Larry and this landscape, so unlike what she was accustomed to that it felt alien.

Of course he'd noticed. She felt him studying her all the time, the way he examined the local insects. Watching. Waiting. Like some predator ready to pounce on a weaker species. But she'd managed to avoid him, for the most part. It meant sleeping upstairs in the heat of the day when she'd have rather been enveloped by the cool basement air. A necessary sacrifice. But it wasn't his way to ask a lot of questions nor hers to answer very many.

Last week he'd come halfway down the basement just before sunrise, when she was still cutting the rough lumber, and stood on the steps. Waiting. "Aren't you coming to bed?" he finally said in a needy voice. When she didn't respond, he stomped upstairs and slammed the door. She knew he didn't feel any more comfortable in the cool dark than she felt in the hot light. They had their differences, and this was a big one.

Her eye scanned the wet wood. The stain would dry overnight. By tomorrow she'd have to decide whether to varnish or shellac. Chemicals preserved better over time and repelled moisture, too, but she preferred the natural look of shellac. Her Nana had favored shellac also, and she'd told Aileen all about the lac scale, an insect in this part of the world, one of the ones Larry studied. How the female excretes resin onto the twig of a fake banyan tree, creating a safe place in which to live. And die.

"It's her home," Nana had said, "like a turtle's shell is home to a turtle." Larry's books had told her more. The sticky glue–like resin protected the lac scale from predators and other dangers in the environment, attracted potential mates, and snared meals. That resin formed the basis of shellac.

The idea appealed to her: a natural substance produced by a creature dwelling in a tree, applied to an object made from a tree trunk. Ultimately the wood would rot and form the new earth in which a new tree might grow. It was a cycle made familiar to her by her Nana: birth, death, rebirth.

The fireball sun seared her flesh and blinded her with its yellow glare. The heat weighed against her body; she felt heavy and clumsy. Sluggish. When it set, she stumbled down to the basement, muscles flaccid, the lining of her brain inflamed.

Aileen breathed shallowly. Each brush stroke of shellac was a torturous labor. Still, she felt vindicated that she had chosen this forgiving substance. Varnish would have required precision she could not muster. Even before the first coat of shellac dried, she began applying the next. Layer upon gummy layer blended together with no differentiation. No division. It was nearly dry in an hour, about the time the floorboards above her head squeaked.

Larry stood at the top of the cellar stairs peering into the dark basement. He watched Aileen, brush in hand, step into the shaft of light filtering down from the kitchen. Her skin was so fair. So unprotected. Unlike him, he knew she had a hard time with the heat and humidity.

He was seriously worried about her. Down here every night. Alone. They were never together anymore, since they'd moved here. When had they last had sex? It wasn't healthy.

Beside her left hip, the light from above illuminated a triangular wedge of shiny wood. The hairs on the back of his neck rose. What in hell was she building, anyway? Light from the kitchen caught the liquid in Aileen's eyes. For a split second, an optical illusion made her eyes appear entirely white. Her bent arm held up the brush like a flag of surrender; he noticed her fragile-looking wrist bone jutting out. Funny how that bone had always turned him on. That and the way her collarbone protruded, delicately exposed where her shirt collar lay open.

Her skin was sweat-slicked. Even through the shellac, he could smell her from here.

"Come up to bed," he coaxed.

Aileen lay the brush down, started slowly up the steps, stopped. She glanced up at him through dark lashes and breathed, "Come down."

Larry hated dark basements. Had since he was a child. Dank air. Gritty earth that clotted his nostrils with the odor of eons of decay. The atmosphere reminded him of cemeteries. The basement itself felt like a crypt.

Her lips twisted into a smile. She backed down the stairs, unbuttoning her blouse. The shadows swallowed her.

"Aileen?" he called.

Wood scraped against wood. The small segment of wood lit by the kitchen light swayed like a tree branch. Unnerved, Larry gripped the railing and took a step down. The air cooled. "Honey? Come on up."

A sound of shuffling. Wood creaking. Aileen's short dark hair flashed through the lighted triangle as she lay back. Within that yellow illumination, like an artistic photograph framed in darkness, one side of her fragile collarbone pressed suggestively against her skin. A round slick breast, the nipple a glistening eye gazing directly into his, mesmerizing him. That little section of flesh rose and fell and quivered as she breathed. The scent from her body mingled with the potent resin to create a sweet musky perfume.

"Close the door," she whispered.

Larry did. Surrounded by darkness, he felt his way down. Her earthy scent guided him.

He reached out, low, and touched cool tacky wood. His fingers crawled up and over the edge to find her. Sticky firm flesh yielded to the pressure of his touch. He wondered what made her sweat so thick.

Aileen pulled him down on top of her. The exotic wood creaked under the double weight but held them. She ripped his shirt away while he worked on his pants. He crawled further up her body, shivering, fear or cold or passion, she could not tell which. There was only a vague predatory instinct emanating from him that she could sense; she felt safe enough.

Her chisel–sharp teeth clamped onto his broad shoulder, piercing clammy skin. He howled and squirmed, but her sticky sweat bonded their flesh and, in truth, he did not really resist. And when they joined, it was perfect, as perfect as Aileen always knew it would be. As her Nana had told her it could be.

Cool pale wood beneath her. The familiar aroma of shellac seeping into her pores. She and Larry encased in this sheltered environment. Now that she had finally adapted, she could stay here the rest of her natural life. In complete comfort and safety. Mating. Eating. Producing the next woodworker.

Alien Love

My lover is an alien. Not a person from another culture, but a being from another planet.

Many women feel that way about men, of course, and vice versa; it's a statement of how disparate the genders often seem to one another. But that's not what I'm talking about. I'm talking about a real alien. A being unlike any other that walks this planet.

I'm not a patient in a mental hospital, writing this on scraps of toilet paper, and I'm not some SoHo performance artist who wants to shock and enlighten. I'm just a woman, an ordinary human being. And because of destiny, I managed to hook up with Thomas, or at least that's the name I call him, since the sounds he makes are enough like that name that I find it comforting.

From the start I'll admit that I've always had a fascination with extraterrestrial life. That may taint some of what I'm about to say. Even though the majority of North Americans, if not citizens of this planet, believe that intelligent life exists in space, admitting to that seems tantamount to implying eccentricity at best and lunacy at worst. I will also acknowledge that I went through a period of time—about a year actually—when my marriage was breaking down where I'd drive around Philadelphia at night in my little silver Toyota, searching the skies. Of course, as Fox Mulder would be the first to tell us, a city is the last place where a space ship would land. The fact that I, like most people, know that didn't stop me from looking.

But then I was close to a breakdown. Whenever I traveled on business or for pleasure, I'd rent a car and drive around—in Atlanta, in Phoenix, in Stanford, Connecticut. I did not see any ships or any aliens. I was not a passenger on one of the commercial aircraft where the pilots saw alien vessels trailing their Boeings. I did not visit that town in the Yukon where the entire population saw lights that were not the aurora borealis streak across the sky for several nights in a row. I have never been aboard an alien craft, either voluntarily or as a kidnap victim. At least not that I remember.

That year of searching the skies was an anomaly in my life. And when the divorce was finalized and I began to heal, I read Carl Jung and something he said, about space ships and extraterrestrial life being symbolic of a search for the divine and a latent desire for wholeness, well, that made sense to me.

Besides Jung, I read a lot of science fiction. There seems to be several theories of why these beings come to Earth. Foremost is to make contact. Another reason is to keep tabs on us, the techno–idiots of the universe. To take us over is a third, and to intermingle and create a new species is last but not least. But there's another reason they come here, at least with Thomas there seems to be.

We met in Toronto. I was there on business, staying at one of the big hotels along Lake Ontario where the computer conference was being held. It was summer, a pleasant evening, and I decided to take a walk along the harbor of this notoriously safe city.

The sun had just set, but the sky was still light. Sailboats dotted the water, and to my left I watched one of the ferry boats carrying people from the mainland to a five mile strip of terra firma called Toronto Island. I walked slowly along the flagstoned harbor path and stopped to rest against the ropes that acted as a barrier between land and water.

We've all had that feeling, of someone staring at our back. In the twilight, I sensed him. And turned to my right. Coming along the path was a man with white hair in a light–colored suit. He was not old, but in his late thirties, my age, or so it seemed to me then, although then as now I cannot clearly recall his face, and he does possess a timeless quality. His body emitted some type of invisible energy that drew my attention. I know that sounds very New Age, but believe me, other than that year of living dangerously close to the border of breakdown, I normally have my feet firmly planted on the ground.

When he reached me he just stopped and turned, so that he, too, stood facing the water. It was as though we were old friends who didn't need words to communicate with one another. We simply stood there, inches apart, shoulders almost the same height.

Now, I do not normally talk with strangers, except in a crowded place, like a bank, or a restaurant lineup, and then it's cursory and polite. I'm not paranoid, simply cautious. Being in a strange city usually inspires extra caution. And since there were no other people along the waterfront, at any other time I would have walked away.

Why did I stay there? I've thought about it a lot. There's the obvious—I was lonely. But loneliness has never been enough reason to cause my good sense to abandon me before, other than my search for space ships, and I think I've explained that. With all the pondering I've done, though, I still can't honestly say what kept me there, other than that I felt something happening that I liked. It was as if the level of iron in my body had been seriously depleted and I hadn't been aware of it. Then, suddenly, my receptors were open and reaching out towards this being to be replenished. I know that sounds vampiric of me, and I suppose that our relationship is like that in a way. But there's more to this relationship. Much more.

But that first evening, we stood at the water's edge until the sky darkened and the new moon rose. I was keenly aware of him, the intensity of the life that pulsated from him. That intensity left me afraid to actually look at him. But when I did turn, he turned also, mirroring me, as if he were a mime. I stared into pale almond eyes that seemed to darken then lighten as I watched them. They enlarged and emitted a warmth that cocooned me from head to toe. Had he touched me physically the sensations could not have been stronger. I found myself gasping, overwhelmed by a kind of passion I had not envisioned existed. It was like orgasming on the sidewalk, and I was both afraid and excited.

Suddenly, he turned. Whatever energy connected us connected us still. As he walked away, I was pulled along, behind him, by invisible bonds.

We walked and walked, as far as the harbor path would take us, then through a park, then to a marina. At the far end finally he boarded what I can only describe as a black metallic vessel that blended with the night, so well, it seemed to be invisible. I trailed behind him up the midnight gangplank, my heels clacking against the metal, still engulfed by these silky yet invisible threads of passion kneading me.

Once down below deck, he shut the door and we were plunged into complete darkness.

It was at this point that I became aware of being very afraid. I've never felt comfortable in the dark, and there I was, in a peculiar, isolated place, with a stranger, in a strange city. I tried to speak but found I couldn't form words. I imagine this is what aphasia feels like: you know the concept you are trying to get across, but can't quite remember how to say the word. Although I was not physically bound, I might as well have been, because I was unable to move.

My eyes became accustomed to the metallic blackness. I couldn't actually see anything identifiable, but I had vague impressions, one of which was this man—for a few moments more I still thought of him as just a man—standing there, facing me, silently. I realized my heart was beating hard, and my lungs filling and expanding rapidly. Chilly sweat coated my body, and my limbs trembled.

I wanted to ask him what he was doing to me that left me immobile. I wanted to know why he had brought me here and what he had planned. I wanted to know who...no, what—because by then I began to realize that he was not quite human—he was. I wanted to ask him why he had no scent. Of all the other questions, that was the one that startled me most when I became aware of it. I simply could not smell him. Stainless steel has a smell. Even plastic has an odor. And certainly anything organic. But he did not. And although my own sense of smell has never been outstanding, it isn't bad and I recognized that scent was the one sense that went missing.

Finally, when I thought my heart might not be able to take the tension any longer, a sudden wave of calm rolled over me. I realized he was flowing closer—that I could sense.

Oddly enough, the closer he got—as he had at the harbor—the more my anxiety turned to pleasure, and the pleasure to passion. When he reached me physically, I gasped. He lit up—that's the only way I can put it—phosphor in a metallic night sky. The light took the shape of his body, but more than his body, as if what the psychics call an 'aura' was visible and his solid molecules actually mingled with the air molecules and I could see that there was no clear division between them. There were colors I recognized, but many I did not, as though he used a different spectrum and my eyes could finally see what they normally were unable to distinguish. Colors that had the intensity of red and yet were more like combinations of blackened silver and yellow and peach, although that does nothing to describe them or do them justice.

I found the visuals fascinating. So much so that I did not at first realize that his body was enfolding mine. The colors that he vibrated encased me and then I felt them enter every pore in my flesh. But they entered me as a scent, like thousands of tiny vapors working their way into every pore. The scent was new to me, more pungent than sweet and tart, greater than anything I had encountered before.

It was a penetration I could not have envisioned and one that kept me on the edge of something akin to climaxing in a delicious, delirious state of almost being sated. A state where time and space became meaningless and all that mattered was this essence that filled my body through my pores as, by way of a poor analogy, the smell of a rose would have filled my nasal cavities and lifted my spirits. And through it all I heard him. And yes, it is likely that in my fragile humanity I reached out and used the sounds to form a name, to find something familiar...

In the morning—and I must skip to morning because I cannot honestly remember details—I found myself lying on the path, at the harbor, where I'd first seen him. There was no sign of him. No sign that he had even been there. And, of course, my sanity returned. With it, anxiety resurged. It wasn't long before I was at a police station, filing a complaint with them, trying to describe a man I could not remember visually with a crime that seemed like rape but which I could not articulate.

I scanned hundreds of photos. The dark metallic ship was gone, of course. The police dusted the harbor ropes for fingerprints and found only mine. And the worst part of it all was that a physical examination revealed no signs of intercourse. I couldn't bring myself to tell them that the entry had been through my pores as well as every orifice of my body, but I did ask for a skin analysis. Nothing unusual showed up. And by the time the DNA results of blood and vaginal secretions finally came through, I was back home. Only my own DNA was present.

That encounter occurred a year ago. I went through much trauma and soul–searching. I even saw a psychiatrist for a few sessions. Until the next new moon.

Every month, at the new moon, Thomas shows up, no matter where I am. I could be home alone in my living room. At a movie with friends. Working overtime. Traveling again. Each time it is the same. I am drawn to him, as if my body needs to recharge. He takes me some-where where we can be alone. And I go willingly. And then he is recharging as well, with what he gets from me, through my pores. Whatever that is. I still don't know.

I have been afraid. Utterly terrified to be precise. Never with him, but between the times when I see him. And what terrifies me most is how much I long for him.

It took me three months to realize it was the moon that determined when he would appear, which leads me to feel that the moon plays on him as it plays on our tides. Perhaps his home is a moon, black and metal-lic. It took time to see the symbolism of that beginning the new moon represents. It took time for me to realize exactly how I have changed.

Needless to say, I am different. Whereas once I was outgoing, now I live only for those hours when I am with Thomas. I am obsessed, yet to my family, friends and colleagues I am the same woman I have always been. I go about my business and interact in familiar patterns. But my life is like an orange with the juice extracted from it. When we are together Thomas gives to me, but he also takes from me and leaves an ever–hollowing shell behind. Oddly enough, I do not hold this against him. Somehow, it makes me love him more.

Physically, I am constantly dehydrated. That, of course, leaves me exhausted, but then, as the new psychiatrist says, I'm depressed; Prosac doesn't help. I have many of the symptoms of HIV and yet the tests are negative and no virus can be isolated. The doctors are stymied by that, and more so by what they have labeled a noxious odor my body emits. These colors with their wondrous fragrance that Thomas leaves inside me seem to transform into something not so pleasant to others. To hear people talk, you would think I was rotting inside, and one day I will wake up and be nothing but decay. But the decay smells sweet to my nostrils, because it reminds me of him.

And Thomas? Each time I see him I know he is stronger. His colors smell brighter, more vivid, and the range has expanded. He lives while I die. It seems unfair, and yet what he gives me is all that has meaning in my life. All that keeps me going. All that matters. And I would gladly give him every drop of my existence for one more breath of that alien scent.

It amazes me now that I spent an entire year searching the heavens for aliens, when one was walking this planet. Is that why he found me, because I searched for him? What he shows me I realize is his home planet, which must be so far away, perhaps in another time or dimension. I do not know exactly why he has left there and come here, but I feel he is the only one of his kind and that he has found a way to survive. I feel, too, his loneliness. Except for me he has no contact, although I could be wrong. It's possible that every night he absorbs the essence of another who acts like a battery providing him energy, until the battery is dead and is either recharged, or a replacement is found.

But I don't think so. I think that it is my essence he wants and needs, and my greatest worry is what he will do when I'm gone. Because I know in my heart that he does not understand death. On his planet, wherever he comes from, life continues in a dark, ever–changing form. It is simply a matter of revitalizing. He cannot know that we poor mortals who strive for wholeness do so in order that we might blend with the whole, with the divine, with what is larger than us and absorbs us when our frail bodies can no longer contain who we are.

What I have come to understand is that as he takes me in, I take him in, and it's possible that internally he is changing as I am. Why do I think that? Because I can now smell him. And he smells sweet. Very very sweet. The sweet essence of all life itself, the life of this planet Earth. It makes sense to me; that's why he has come here. To take us in.

What Matters

That he drank blood for a living, that sunlight scorched him, that daily he rested in a coffin, none of it mattered to Beth. Because when they were alone together, snuggled in that white–light coffin, she locked in his embrace, his fingers heating her nipples, his rough tongue—framed by razor–sharp fangs—toying with hers, when he pierced her with his thrilling hot hardness, and drove her to heights of ecstasy that formerly she had only dared dream about...

The fact that he was a vampire didn't matter.

"How long can this go on?" she asked him one night. "I mean, you'll live forever, I'll grow old and die."

"We can change that," he said, his voice sparks flickering through her veins.

"You want me to become like you?"

He said nothing, but the distressed look on his face spoke volumes. He kissed her then, a long, deep kiss, layers of passion coiled around promise. And when her body burned, ready to incinerate, he took her with a controlled violence that left her gasping for air, trembling, sobbing with the release of so much unfulfilled need that had now, suddenly, in an eternal instant, exploded.

But it troubled her. Losing him. She would be forty soon. Not young. Not old. Aging. At her peak but that meant decline to come. And he, looking her age, would soon look younger, while she would always be younger than his two hundred years. She had lived a full life, but one partially unfulfilled. Early marriage, late divorce. A son, now in college. A career that had been challenging, once. But the inner longings that smoldered in silence he had ignited. And now there was no suffocating that fire.

"I'm ready," she said, meaning it. Ready for whatever.

She slid her hand down his back, the muscles solid, powerful, her palm reaching his right cheek and resting there. The swell of his butt flesh beneath her hand made her moist again. The swell of his penis turned the hot dew in her vagina to a boiling river. As heat swelled within her body, she gazed into his eyes, so fiery yellow that they appeared to be flickering.

"It is painful," he said.

She nodded. She would suffer to be with him.

He tore a line across his throat with a fingernail and blood gushed. Before she could think clearly about it, he moved her lips to the wound, and she sucked hot blood. At that moment, he penetrated her, the firm flesh making her gasp, and the gasp causing awareness of the blood scalding her throat.

Pain rocked her as his teeth tore into her wrist. His mouth clamped firmly, the suction intense. He thrust deep and hard into her, stoking the fire, building the blaze. Her body soared in the inferno until she could no longer bear it, yet wanted more.

And then, in an instant, she burst into flame.

The change startled her. She had not expected this. "We'll grow old together," he whispered. They would grow old together, now that he was human.

And it didn't matter at all to Beth that he had once been a vampire.

Heartbeat

It was the beat that got to him. Now, looking back, Greg tried to reconstruct what had happened, to analyze events. He realized he'd never heard rhythms like that before, not within conscious memory anyway.

It made sense. His roots, at least on his mom's side, were Haitian. But his mother had moved with his Irish father to Canada before Greg was born, and the ties to her culture and history were out of place in the lonely, yellow land of Saskatchewan.

Why they chose the dry, desolate, sparsely populated prairies, Greg did not know. Growing up in the tiny town of Tisdale, 150 miles north of Saskatoon, the small city where he had gone to university, Greg had not encountered music like this, even on the radio. Music that pounded through him as naturally as his heartbeat.

That morning at the harbor, Greg remembered turning, to glance at the glass and chrome skyscrapers behind him. This was his first time in a large city. He came to Toronto a month early for purely practical reasons: to find a place to live, to learn how the streets were laid out, to get organized with the university before starting on his PhD thesis.

After breakfast, he'd decided to walk along the flag–stoned shore of Lake Ontario at the south end of the city. Out on the water he saw a long island, with an airport at one end. Expensive cruisers and historic schooners sailed the harbor; he snapped pictures of the tall ships on display, with the gulls circling their masts.

Suddenly he realized that over the hours the lakeshore had become crowded. Droves of people headed in the same direction, seemingly drawn by a tinny sounding music. He could see the parade route two blocks away, something colorful swaying above the heads of the throngs in the distance.

Women, gorgeous women of all skin colors and ethnic origins, passed him, laughing, dancing to the rhythm of this sound, their long colorful skirts swinging as their hips moved so naturally. Some wore tight jeans or spandex, others shorts. Feet sandaled, midriffs bare, heads decorated with big straw hats or multi–colored bandannas. The men surrounding him seemed relaxed beneath the brilliant summer sun. Black–skinned and white–skinned walked together like brothers. There were Orientals, East Indians, South Americans, and even a few North American natives, all talking and grinning as though the United Nations had declared a day of world peace. It was astonishing to see so many people getting along well, and he decided to walk a little toward the sound to investigate what this parade was all about.

Of course, being a member of the only mixed–race family in Tisdale, a tiny, isolated community, Greg hadn't been aware of much prejudice. He had met with some in Saskatoon, but he'd been virtually cloistered there, living on–campus. Still, he read the papers, and subscribed to magazines. He watched the news on tv, and caught the gist of the larger world in movies. By the time he'd acquired his MA in quantum physics, he considered himself worldly. But nothing had prepared him for this.

"You a visitor, yes?"

He turned, startled. A short woman with very black skin walked in step beside him. Her midnight hair held fiery red highlights, braided and beaded, and her eyes were an arresting green. What an odd combination, he thought. Intriguing. A bit unnerving. Her colorful cotton skirt hung to her thighs in front, and to her heels in back, and rustled around her as she moved so gracefully. A rope holding a carved gourd was slung across her chest—he suspected the gourd acted as a purse. A black, red and yellow African cap perched at an angle on her head, and a low–cut top composed of several silk scarves, wrapped and knotted in a creative fashion, allowed her breasts natural movement. He found this attractive but disconcerting.

"I'm...I'm from Saskatchewan," he said, adding, "I'm going to school. Graduate school." He wondered why he felt as shy as a freshman. "What about you?" he managed.

"Me? I be a witch, doncha know?"

The exquisite woman smiled up at him, her knowing green eyes shining, teeth brilliant. So white, the color temporarily blinded him.

Greg was aware of leaning against a wooden barrier, pressed in by people behind and on both sides. Across the street were more people, hundreds, thousands, eagerly waiting. Distant music wafted through the air like scent.

"Caribana is an annual event," he heard one woman explaining to someone. "Draws about a million people. Amazing lack of violence, considering the numbers."

He did not recall walking the last couple of blocks. How odd! Maybe it was this humid heat; he was accustomed to dry prairie summers. He shook his head to clear it and took a deep breath. Across the asphalt, behind a barrier directly in front of him, he saw the gorgeous woman. Their eyes locked. She waved and smiled, her emerald irises glittering in the brilliant sunlight.

He waved back, wondering if he should run across the street and join her. He'd like to. But they were together before; how did they get on opposite sides? Maybe she didn't want to be with him.

As a band rounded the corner to his right, the street exploded with sound and movement. Two skimpily–clad women, one black, one white, carried a banner that read "Music Mahn Records Presents:" and the name of their act: "Trinidad–Tobago—Drums of Fantasy."

Three dozen dancers wore silver and gold costumes, both the men and women in short skirts, or string bikini bottoms that exposed quite a bit of flesh. Their tops were shaped like twinkling gold stars. The hats glittered with stars or moons. The lead dancer, encased in a kind of costumed cart on wheels, carried an enormous headdress—half a story high—composed of both stars and a giant new moon in the center. The entire costume was a sky of gold and silver sequins, beadwork and feathers that sparkled and swayed beneath the hot sun.

They danced and thrust forward in the small–stepped style of Caribbean folk dance to the music of the steel band following on a flatbed.

Greg glanced across the street. The green–eyed woman's body gyrated so naturally to the beat. Suddenly she snapped her head in his direction and smiled. He could not help but grin.

As the band neared, the music became ear–splitting, and Greg had an urge to cover his ears. Sound pounded against his eardrums painfully. All around him people danced and strutted and clapped. He had never seen so many grinning fools! Not that he minded people having a good time. But exhibitionism bothered him. It lacked decorum.

He checked his watch. Nearly lunchtime. He had to find a store where he could rent a computer before Monday.

The sound swelled to nearly overwhelming. He felt pressure in his chest, as though the bass shoved against his heart and forced it to beat at a different rhythm. Greg began to feel afraid. He was not used to this much stimulation. He turned to make his way through the jiggling bodies before the fear could get too much of a grip.

"Don't go. It's not yet begun." She was behind him.

"How did you get across the street?" he blurted.

Her hand lightly touched his arm. The feel of her warm, moist skin on his flesh was electric current through water. Each of her finger-nails—well over an inch long—had been filed almost to a point, and painted such a blood red he was not at all sure the color wasn't really black. His reaction to what his eyes saw was far different than to what his skin tasted.

When she took her hand away, he felt dismayed by the emptiness that hit in the pit of his stomach.

Her eyes brightened as she pointed one of those daggered fingers down the street. Another band approached the turn–off. The stars and moons band was almost past, and the sound had reached a level he could tolerate. He decided to wait a bit.

She leaned to the left, close up against him, her body both soft and firm. She smelled of exotic sweet flowers, and the scent filled his nostrils, cutting out the odors of ginger beer, meat patties, sunscreen. Two heads taller, he looked down at her hair flying from beneath the cap that could not restrain it, streaking her smooth dark shoulders. He wondered at the red strands. Of course, women color their hair. The red highlights were probably from a bottle.

She snapped her head around and up. Those green eyes narrowed, and her full lips pressed together tightly. "My mama, she Irish, my father Haiti. I know the pagan practices from both lands. It make me special. Like you, mahn."

He could only dwell briefly on the fact that she seemed to have read his mind. And that she was going on about this witch nonsense. What startled him was her ancestry, the same ethnic mix as his.

Before he could say or do anything more, she gripped his arm, sending more shocks through his skin that left him speechless. "This band for you," she cried through the increasing sound surrounding them, gesticulating lavishly at the approaching dancers.

As the band turned the corner, the crowd roared. More than with the previous group, these costumes were spectacular on an entirely new level. The dancers, in black and white, each wore a thin two–toned mask, nearly obscured by a hood attached to a long cape. Only the feet shuffling forward to the beat betrayed race, and again it was a mix. Greg wondered how they could stand to wear capes in this heat.

The lead's headdress draped behind in a long train carried on two carts with wheels. It reached higher than the other, at least one story of a building. The crowd went wild, screaming, clapping, cheering, bodies swaying.

As the band neared, Greg saw that this masterpiece of a headdress was dotted with many small masks, made from sequins and beads, duplicating the obscured faces the caped dancers wore. Long black and white plumes alternated, and movement let these feathers sway and bend like the leaves of a palm tree, or fingers beckoning. Black and white, black and white, black and white. Each mask depicted a different emotion. The opposites glittered and sparkled, the satin shimmered, all of it blended together to weave a hazy world between light and dark, one that had the crowd ecstatic.

The flatbed truck pulled up; steel drums sang and horns blared through ten enormous speakers. "Haitian Drums—Synergize."

As the music swelled, Greg felt almost knocked off his feet. The vibration pounded in his head, his chest. He lost track of his heartbeat, which capitulated to this intense beat. The relentless sun, the scent of exotic flowers, the volume of sound like a tidal wave...Greg felt himself slipping down, slipping away...

Warm flesh curled around his bare arm like five strips of fire. He glanced down and saw the blood–red claws press against his skin. The woman with the green eyes smiled in the most seductive way, a smile that visually represented the sound that made his body quake. As sunlight hit those emerald orbs, the dark dots in the center shrank to pinpoints that transfixed him.

Before he could stop her, she pulled him beyond the barrier and into the midst of the dancers.

She faced him, shoulders rotating, hips swaying, head bobbing, her smile luscious. Her body began to undulate. He could not feel his body moving. He could not feel his body at all. But when he looked down, he saw his feet step forward one at a time, imitating the slow shuffle happening all around him.

The music controlled him, turning him into only sound. Around him, the crowd had moved into the street and the line between observer and observed vanished. People of all skin tones trembled violently, as if throwing a fit. Several couples did an erotic dance, a kind of hopping close together, the woman in front, the man behind, their faces joyous as they melded with the music. Before he realized it, he was doing this dance with the green–eyed woman.

Her dark hair with the beaded red plaits whipped his chest as her head snapped back and forth to the beat. The sultry scent of her permeated every pore of his body. He felt her body meet his, from head to toe, as if they were one flesh, not two. It was no longer just the music. He was losing himself, blending, disappearing...

Greg broke away from her and ran!

The music of steel drums dogged him. He tripped and fell, got up and raced down the street, fighting unconsciousness. Another band was turning the corner. He saw the sign "Jamaica—Black/White Mahn/Womahn Reggae" and felt desperate.

People barely parted as he rammed between them, stumbling over curbs, running into traffic to blaring horns, falling onto the grass, getting up, running against the curious faces coming toward him, until finally the crowd thinned.

The sun pressed him down. The air felt dense and he could not breathe easily. He gulped in breaths and felt sweat trickle down his face, sticking his clothes to his body. He looked around—he was at the spot along the harbor where he had begun. A semblance of normality was returning. But the music that had invaded his chest still beat where his heartbeat should be. And the ringing in his ears cut off the outer world.

He slowed, gasping, wiping sweat from his eyes. His heart did not slow. The steel drums felt imbedded in there, pounding a tinny rhythm that was too voluminous and too fast. This was too much life for him to contain.

A thought gripped him—he needed to get to a hospital. Maybe he was having a heart attack. Or a seizure.

The next few hours were a blur, like a nightmare that leaves a taste of terror afterwards. He remembered hailing a taxi. Sitting in the emergency room. Undergoing an EKG. A young resident, an Oriental woman with ancient eyes, telling him nothing was wrong, handing him a prescription for Adivan. Greg heard the words, "Heat stroke" and "Call your doctor."

The drug helped some. But in the middle of the night, the pounding of his heart kept him from sleeping. His body vibrated and throbbed. But when he looked at his hands, they were not shaking. In the mirror he could see his body was not trembling, although it felt that way. His eyes looked desperate, frightened, and he had never felt so alone.

By instinct, with no plan to guide him, Greg made his way to the lakeshore, to the parade route. Traffic gone, the street was eerily silent. Sanitation workers had removed all but the odd sequin and feather. The barriers had disappeared.

Greg did not know why he had come here. Above, the moon shone full and expectant. It was quiet enough to hear water lapping against the dock when a boat passed in the harbor, although the ringing in his ears continued. The air was hot and heavy for this late at night, and a mist rolled in off the lake. He caught the scent of flowers and turned.

"What have you done to me?" he cried.

The green–eyed woman moved and swayed toward him like a shadow in the night. When she reached him, she raised her arms, as if to caress him, but he pulled back.

"You fear me, you fear you, doncha know?" she said.

He watched, paralyzed, as if what was happening occurred in slow motion. She unbuttoned his shirt. She laid her black palm against his bare chest. He watched her sharp fingernails press against his skin. And enter his body.

His heart beat wildly, erratically. Her touch exaggerated the pulse of the muscle on which his very life hinged. Suddenly, the beat of the steel drums settled in again, as strong as it had been in the afternoon.

"Make it stop!" he cried, his chest heaving. Tears spilled over his eyelids; he could not recall the last time he had cried.

"It not stop now, mahn. No, never," she said, backing away just a little. "You grow used to it. This drumbeat, it be your heartbeat, and these tears you weep so sadly, they will seal them beats together. Oh, you get used to it!" Her eyes danced, sparkling like green stars, like the Caribbean Ocean, like the Emerald Isle. Like the color of his steel–drum heart.

Megan's Spirit

The cup had just touched Megan's lower lip when the ghost drifted into the living room. Her hand jerked, splashing Colombian coffee onto her flannelette pajamas.

The nearly transparent man in worn Levis, black tank top and open black leather jacket had the sensitive face of a thirtyish Gordon Lightfoot. His blond hair was slicked back into what used to be referred to as a 'duck's ass.' He paused. Megan set the cup and saucer on top of the unopened carton precisely marked *Living Room—Entertainment Unit—Third Shelf—CDs.* She held her breath.

The apparition eyed Megan slowly from head to toe, his pale masculine eyes troubled. Then he strode through the room as if in a hurry, his knee–high boots silent against the rugless hardwood. As he passed through the wall into the awkward space she used as a dining room, Megan wondered why he didn't just go through the door.

She ran into the room. No sign of him. She entered the stainless steel kitchen—empty. This was the second time she'd seen him. Yesterday, when she was moving in, he'd made his presence known as if staking out territory. While normally she wasn't prone to hallucinations, the stress of moving made her write the incident off as just that—stress related.

But seeing the ghost again was a shock, an intrusion into her orderly existence, and she was concerned that she might begin responding to him as if he were a normal part of her routine. Then she chided herself. "Not on your number–crunching life!" She was practical, not the imaginative type. Alan, her ex, had confirmed that self–assessment often enough, as did Frank, the head accountant at work. Seeing a ghost was not like her at all.

But others had seen 'Gordie', the nickname she'd conferred on her personal apparition. The two guys who moved her; they wrote Gordie off to the fog that came with the rain. She was happy to do the same thing until she discovered that the previous owners knew about him.

When Megan phoned about the key for the basement door, she'd casually brought up the apparition. Helen MacIntyre dodged her questions but finally confessed that she and her husband had researched past owners, and hadn't uncovered much. "They say, though, that the place has always been a wee bit haunted. But don't you be worrying yourself. We've seen nothing. And besides, I think he likes women," and she hung up.

Megan was furious. She'd worked hard to get out from under the debts Alan had saddled her with. Finally she could afford the minimum down payment on this tiny house—her first—and she didn't want to share it with any male, living or in any other state. *It doesn't matter,* she'd almost convinced herself.

But honesty forced acknowledgment that had she known, she probably would have passed on the place, even though it was perfect in every other way. At least now she understood why the price was so low. And why the MacIntyres were in such a hurry to sell.

She unwrapped the kitchen clock and hung it above the refrigerator. The ghost had come at twelve both days and she suspected he wouldn't be back until noon tomorrow. *At least Gordie's reliable,* she thought. A lot of men aren't.

"You think I should call a ghostbuster?" Megan asked.

Frank crossed his arms over his chest. "All I said was, Alice and I saw this tv show about a local guy who dehaunts houses. If old Gordie's such a threat, do something about it. Look, if you had termites, you'd bring in an exterminator, right?"

"A dehaunter? I think I should call a debunker," Megan snapped. She'd been so upset she'd blurted everything out to Frank, something she ordinarily would have been too circumspect to do. Now she regretted it. She'd forgotten how annoyed he got when anyone resisted his ideas. Still, he was her boss. They had to work together.

"I'm sorry, Frank. It's just that this is so wacky. A ghost exterminator. It's like something you'd read about in a flaky New Age magazine."

"So is having a ghost."

"Good point." She raised her mug in his direction, hoping to change the subject. He nodded and handed her his cup.

As Megan walked to the coffee maker for refills, she tossed Frank's suggestion back and forth in her mind. Quirky as it was having a cute and innocuous specter who appeared on schedule, Megan knew she wanted him out. It was her house. Her home. The world outside her door was frightening and uncontrollable enough, everything from murders and sexual assaults to AIDS—is there such a thing as safe sex, she'd often wondered? She was a woman, alone now, not that she really hadn't been alone through the long and painful years of her marriage. Everyone, she reminded herself, is entitled to a secure retreat. She needed to lock the door, close the blinds and block it all out. This dehaunter, or whatever he called himself, was expensive, although it might be worth the price if she could be free of Gordie, not that she thought it would work.

As she handed Frank his coffee, he said, "I'll pay. Consider it a house–warming present."

'Doctor' Randolph arrived Saturday. "You may call me Latern," he said in a British House–of–Lords accent. Then, "My associate, Mrs. Reisman."

Megan shook hands with both of them. Latern, sixty–something, reminded her of Alistair Cooke. Megan thought Mrs. Reisman, older, greyer, much shorter, could double for Dr. Ruth when she wasn't erad- icating spooks from people's homes.

Latern carried an old–fashioned black doctor's bag, but Megan had the feeling the title in front of his name was honorary. "Where does the lingering soul manifest?" he asked, looking around soberly. Mrs. Reisman appeared to be preoccupied.

"He always comes through the wall on that side of the house and walks through this room, then through this wall." She led them into the main room.

The Phenomenologist, as his card identified him, tapped the wall beside the dining room door. "Undoubtedly this was, at one time, a larger doorway. Perhaps leading to a second bedroom. Not unusual in a modest, older home."

Mrs. Reisman moved around the living room, one hand stretched before her as if she were blind and feeling for objects in her path. A weak sound came from her lips, something between a hiss and a sigh.

"She perceives his essence. On the astral plane, of course," Latern said.

Megan wished she'd had the nerve to insist that Frank be here. After all, it was his 'gift,' having these people invade her privacy.

Latern sat his case on the coffee table and opened it. Megan peeked inside. Fat beeswax candles and thin colored ones, bunches of dried herbs—she didn't have a clue what—wooden tongue depressors, string, a large box of table salt.

Latern removed a white candle and a branch of one of the herbs and lit both with a pocket lighter. The aroma of sage filled the air, reminding Megan of Thanksgiving.

"Can I get you anything?" she asked, feeling cynical. "Coffee or tea? A candle holder?"

He shook his head. Megan got the feeling she was in the way. Latern followed on Mrs. Reisman's heels. They wandered the length of each freshly–painted wall, Latern holding the candle above his head and blowing the strong–smelling herb down in front of Mrs. Reisman's face.

Megan perched on the couch watching, feeling a bit like a voyeur. At one point Latern said, "It is imperative we purify the corrupted space. Male apparitions frequently enjoy tormenting a woman without a mate, if I make myself clear. The herbs will, shall we say, dampen his fervor." Megan nodded, although she had no idea what he meant— Gordie had been about the most polite ghost she could have wanted, if she'd wanted a ghost, which she didn't.

At two minutes to twelve, Mrs. Reisman began to hyperventilate. Both hands trembled as they extended in front of her. Megan jumped up, alarmed, but Latern waved her back. "He's near, oh yes he is. Can you hear me, then?" he called in a loud and somber voice.

"I hear ya!" It was Mrs. Reisman, but not her voice, at least Megan didn't think so. So far Mrs. Reisman had only made sounds; the nasal tone might in fact be perfectly natural.

"She channels, a living necroscope, if you will. I am merely the reassuring voice with which the near–departed communicate," Latern advised in a stage whisper.

Megan checked her watch. "It's only—"

"Shush!" he instructed.

Mrs. Reisman's eyes rolled up into her head, which fell back. Her body began to convulse.

"What is your name?" Latern asked.

"Hershel. Hershel Seinfeld," Mrs. Reisman replied.

Megan's eyebrows shot up. Gordie might not be her ghost's name, but she definitely couldn't see him as either a Hershel or a Seinfeld.

"Why are you haunting this house, Hershel?" Latern asked.

"I live here, if that's okay with you!"

"I'm afraid it is not. This is not your home anymore. It's Megan's. And you are no longer living. You're dead, and you are frightening Megan. Your being here is an impropriety."

Mrs. Reisman's voice grew loud and panicked. "Dead! You say I'm dead? Kaput? Can't be!"

"Yes, Hershel, you have become spirit, not flesh. You have passed on and must continue into the beyond. The astral plane. Along the tunnel and into the light."

"Nah! Not the light. I'm scared of the light. It makes me *meshuga*!" Mrs. Reisman's arm jerked up to protect her eyes.

"The light is nothing to fear. There, pleasures await you. Anything you desire, Hershel. More than you could obtain in this accursed mortal realm. Isn't there something you've always longed for?"

Mrs. Reisman and/or Hershel thought for a moment. "A new Harley. Yeah! 900 cc's. Mine was trashed in a crash."

Megan sighed. She had described to Latern on the phone how her ghost dressed. He was obviously a rebel. She supposed he could be a biker, but it was disappointing. She thought Gordie—*Hershel*—had more class.

"What else do you want, Hershel?" Latern asked.

"Beer's my poison. Bud!"

"It shall be yours. Is there more, Hershel?"

"Blondes. Like Megan. But dozens of 'em. Shapely. Not too bright. Fun to be with, know what I mean?"

While this conversation continued, Gordie appeared. Dressed as always, he strode into the room purposefully, glanced at Mrs. Reisman and Latern who did not notice him, then turned his sad and frightened eyes on Megan. She felt accused.

"Walk into the light!" Latern ordered, pointing toward the bay window. "There ye shall find all that ye seek."

"Yeah, the light. It ain't so bad, I guess. It's, like, callin' me. Hey, there's my shiny new bike! And a couple cases of brew. I'm goin'," Mrs. Reisman called, her voice growing softer, as if she was farther away.

Gordie turned toward the dining room.

"I'm goin'," Mrs. Reisman whispered, heading toward the window.

Gordie passed through the wall.

"I'm gone." Barely audible. Mrs. Reisman's fingers touched the glass.

There was silence. Megan tried to digest what had just occurred.

Latern led the exhausted Mrs. Reisman to a chair. She looked drained, lips pale, brows furrowed, but she'd come out of the self–induced trance. "Would you be so good as to bring Mrs. Reisman a cup of tea?" he asked. "Chamomile, if you have it. Loose, not bagged."

"Sure." Megan headed to the kitchen.

Gordie stood in the doorway to the kitchen. Her first thought was to call for help. Her second to run. He stared at her with those forlorn eyes. Eyes that talked about loneliness and pain. About betrayal. About loss. Although she had never been this close to him before, she didn't feel frightened. He looked like a hologram.

Tentatively, Megan reached out. Instead of meeting his face, her hand passed through empty air. That unnerved her and she jerked her arm back. But he looked so vulnerable that she relaxed and tried again. This time the air felt textured. Emotional.

Emotional? she thought. *What made me think that?*

"Can you speak?" she asked. His lips did not move—it was as though he couldn't hear her. "What about writing?" She edged past him and took a pen from the holder by the sink, tore a sheet of paper from the pad magnetized to the refrigerator door, and handed both to him. He reached out, but his fingers went right through the solid objects.

Frustrated, she tossed the pen and paper onto the counter behind her. "Great!" She turned back to him, saying, "How can we have a relationship?"

Latern, clearly visible, walked through Gordie's subtle body. Apparently he did not see the ghost. "Perhaps we are dealing with a resident incubus," he said.

Gordie vanished like steam from a kettle.

"Why don't you try sign language?" Frank suggested.

"I guess I could," Megan said tentatively, wishing he hadn't brought this up again—of course, Frank had wanted all the details, figuring, no doubt, that he'd paid for them. "It would have to be simple signs."

"Me living," Frank pointed to himself, "you dead," he pointed at her. Megan felt belittled.

"Maybe," Frank was really getting into this, "you can coax him to merge with the chips inside your PC. He can send you insider messages in DOS about the stock markets of the other world."

Boss or no boss, she didn't have to put up with this. "You're not taking me seriously."

"What was your first clue?"

"You think I'm losing it, or making all this up, don't you?"

Frank, who'd been pressing his desk calculator's ON/OFF button, sat back in his swivel chair and stared at Megan. "I think you think you're seeing the ghost of Gordon Lightfoot who, I should remind you, is still living—"

"I didn't say he was Gordon Lightfoot. I said he looks a little like a younger version of him."

"Looks like, is, what's the difference, Megan? You're talking about a supernatural being. You're playing a game with yourself; you need to get out more. It's been a year since Alan. You're probably lonely. And after everything that's happened, nobody would blame you for being gun shy. It's natural. But you're an attractive woman. Very attractive. You shouldn't be alone."

Megan found all of this attention embarrassing and intrusive. She made some excuse about an unbalanced balance sheet and escaped.

Gordie was staying longer. Yesterday he'd been in the dining room—obviously his favorite room—for two and a half hours before he'd entered the kitchen and faded. Today, the clock over the stove in the kitchen said four PM and he showed no signs of evaporating.

Megan had tried various methods of communication: hand signs; written notes; words on the computer screen. She had no idea whether he couldn't read or couldn't see the letters. Maybe she and her world were as hazy to him as he and his world were to her.

She wasn't sure if he heard her, because he did not respond, but Megan told him about herself. Of twelve painful years of marriage to a man who not only nearly destroyed her financially but had been unfaithful on more occasions than she cared to count. The divorce had made all that public and humiliated her.

She also told Gordie about her fear of having to face the world alone. A world that had altered considerably from when she had been a young single woman. And of her terror of nudging forty and no longer being as attractive as she had been. She certainly was not as naive and trusting.

As she spoke, Megan reached out slowly. Her fingertips were becoming fine-tuned to his ethereal body. She sensed the cool electric energy as if it were solid. Her hand moved into his chest. The translucent particles vibrated and parted, and her skin tingled up to her arm.

It was like running underwater in slow motion, the liquid charged. Alive. Solid in an odd way. Struggling to stay separate and yet to meld with her skin.

His melancholy eyes sang to her. He was lonely too, trapped; she felt that to the core of her being. She moved her hand down his chest, further inside him. Heart-level, vaporous light pulsed and radiated, making the texture of her hand more porous and changing the color of her flesh to a pinker shade. The particles warmed her skin like dry ice.

Megan became aware that she had been holding her breath. As she let it out, fear filled her. The sensations felt too erotic. Too real. This is not right, she told herself. I'm spending all my free time with the dead. Caressing the incorporeal. This isn't healthy. He's a ghost. Fear swirled up her backbone as the implications of that word crystallized in her mind. She became acutely aware of a solid, other-worldly silence. The texture of the air sharpened.

She backed away, and he reached out. Megan panicked. It was the first time he had touched her. Terror of the unexplainable glued her in place. His arms encircled her body, passing through her shoulders, his chest melted into hers. *Flesh dusted by a purple passion plant*, she thought. Her body quivered slightly, a leaf touched by a breeze. A leaf that had not been touched in a long long time.

No! This is crazy, she thought. *Very sick. I'm losing my mind completely. I need help. Fast!* She backed across the room trembling.

Suddenly the temperature plummeted. An odor clogged her nostrils—hair cream. Frightened, her body turned clammy and her skin sprouted goosebumps. The silence became a living entity and crushed hard against her eardrums. She clamped her hands over her ears and squeezed her eyes shut, terrified. Every orifice felt assaulted. Something was trying to invade her.

She wanted to flee the house, race out into the streets and scream for help. But the twilight outside her door felt more threatening than being inside, and that paralyzed her.

And then a sound—like wind sighing. A not-quite human breath, seeping through the barrier between worlds. A breath that sent a shiver up her spine, that carried a word—*Megan!*

She stared at Gordie, startled. His form was like a pulsing mist, on the verge of dissipating, or solidifying. On the verge of erupting. His spectral face held a terrifying predatory quality. He was hungry; starving. He reached out for her again.

Megan darted from the room and raced upstairs to her bedroom. She locked the door. In bed, she drew her knees to her chest and pulled the duvet over her head. Tears of rage and fear welled out of her. She felt caught between a sob and a laugh. *I am fated to be alone. Lonely. Vulnerable. My life insubstantial. I am barely a shadow, fearfully skirting life. Never experiencing warmth and love and companionship. Destined to live with phantoms. A phantom myself.*

She cried loud and long, cursing fate, despising the fears that kept her locked inside. Finally she tumbled into the black hole where dreams usurp reality.

The impression of stillness. Her flesh throbbed, a large mouth hungry for life. Diffuse brilliance from every direction coated her, from nowhere she could identify. Density crushed her body, the weight of a leaf floating on air. She could not breathe; a scent both comforting and intimidating filled her.

A wispy cloud passed along the skin of her breasts and paused at her nipples. She trembled in fearful ecstasy. Something wafted down, through the skin and muscle of her belly, penetrating organs and swirling deep into the cradle of her pelvis. Her marrow opened to buoyant clarity. Fire swelled down to her groin and roared back up, scorching her. It was as if she were in the grip of an inferno. Suddenly, she burst into white flame and cried out.

Suspended in the white light, Megan felt Gordie in and around her. She had never experienced such luminescence or felt so secure. Instinctively she understood everything: he could be there for her, as no man had ever been. As no man could be. He would live inside her, and she would give him the world, through her eyes, her ears, her flesh. In protecting themselves, they would protect each other. By opening, they could both be free.

Two minds fused realities: *the world in which you exist is only frightening if you're alone. You'll never be alone again. We're one now.* His voice, so clear, deeper, more confident than she imagined it, brought her to awareness of their joining. She felt caught in this new half–life like an insect in amber. Already, her needs and desires were far more intense than in the full life she had now. She sensed merging with her was more concrete for Gordie than his ethereal soul–prison. A prison that, in a sudden horrible flash she knew had come about because of no sad act of fate, but was a form of punishment he had been relegated to. A punishment for what, she did not know, but her intuition told her that she might soon find out.

Megan struggled, but it was too late to resist him.

Everywhere. Always. Together. You'd better get used to it!

As if her body were being moved by invisible strings, Megan watched herself climb out of bed. She stripped off her clothing and stood before the full–length mirror. Her body looked slimmer, more *male*. The hands fondling her so roughly felt unlike her own. The thought came to her that she would need new clothes. A leather jacket, boots. She pulled back her hair to see how it would look cut short, just a tail at the nap of the neck. She would need to buy hair cream.

Megan felt herself crying and looked again in the mirror; the tear ducts were blocked by spectral plugs and no liquid leaked from her haunted, terror–streaked eyes. But that, she knew, was irrelevant, because the voice swirling through her could not have been more adamant, more possessive: *You'll learn to play, Megan. My games!*

When Shadows Come Back

Fe's earliest memories were of her mother's gnarled, heavily veined hands twisting into unidentifiable shapes. Shapes that resembled nothing until the pale hands moved behind the light bulb. Then, suddenly, a form sprang to life and attached itself to the wall. Dark. Shifting. Fe remembered shrieking with delight at the familiar and benign animals—horse, dog or rabbit.

But sometimes her mother created scary things. Vague, swarthy beings that throbbed and writhed through the wallpaper flowers. It was during those moments, when the blackness contorted, threatening to come alive, that Fe looked to the wall and then to her mother's tense fists. The wall. The fists. She could find no connection. "They come back," her mother whispered. "Whenever you need them." And finally Fe would search her mother's eyes, pleading. Always a mistake.

Fe stored her childhood memories the way she had finally packed up her dolls and sealed them in the toy chest in the basement. The fears vanished too, or so she had wanted to believe.

"Huge house," Philip said.

"As big as I remember." Fe reached for his cigarettes on the dash and quickly lit one. After the first drag he took it out of her hands. "I'm not starting again," she protested, but he'd already stubbed it out.

The red–brick row house where Fe had lived with only her mother until she was seventeen could hardly be distinguished from its neighbors. Four stylized whitened cement strips across the tops of the windows looked like eyebrows. They made the two windows on each of the first and second floors resemble eyes. Beneath the peaked roof the attic had only one eyebrowless window. Its dark shade was drawn. A third eye, permanently shut.

Philip cupped her chin and turned her face. "Want to go in?" He was the best thing she'd run across. He cared about her dreams; protected her, sometimes from herself; kept the loneliness at bay—he was solid like no one else she'd known. If a man can be maternal, she'd often thought. His face in the sunlight gave her courage—squared jaw, licorice eyes, mouth permanently crinkled at the corners because his full lips turned up so easily.

"Let's do it," she said. The empty street at noon felt the way she remembered it. Kids in school. Mothers and fathers away from home. Fathers away.

At the top of the three wide marble steps she rummaged in her straw bag for the key. Weather had rusted the lock. She fumbled and her hand trembled but she opened the door.

They stepped into the short hallway and collided with moldy gloom. "Whoa!" Philip yelled. "Didn't your mother ever clean?"

"Not often." She felt hurt. He knew her situation.

He turned and slipped an arm around her waist and kissed her forehead, running a hand through her hair, as if to say, *I'm a jerk.* Philip empathized automatically; it was one of the things she loved about him. She returned his kiss.

The living and dining rooms were bare. It had been a long time since anyone had used most of the house. During the four years Fe had been away at school in another city and while her mother lay dying, illness had forced her mom to retreat here, to the enclosed back porch, the kitchen, and a bathroom in the basement. Where she'd wasted away. The windows were blocked with black oilcloth and Fe ripped it off. Soot–filtered sunlight revealed charred pots stacked by the sink that she had hastily scrubbed after the funeral. She opened the refrigerator. Inside the door a bottle of thick ruby liquid, a jar with emerald contents, each half full, fungus flourishing in both. The furniture in the back room was dusty—the daybed's damask pattern hardly visible, the walnut coffee table grimy. A dead pothos had collapsed over the edges of a hanging pot; sunlight cast the dry brown leaves into silhouette against the cupboard door. Fe glanced at the twisted shadow; it did not resemble the plant. It didn't look like anything identifiable. She turned away fast.

"Let's go up," Philip said.

They climbed the stairs to the second floor, their soles printing tracks in the dust. As she opened each door, the rooms lay empty, barren wallpapered wombs that could not support life. The sewing room. The bathroom. The guest bedroom, dark for lack of a window, where no guest had ever slept. Her room at the front. The windows, from inside, like huge cataracted eyes.

"You'll have to get somebody in to clean if you want to put it on the market," Philip said. "And we should strip the walls and floors. Get a better price." He flipped a light switch in the hallway and a dim bulb high in the ceiling sputtered to life. "Maybe we should live here ourselves."

Of course, he was joking. Still, terror snaked the length of her spine. She must have been holding her breath because he clutched her around the waist, looked seriously into her eyes and said, "Breathe," then smiled.

Fe sucked in stale air. As she exhaled they both heard a little wheeze. "The dust," she told him.

"The cigarette."

"I'm okay," she said, and Philip nodded.

He started up the narrow stairs to the attic but stopped. "Any ghosts?" He inclined his head upward, his voice again mock–serious. "Maybe you should go first. Not that I'm scared. No way. It's just that, well, you'd better introduce me. After all, it's *your* family."

Fe was only half listening. Behind Philip, against the wall, a reflection crouched. The wattage of the light bulb barely allowed her to make out the shape. Philip but not Philip. Smaller. Darker. Lurking close to the steps. Lying in wait.

He glanced to where she looked. "What?"

"Nothing. The dust is getting to me, that's all."

"We can come back."

She didn't want to come back. Ever. She pushed up the steps, past him, and he waved her ahead.

Fe ascended to her mother's bedroom, the room she had not been permitted to enter without her mother. The room she had entered alone only once. Memories devoured the present.

The steps creaked. Every night. Phoebe followed her mother up for the bedtime ritual. When THEY *came back. The steps had creaked on the night Phoebe entered Momma's room alone.*

Fe stood at the top of the stairs, before the small crimson door, and shivered. It was too dark to actually see, but the color had imbedded in her memory from the many lonely nights she had come this far, only to retreat downstairs into light and quiet and safety. She did not turn the handle.

"We going in or what?" Philip wanted to know.

Her voice snapped through the dense air, "In a minute!"

He touched her shoulder and she jumped. "Take your time."

They're gone, she told herself. Mother took them with her. She promised she would. Sweat slid down Fe's backbone. The knob, cut glass, pressed into her wet palm. She turned it and pushed.

The door opened silently and blackness rushed to greet her. Dead air. The pressure of silence heavy against her eardrums. Fe's legs locked and she could not catch her breath.

"How about a little light," a voice behind prodded. A voice harsh with impatience.

She felt along the wall. Paper rough and torn. She imagined the pattern, giant raven flowers with grey leaves and lead stems, "Alice in Nightmareland," her mother had laughed. Then she remembered: there *was* no overhead light.

Fe felt her way across the room to the night table. The switch clicked but the lamp refused to go on.

"Probably the bulb. I'll get one from downstairs." He paused. "Want to come?"

But the tone did not sound inviting and she heard herself say, "You'll hurry back?"

Footsteps descending. Fainter. Silence.

Fe's heart pumped triple time. But all the adrenaline in the world could not translate into action. She felt trapped in the heart of darkness. A darkness that absorbed everything.

"I've gotta go down to the kitchen—these ceilings are too high to reach," Philip called.

In desperation Fe pushed the switch again. White light exploded, blinding her. When her eyes adjusted, she cried, "It works!" but Philip must have been out of earshot.

The little room was unnervingly the same. The peaked roof sliced it into an 'A'. Inky swags guarded the shaded window, killing stray light. The ebony loveseat, matching parson's table and vanity nestled against one low wall, mother's bed clung to the other. And everywhere sketches, figures like ink blots, easily twisted and bent to be anything Fe wanted to see.

She had an urge to run. "Philip?" But he did not answer.

The box on the table under the lamp caught her eye. She lifted the onyx lid and music bubbled out. Inside, the tiny white female and black male figures spun together to the melancholy tune. The tune that she recognized as having become the melody of her life. Each note lulled her, blossoming into memories.

"Come here, Phoebe. I want to show you something."

Phoebe ran to her mother. The black box was playing that pretty music again. The couple inside swayed. Mother stretched out her arms. Phoebe crawled onto the bed and was enveloped.

"Watch carefully," Mother said, "and remember."

Hands, so delicate. Vulnerable. They joined, pale, nervous fingers interlocking, bending oddly. Phoebe watched the fragile blue wiggle beneath the skin.

"The wall," Mother directed.

A slithering through the dark flowers. Phoebe shrieked, "Snake!" half in hope, half in fear. Mother shook her head.

She struggled to catch a glimpse of what she could not see. As it skillfully darted for cover, the room shifted.

Phoebe looked around. She was alone in the dark forest. "Momma?"

An iron-gray leaf quivered at the sound of her voice. Something hid behind it. Watching her. The music grew loud, the foliage dense and moist. Phoebe screamed, "Momma, make them go away!"

A crash below brought Fe to her senses. She raced to the door and down to the second floor. "Are you alright?"

A distant and muffled curse. Moments passed. He came to the first floor stairs as Fe looked over the banister. "The chair leg broke when I was unscrewing the goddamn light bulb. I'll be up in a minute."

"Want me to come down?"

"Stay there!"

The music box was still playing and she intended to go up and close the lid then leave. But as she picked up the box she noticed the female within, gracefully sculpted in virgin white marble, gazing adoringly upward. Her features were finely detailed, the face almost recognizable.

But the dark male was disturbing. Rigid posture. Hair severe, tied back in a classical style. Brows arched. Haughty. The eyes hollows that swirled inward like obsidian pools. Pools with a threatening undertow. Why had she never noticed? But suddenly Fe remembered.

Mother was out. The knob on the door at the top of the stairs turned easily. Phoebe entered Mother's room.

The box that played music rested next to the bed. She would just listen a little, then hurry back downstairs before mother got home. She opened the lid.

Notes tinkled, a high one then a low one, the melody bitter-sweet and rhythmic. The man had the woman locked in his arms and they swirled in time. Phoebe leaned back against Mother's pillows and closed her eyes. She dreamed she was dancing in the forest of shades with a darkly handsome prince. They dipped and swayed as the song lilted and plunged, lilted and plunged. The music wound in circles and they spiraled together.

Phoebe looked up at her partner. His hair was tied and black, dark as the drawings mother made with India ink. As severe as his skin and clothes. As his shadoweyes.

Even as those eyes hardened to black diamonds and pierced her, they melted to ebony pools which would float her to his land. The land where black flowers grow and never die.

"Like the dark?"

She dropped the lid shut at the sound of Philip's voice. When had the light gone out?

He moved through the darkness until she sensed him near. "The lamp." His demand jolted her to action and she guided his hand.

Light followed a click. His shadow appeared on the wall, at home among the midnight flowers.

"You came back," Fe whispered. Delighted. Terrified. She opened the box and the music flowed between them, connecting them. Suddenly she felt like dancing.

He walked to the door, closed then locked it. She watched his enormous silhouette stalk through the flowers until it reached the bed. The dark form towering above grabbed her in his arms. "Whenever you need me," he said.

His black ice eyes melted into licorice pools and Fe sank into that bitter–sweet darkness.

Snow Angel

They'd been warned in Whitehorse. By several people. And again in Dawson City. But Joe never listened. He called himself a "free–floating spirit." Coleen thought of him as somebody who needed to be nailed down to the earth.

Joe's death had come as a complete shock. Coleen was just finishing drying and putting away dinner dishes in the Winnebago's little cupboards. He stepped out of the one–man shower that also functioned as the toilet. She pushed aside the pink and white curtain above the sink to watch the odd snowflake drift onto the frozen tundra, thinking again how much she did not share his love of or trust in this barren land. It had been his idea to come way up here in the fall, "when there's no tourists," he'd said, adding in his poetic way, "so we can nourish the snow spirits and they can nourish us."

She folded the dishtowel. "We're almost out of food, Joey. We'd better head back to Dawson City—that'll take us half a day. Didn't that guy on the CB say something about a low pressure system building?"

When he didn't answer, Coleen turned. Joe sat on one of the benches at the table, a deck of cards before him. His chunky six–foot frame slumped back towards the front of the vehicle. His pale green eyes looked as cold as the crevices in a glacier. In his right hand he held two mismatched socks.

Coleen performed mouth to mouth resuscitation. It didn't work. She got out the first aid kit and found some smelling salts. When everything else failed, she pounded hard on his chest, first in desperation, then in hysteria.

All that had happened yesterday. Today she had a different problem—what to do with her husband's rotting corpse.

She stared out the window. The storm she feared had magically eaten its way across the landscape while she'd struggled last night to revive Joe. She had judged the weather too bad to drive in but now she realized she'd made a mistake by not trying. Eight hours had done damage. Swirling gusts of snow clouded her view beyond a couple of yards. Every so often the wind banshee–howled as it buffeted the two–ton camper, threatening to hurl everything far above the permafrost and into another dimension. It made her think of Dorothy being swept away by the tornado and ending up disoriented in Oz.

Coleen's eyes automatically went to Joe's body. She had wrapped him in the two sheets they'd brought along and secured the sheets with rope. He lay on the floor like a tacky Halloween ghost, or a silly husband playing ghost. Any moment she expected him to rise with a "Boo!" Then he'd laugh and admit to another of his practical jokes. But the form refused to play its part. It did not sit up. She had an urge to kick it in the side.

"It's all your fault." Furious tears streaked down her face. She snatched at the box of Kleenex and blew her nose long and loudly. "You wanted to go into debt to buy this stupid camper. You wanted to drive all the way to the Arctic Circle. You wanted to stop at this dumb lake. You never plan anything. Why do you have to be so damn spontaneous?" She yanked open the small door beneath the sink and hurled the tissue into a paper bag of burnable trash.

Suddenly her shoulders caved in and she let loose. The weeping turned to a wailing that frightened her all the more because it made her aware that she was alone. She stopped abruptly and the silence hurt her eardrums. When had the snow and wind expired? Outside it looked like some kind of perverse fairy land, white on white merging with a colorless sky. Although the Winnebago was warm, she shivered. This place. It was so...empty. Nothing could live here.

Coleen knew she needed to act to break this mood. She washed her face in the kitchen sink, dried it with her shirt tail and tried the radio again.

Last night the storm had smothered signals coming and probably going too. For the first time since Joe's death, she was getting some static; she reread the part in the manual about broadcasting. She picked up the microphone and sent out a distress call and gave their location, as recorded by her in the log—three hundred kilometers northeast of Dawson City, on Hungry Lake. She repeated the call for over an hour until she needed a break. Coleen sat at the table with her coffee. She felt disheartened and lifted the cup to inhale the comforting sweet–roasted scent. Sweet–sour noxiousness clotted her nostrils and she gagged. "Oh my God." Setting the cup down spilled its contents. Joe was starting to stink.

Primal fear raked a nerve. She jumped up and lifted the seat of the bench. Among the tools inside she found a small shovel and the ice ax she'd insisted on buying. She threw on her parka, stepped into her boots and grabbed the fur–lined mitts. Once she was dressed she turned the knob of the back door. The door wouldn't budge. The glass had frosted so she couldn't see the problem. Panicked, Coleen threw her weight against the door, finally creating an inch gap that let in freezing air. She peered through the slender opening. Snowdrifts had climbed halfway up the camper. She jammed the shovel handle between the door and the frame and used it as a lever to pry another inch, then another; finally it was wide enough to get the ax through. Hacking and plowing gave her a one–foot opening she could lean around.

Crystalline whiteness extended as far as she could see. The banks must have been four feet high, the lowest drifts two feet deep. The realization dawned that the truck would not get through this. Even if she managed to connect the chains to the snow tires—and there was a good chance she couldn't do it by herself—no way would the camper make it.

Despite warm clothing, the air nipped at the skin on her face until it numbed. A bad sign, she knew. She pulled the door shut and made herself another cup of coffee.

While Coleen drank it, she thought about her situation. The weather might warm. The snow could melt enough in a week or so that she could drive. She'd keep working the radio; eventually somebody would hear her. The thought came, maybe a snowmobile will drive by, or a dogsled, but she knew that's the way Joe would think. There were only 25,000 people in the whole of the Yukon and Hungry Lake was a good hundred kilometers from the nearest highway.

Thank God she'd bought that book on surviving in the Yukon when they'd passed through Dawson City. Joe, of course, had laughed at her. There was a checklist at the front—"What to do While Waiting for Help to Arrive." She'd torn it out and tacked it to the wall. Joe had found such practicality even more amusing.

Joe. She knew she'd been avoiding thinking about him. She sighed but it sounded more like a moan. Her heart felt both too full and empty. She looked at the body on the floor, wrapped like a mummy. Even now the smell was there, under everything, seeping into the air like poison spreading through water. She'd have to take him outside.

After trying the radio again, Coleen dressed in the heavy clothes—this time wearing a ski mask as well. She continued chopping and digging into the crusty snow. By five o'clock she had the door wide open and the bar locked so it would stay that way. The landscape looked the same now as it had at ten AM, as it would look at ten PM. With only six hours of darkness, even the underside of the clouds reflected white luminosity—snowblink, they called it. This almost endless brightness was unnatural. She remembered near–death stories she'd read about, of white light and how departed souls float down the tunnel towards that blinding light. Coleen wondered if Joe had gone down a tunnel. She squinted. She couldn't imagine anything brighter than this.

Dense cold filled the Winnebago, which numbed her nose and anesthetized her emotions, making the second part of the job easier.

She grabbed Joe's ankles. Despite the gloves, she was aware of the hardness of his cadaver. Coleen clamped her teeth together; this was no time to let grief and fear overwhelm her. Grunting, heaving, she dragged his dead weight along the brick–red linoleum to the back door.

There were snowshoes—she'd seen to that—and she strapped a pair onto her boots. She'd never walked in them and had no idea how she'd manage. They weren't like skis; they were feather light but the racket part up front was so wide that she couldn't help tripping herself.

Her big fear was that the snow wouldn't be solid enough to hold her up, but it did. She backed out of the camper and, once sure she was balanced, bent over and grabbed Joe's feet again.

She pulled and the rigid body slid over the door frame easily. All but the head. It caught on the frame. When she yanked, it plummeted into the trench she'd created around the door.

Joe was so stiff that when his head went down into that pit, it jarred her hold and the rest of his body popped straight up into the air.

Look, Collie, a human popsicle!

Fear slid up her spine. Coleen looked around. Nothing. No one. Only the corpse.

She knew he was dead but still she said, "Joey?" and waited. It had to have been the wind. She steeled herself and jumped up to grab his feet. Her body weight pulled them down. He leveled like a board and, stepping backwards carefully, she slid him along the compacted snow.

Somehow she didn't want to leave him just outside the door. The dry cold was exhausting, and deceptive—she knew it was colder than it felt and she had to be careful of frostbite—but she dragged him away from the camper, tripping once, having a hell of a time getting back up on the snowshoes. The air burned its way down her throat and the pain in her lungs became ferocious, making her fear pneumonia.

Finally he was far enough away that she wouldn't smell him every time she opened the door, yet he'd still be within sight. Coleen struggled back. By the time she got inside, her entire body was numb. That desensitization was preferable to the defrosting that followed. A hot shower brought pins–and–needles pain that made her cry out loud. Trembling, she bundled up in Joe's two bulky sweaters, pulled open the bed and crawled in. She couldn't see Joe from here. She drifted into what turned out to be a nightmare. A frozen animal carcass with Joe's face grinned down at her. He was sucking on a decaying popsicle.

When Coleen woke it was still light outside. She checked the battery–operated clock radio and could hardly believe she'd slept nearly twenty–four hours until she moved and her muscles screamed and she remembered having been up for thirty–six hours doing exhausting work in sub–zero temperatures.

Joe's death, her being stranded, all of it suffocated her with despair. It was only the thought, *I could die here,* that got her out of bed.

She ate, played with the radio—now even the static was gone—reread the survival list, and went about doing what was necessary. She checked all propane hookups and turned the heater down—she'd have to use the gas sparingly. Thanks to Joe, the extra tank had been gobbled up when he'd insisted they extend their stay.

Next she tried the engine. It wouldn't kick over; the fuel line had to be de–iced first. She'd need to do that twice a day to keep the battery charged. The gas gauge needle pointed to three–quarters full and there was a five–gallon container for emergencies. Two of the three hundred kilometers back to Dawson City would be through the mountains where the snow could avalanche and put out the road. But at least there was a road. Making it to Highway No. 5 was the problem. They'd had a hell of a time getting through the spruce and poplars to the lake from there and, under these conditions, there'd be double hell to pay to get out. And all of it depended on enough of a thaw to drive the camper.

The snow, she realized with a bitter laugh, had at least one benefit—there would be plenty of snowbroth; fresh water wouldn't be a problem. She checked flashlight batteries, matches, candles, flares and medical supplies. The cupboard held a big jar of instant coffee and a box of tea bags, but even at half rations, the food would only last one person one day. They should have been back in Dawson City five days ago but Joe had insisted on this side trip. She'd argued against it but he'd fixed on some crazy idea he'd read about in a magazine that he could fish in the lake and catch char and they'd "negotiate with the Eskimo gods to live off the land," a concept that now struck her as insane.

Most of their fifteen–year marriage she had, in her way, loved Joe, although their relationship was not the fulfilling one she'd hoped for. She had to admit that because of him she'd been places and done things she wouldn't have, left to her own devices. Early on she'd seen him as a welcome contrast: devilish to her seriousness, adventurous to her timidity. But it wasn't long before she admitted that what had once been charming traits in Joe turned to juvenile habits that gnawed away at her patience; divorce had crossed her mind.

Still, he was her husband, till death did them part. He had died, if not in her arms, at least in her presence, and he had died as he'd lived—impulsively. On some level she missed him dearly.

But she was also angry. Angry that he'd brought her to this God–forsaken place and left her, maybe to slowly starve, or freeze to death like a character in a Jack London story. And why? Because he claimed his destiny was to see the "Good and Great White North."

And he had too much childish faith that life would support him to worry about freak storms. If he wasn't already dead, she might have entertained murderous thoughts.

She pressed her face against the chilled glass in the back door. White. Everywhere. So pure, so foreboding. The wind had erased her tracks. She couldn't see Joe's body. Suddenly she felt guilty for leaving him out there all alone in an icy grave. The thought struck, maybe he's not dead. Maybe he's in a coma or something. She tried to talk herself out of that notion but soon Coleen was putting on the parka and the snowshoes and trudging across the hardened snow in the direction she thought she'd taken her husband.

The air had a peculiar and enticing quality. The cold felt almost warm. As she crunched along, the beauty of the snowscape struck her. Everything was elementally pure, pristine. Blameless. Almost spiritual. In the darkening sky a faint aurora borealis flickered green and blue, like some kind of signals emanating from heaven. She understood how Joe's soul could soar here. Suddenly, the incredible glare on the horizon temporarily snowblinded her.

From behind, the wind resurrected itself and knocked Coleen off her feet. She plunged straight forward as if her body were jointless. Her face crashed into the frost and knocked out her breath. As she struggled to her knees, little puppy yaps came out of her mouth. Pain shot through her nose and forehead. She squeezed her eyes shut hard and opened them slowly to regain her vision. The snow beneath her was red. She touched the ski mask over her nose; the glove was stained.

Coleen looked around wildly, trying to orient herself. Joe's body lay six feet away. She started to think, why didn't I notice it before…and then stopped. The body looked the same, but the snow surrounding it appeared scraped. It reminded her of being a child and lying flat, making snow angels by opening and closing her legs, and raising and lowering her arms above her head. *He can't be alive,* she thought. *The sheets are still tied around his body. There's no way he could move his arms and legs.*

Coleen crawled to the body. Instinctively she felt afraid to touch it, but forced herself. It was iceberg hard. When she tried to shake him, she discovered that the sheets had adhered to the snow crust.

"Joe! Joey!"

Freezing in Spirit Land, honey.

"My God!" She tore at the sheets but her gloves were too bulky so she yanked them off. Still, the cotton was more like ice and she had to use a key to gouge through it. She wedged her fingers between the fabric and his neck and ripped the fabric up over his chin. The cotton peeled away from the familiar face to reveal chunks of torn flesh and exposed frozen muscle.

Coleen gasped, horrified. His face was a pallid death mask. "Joe!"

Her hands had numbed and were turning blue and she stuffed them back into the gloves before slapping his cheeks. "Can you hear me?"

She sobbed and gulped stabbing air. The storm was getting bad again; she could hardly see the Winnebago through the frozen fog of ice crystals. If she didn't go back now she might be stranded here. She glanced down at Joe. If he hadn't been dead when she'd brought him out, he certainly had suffered hypothermia and died of exposure. The wind whispered and Coleen accepted the fact that Joe had not spoken to her.

She left him and clumped her way back. By the time she shut the door and peered through the glass, the camper was enshrouded in white air.

Coleen devoured the rest of a tin of sardines in mustard with the last two saltines and drank another cup of coffee. The coffee had her edgy and she decided to switch to tea, although she didn't like it as well. But now that the solid food was gone, she'd need to keep her head.

All day she'd tried the radio and reread the *Survival in the Yukon Guide*. She'd just finished an improbable chapter on snaring rabbits by locating their breath holes in the snow and was about to close the book when the section on leaving food outdoors caught her eye. The three paragraphs warned about wolves, bears, caribou and other wild animals being attracted to food. She lay the book in her lap for a moment and rubbed her sore eyes.

Human bodies were food.

She recalled seeing the movie *Alive* and how the survivors turned to cannibalism. She shivered and hugged herself.

Coleen went to the door. Snow, the voracious deity of this land, lay quiet and pallid, waiting. Somewhere out there was her husband's body. Those marks in the snow crust could have been made by something that was hungry. Something that might at this moment be gnawing on Joe's remains.

She shuddered. He deserved better than that. Maybe she should bring him back indoors. But that thought was so bizarre it led to the toilet and her vomiting up sardines.

By the time Coleen felt steady enough to put on the heavy outdoor clothing, she knew what she had to do. She gathered the supplies she'd need and went to Joe.

The snowscape had turned into an icescape—the Winnebago was icebound. That should have scared her but she felt strangely invincible and coherent, her mind as crystal clear as the air. There were no tracks; she found him by instinct.

She opened the cap on the lighter fluid and doused his body. It was hard to believe that under this frozen earth lay huge oil deposits; the nauseatingly sweet combustible reeked. She struck a match and dropped it onto the pyre. Flames sprang upward and black smoke fouled the air. She hoped the snow gods did not feel defiled.

Coleen stared at the fire charring her husband's remains. Flesh crackled and a familiar scent wafted up; she realized that she had never known anyone who'd been cremated. It came to her that maybe his spirit was trapped in his frozen flesh. If any body possessed a spirit, it would have been Joey's.

As the inky cloud danced heavenward, she panicked. Maybe she was doing the wrong thing. Maybe the flames would not just cook his flesh but would burn his soul. Maybe hell was...but something caught her eye.

A pale specter appeared in the dark smoke. The face was luminous, the form familiar. She watched Joe ascend like a snow angel. He smiled down at her and waved. Coleen sobbed and waved back. Tears welled over her eyelids and froze on her lower lashes and she stepped closer to the fire's warmth. *We all do what we have to, Collie.* He'd said that often enough, but this was the first time she understood it.

She felt bone chilled. The wind confided in her—the northern demons were still hungry.

Coleen shoveled snow onto the flames and they sizzled into silence. As darkness crawled up the sky, she worked quickly with the ice ax. There was plenty of meat. It would take time to pack it in ice and store it safely before the storm returned.

Brina

"Brina was right, as usual," Cindy said. "We're perfect for each other!"

Paul couldn't help himself; he loved everything about this girl–woman. Under the cafe's track lighting, Cindy's long blonde hair glittered as if dusted with tiny stars. And those twinkling green eyes were reminiscent of new grass sprinkled with dew drops. Cindy was a pixie, with a cute pointed chin and exquisite cheekbones, and the most adorable expressions—Paul felt delighted by and protective of her. But beyond all that, Cindy was one of the sweetest, most gentle, naive women, certainly more so than the series of controlling bitches in the past. He hadn't seen any meanness in Cindy, just pure kindness and love, enthusiasm, imagination…

Paul leaned across the cafe table and kissed her cheek. Immediately Cindy's emerald eyes widened and sparkled and her full lips curved upward. She picked up the pussy willow branch she'd brought him as a gift and delicately ran the soft gray buds across the tip of Paul's nose. His nostrils caught a bit of earthy fragrance. He wanted Cindy, more than he'd ever wanted anyone before. He took her hand and kissed the palm, letting his lips linger on the warm, moist skin. "Sleep at my place tonight. Or I'll stay at yours."

Cindy's youthful features contorted into a look of ancient sadness. She pulled her hand away. "Not yet, Paul. I told you, it's not the right time."

Paul's back muscles tensed. "It's been three months. You say you love me—"

"I do!"

"And that you don't have a problem with sex outside marriage—"

"It's only the timing—"

"I won't be teased!"

Cindy obviously picked up on his tension, bypassing the anger and going right to the wound. "I'm sorry. I want to sleep with you. Every night I dream about it. But I told you, I've never done it before and I can't until my guardian gives me the okay."

Fury surged in Paul. Although he loved Cindy's child–like qualities, sometimes they went too far. "Look, you're twenty years old. You don't need a guardian. Isn't it time you started living your own life?"

"But, Paul, Brina is my guardian, and she says—"

"I don't care what Brina says!"

Cindy's lips parted and formed a large 'O'; her eyes looked startled. Suddenly her features shifted as if the emotion she'd just felt had been erased from her memory. "You know, Brina is the Celtic name for protector, and—"

"Wait!" Paul held up a hand. "I know you and Brina are close. She's taken care of you, brought you up. She's been there when you needed her. But I feel those things for you too, if you'll only give me a chance."

Cindy's features went blank. She looked down. Her voice was calm, distant. "Did you know that the *salix discolor*—that's the Latin name for pussy willow—is one of the most flexible branches that exists?" Paul watched her fingertips stroke the long stem of the pussy willow, up and back, then fondle one of the soft buds. His body responded as if he were being caressed. Cindy's lips relaxed into the smile that usually lived there. When she looked up, her eyes were bright and liquid. Inviting. "Paul, I love you."

"And I love you." He reached for Cindy's hand again.

"What the...?" Pain stung his wrist. He jerked his hand back sharply. Something on the branch had slashed him, right across the bulging blue vein under the skin—any deeper and the vein would have been opened. A string of blood formed and the wound burned. He examined the branch but couldn't see anything pointed enough to cut skin, and there was no insect he knew of that could have bitten like this.

"Shit!" he said, standing. "I'll be right back."

Before he could move toward the washroom, Cindy stood too. Her elfin face was a mask of fear. She grabbed his arm, picked up a napkin, dipped it in her glass of water and quickly pressed it over the gash. "Come home with me," she said, her voice airy, her eyes timid but enticing. "I have something that will heal your wound."

Cindy lived at the end of a dead–end street, on the bank of the river. Three sides of the small house were protected by a garden of tall wildflowers, and large overhanging willow trees that acted as a buffer from temperature extremes. Paul had never even seen Cindy's house before, let alone been inside. More than anything he was struck by an overwhelming sense the moment he entered the yard that time had come to a complete stop.

The interior of the house was mostly wood, dark, unstained, finished in shellac, which gave it a natural look and allowed the grain to show. Kitchenette, dining area, living room. A couch, two chairs, a tv and CD player. The place couldn't have been more ordinary—except for the enormous willow growing up past the floor boards and through the ceiling to the second floor.

He stared at Cindy's sweet, childlike face, then at the tree, its branches alive with narrow lance–shaped leaves and silky catkins ready to burst into flower. The green–brown branches drooped in the way of willows, languid, patient. For some unknown reason, the words *reserving judgment* came to Paul.

"How...I mean, why...?" But he couldn't articulate all the questions running through his mind.

Cindy laughed. Paul knew he must look stunned. "Come on," she said. "I'll wash that cut and show you the upstairs."

Confused, Paul followed her to the second floor, which turned out to be one big loft, a bathroom at the back. The tree had grown through a large hole cut in the floor and stopped just short of the skylight ceiling.

While Cindy chatted about the amazing amount of light the skylight provided, and the deck at the back of the house, and how she'd inherited this place, Paul could only stare at the tree.

He knew Cindy worked in a greenhouse, and loved all things that grow in the earth, but a tree in the house? Wasn't it unsanitary, to say the least? While Cindy chatted, he scanned the willow. Despite its overall relaxed appearance, each leaf reminded him of a green blade, sharp enough to cut. Even though the branches curved, still, they appeared tough and hard.

"Come on, let's clean that," Cindy said, and led him to the bathroom sink where she washed the cut with soap and water, then applied a thick pale brown gel, which stopped the burning.

"What's this stuff?" Paul asked.

"Willow bark. Salicylic acid. You know, what they make aspirin from. It works directly too. I use it a lot. Brina taught me how to make it."

They ended up sitting on her futon on a low platform, next to the tree, so close that leaves brushed the back of Paul's head, sending a shiver rippling up his spine. Instinctively he inched away.

"Sometimes it's as though the branches pull me in," Cindy said, running a hand over leaves, "until I'm hugging the trunk, enfolded by the leaves, and there's no more light or air, and the rest of the world disappears. And sometimes, in the middle of the night, when the moon shines through the skylight, and I'm half asleep, I can feel every inch of my body caressed and my skin tingles until I can hardly stand it."

She sighed and let go of the leaves. He thought the branch trembled a bit too long.

"Cindy, why do you have a tree growing in your house?"

She laughed. "They say a fairy tree grew from the grave of Cinderella's dead mother. The spirit of the tree became her fairy godmother, and raised her as her mother would have, protecting her, teaching her the things a mother would, like right from wrong. I guess I got a fairy step–mother." Her face altered and became a mask again, this one blank, the emotion leeched away.

He pulled her close, feeling the warmth of her body, the softness of her lips.

Something sharp hit Paul's back and he jumped. Behind him, a branch was quivering. He must have leaned into it. He moved further away.

Cindy smiled her adorable smile, and it was as though the sun had come out. "You know, if it wasn't for Brina, I wouldn't have met you."

"How do you figure that?"

"That day I was supposed to go buy vegetables, and I was putting it off, and Brina made me go to the market right away. She said I'd meet someone we could both live with," she giggled. "I knew it was you she meant, because you were wearing a green t–shirt and brown pants. You looked just like a tree!"

He shook his head, not even sure what he was confused about. "Where is Brina?" he asked suddenly.

"Here."

Paul looked around and shook his head again. "All I see is you, me and a tree."

Cindy stared at him as though he couldn't see the obvious. "It's not just a tree, it's Brina. I just told you that. She looks out for me. Helps me understand what's the right thing to do. You see her, don't you?" she said, her voice low, struggling to suppress a tinge of what might have been fear clinging to the edges. Her large eyes filled with both longing and worry. "My step–mother died here, you know. Down-stairs. On the spot where Brina grows."

Another chill passed up Paul's spine, more intense. Early in their relationship, Cindy had sketched out her traumatic childhood: her mother died in childbirth, her dad died just after he remarried, and then the step–mother—the only mother she knew—died too. But Cindy hadn't revealed the circumstances, and Paul wasn't sure he wanted to hear all the details now. He glanced at the tree. A deep scar in the bark looked like a miniature being, with wings.

"Who…brought you up?" He was afraid of the answer.

"Well, after my step–mother died when I was thirteen, there was just Brina."

"Cindy, that's crazy. This is a tree. Surely there was a person—"

"Brina."

But the more Paul looked at the tree, the more he could understand how Cindy saw. The image imbedded in the bark, now that he knew her way of thinking, began to resemble a small winged creature hold-ing a wand. Cindy would have seen this tiny fairy–like image and it was a short leap to fairy godmother, a substitute for her step–mother.

My God, he thought, *she raised herself!* To have concocted such a fantasy of a loving mother figure, she must have felt very alone.

"Oh Paul!" Cindy cried. "Hold me! Please, hold me!"

He took her in his arms. Compassion turned to passion. Their mouths connected softly, then fiercely. Paul's hands slid up under her sweater. She worked with him to pull the wool garment from her body. Her breasts were full, the pink nipples eager. Cindy's skin held a faint shine. Inviting. Her lips parted in anticipation. He felt drawn to the heat emanating from her body.

He slipped out of his clothes, and helped Cindy shed the rest of hers. Warm skin, a bit moist, silky. He stroked her hips, the swell of her bottom. The flesh gave beneath his touch one moment, and the next moment rose up to meet his hand as if begging for more.

He was being watched!

He snapped his head around and stared at the tree. The trunk curved like a woman's body—willowy came to mind—and the leaves reminded him of long hair. He noticed details in the scar in the trunk, creating a kind of face.

Cindy pulled him back until their lips met again. Not hesitant in the least now, she opened her mouth wide and his tongue probed deep.

Suddenly she lay back, knees tightly drawn together, closing off. But her face seemed so vulnerable. "Paul, not yet. Brina will be mad."

He struggled to smile, to cover a surge of anger. "I thought Brina looks out for you."

"She does, but—"

"Then she wants what's best for you. And I'm best for you. She's the one who brought us together, remember? Don't you want me?"

"Yes," she breathed.

He spread her legs at the ankles and crawled up her body. He reached for Cindy's breasts as he started to bend down. Terror creased her beautiful face. "If I don't obey Brina, she'll punish me."

He paused. "Punish you? Christ, Cindy, what are you talking about? It's just a tree."

She turned her head away. Large tears rolled out from the corners of her eyes and made her cheeks glisten. "I thought you understood," she sobbed softly.

He took the tortured face in his hands and made her look at him. "What I understand is that I want you. I love you. I won't leave you. I'll be here, and you won't need to invent any fairy step–mothers anymore. You'll have a real person who cares about you to love and protect you."

Her sobbing stopped. She looked up at him with wide, moist eyes as though she wanted to believe. Paul's lips caught her mouth. His body lowered onto hers and they writhed against one another. And finally he pressed into her, slowly, watching the fine mix of emotion on her face, taking in the intoxicating scent of her, drinking in the sounds coming from her lips, feeling his desire mount. Her passion–heat rose to meet his own. Her body was so hungry. Her legs clamped around his hips and her arms surrounded his neck; she lifted herself off the futon, clinging to him.

Paul wasn't sure when he noticed the air current shift. The temperature dropped. A cool breeze built quickly in the room. His skin prickled; he sensed a presence. He hesitated, afraid to look, afraid of what he would see.

"Brina says she's always understood what I needed, and she knows what you need too," Cindy whispered, her breath coming in gasps. Paul was afraid to move. "She says you need to learn patience," Cindy continued. "That's why she brought you here. She'll be your fairy step–godmother too, and teach you the way she teaches me."

Paul's heart hammered. He turned his head slowly. God help him, but he expected to see a fairy, a small supernatural being, maybe like Tinkerbell, hovering in midair, ears pointing, wings fluttering, face smiling, magic wand poised to bestow starshine. And strange as seeing that would be, he could live with it. A benevolent fairy step–godmother.

What towered over him certainly reminded Paul of images he'd seen of fairies, except in color and size. His mind boggled with mundane questions: A fairy can't be green and brown, can it? The size of a tree? Wings flapping like wispy leaves in a storm?

Before he could react, branches snaked out and those long thin leaves knotted tightly around his wrists and ankles.

"Wait!" he cried. A branch lifted high in the air like a wand. It descended with a loud whoosh! Knife–like leaves slashed the bare flesh of his back mercilessly, cutting deep.

Agony exploded through Paul's body. He cried out and struggled, but that only tightened the knots of his bonds.

"Brina says when the time's right, she'll let you know." Cindy's voice was impossibly level and clear. The impish face Paul loved had frozen in time and space, as if her will had decomposed, or turned to petrified wood.

The branch seemed to lift into the air, and Paul's body tensed for another piercing blow. But feather–like leaves caressed him from head to toe, circling his nipples, rubbing the tips first with the flat part, then the sharper edges, softly here, firmer where needed, reaching between his legs to stroke him slowly and patiently back to a state of arousal. His mind could not accept that, but against his will his body responded.

Suddenly the branch whipped across his flesh once more. Through the swells of agony and ecstasy, he heard Cindy whisper, "Oh, and Paul? Brina says to tell you not to worry. You'll be living here with us now. Your new fairy step–godmother will look after you too. Forever."

The Children of Gael

(co–authored with Benoit Bisson)

Patrick pulled his BMW into the small parking lot, tires spinning on the loose gravel before stopping. He stepped out and slammed the door, impatient, wishing he was anywhere else but here.

He walked briskly to the small ticket counter, paid the fare and boarded. On the dock, men released the moorings and the boat lurched forward. He glanced across the deck: tourists in sunhats and sunscreen and multi–colored summer clothing. Many surreptitiously stared at him; he knew his Armani suit was out of place, but he also suspected they were impressed by the quality.

The tour boat severed the chilly water into distinct worlds. Patrick looked starboard, towards the mouth of the St. Lawrence River, dotted with islands. Lovely properties, he thought. I'll bet I could buy them fairly cheaply, then sell them profitably through a New York affiliate to Americans looking for an affordable getaway.

The voice of the tour operator pulled him out of his thoughts. "The Irish traveled out of desperation, using anything from rag–tag sailboats to four–masters. Most were trying to escape the potato famine and hoping to find a new Emerald Isle. But life on board was a living hell: overcrowded ships, lack of food, rough seas, sickness. In the end for many, their quest drowned in disease and death."

As if to emphasize this, the boat veered to the left, aiming straight for Grosse île. Rough. Green. So ordinary–Canadian–looking. Hard to believe that this was the 'Gateway to the New World' of the last century. Of course, there was irony in that, since for thousands the New World turned out to be death.

Patrick remembered his father talking about how his great grandfather had come here in 1847 because of the famine, in the midst of a cholera epidemic, and had been one of the few smart enough to survive. "If they had not made the voyage," the guide said, "they would not have died."

And you wouldn't exist.

"What?" Patrick glanced around. Who had said that? There was no one close to him. A dark cloud passed over the sun, wiping color from the bright day. With it came a gust of cool air that sent a shiver down his spine, through his legs, his arms, his stomach. His body trembled, as if he'd fallen into the chilly waters. He glanced over the railing, feeling drawn by some invisible force. He stared into the darkness; the hypnotic pull of the waves. He thought he could see faces there, some grinning, some howling, some just staring back at him...

"*Nous arrivons*! Please watch your step."

Patrick shook himself, clearing his head of silliness. He had never liked crossing water. Boats made him seasick. And who hadn't envisioned drowning? Obviously, the unexpected wind had made a sound, which he had interpreted, but which was actually his own thought.

Impatient with himself, he strode toward the dock and leapt onto solid ground.

The boatload of tourists was met by a handful of park guards, ready to guide them to the high points of the island in both official languages. Patrick aligned himself with a smaller group. The young blonde bilingual guide chirped and bounced, managing to convey the facts without much emotion, which suited Patrick just fine. He hadn't come here for distortions of history or emotional renditions of the past.

Thinking about why he left Montréal three hours ago, on a business day, and drove to this island, his jaw tensed. It was just not like him to do such a thing. The death–bed promise to his demented father was ridiculous. The old man had lost his mind and become a raving lunatic. But despite knowing that, and in spite of the nagging voice that kept telling him that what he had sworn to do was idiotic and a complete waste of time, Patrick knew making pledges to the dead was one of those things that had to be carried out if the living were to have any peace.

And even though he hated to admit it, something else nagged at him as well: this sickness seemed to be hereditary. His father, grandfather and great grandfather had all died agonizing deaths, lost in insanity. Patrick was afraid he would end up the same way. And he was terrified that he would be as helpless and as out of control as he'd seen his father.

"And first," the guide named Francine said brightly, "I'd like to ask each of you what brings you to Grosse île."

Patrick listened to the reedy man from Nova Scotia ramble on about his ancestors, whom he didn't know, really, and how they seemed to have come from Ireland, although he wasn't exactly sure of that either.

Then there was a stuttering journalist from Winnipeg doing a travel guide on Canadian parks, then two short, round women with brush–cuts, one from Toronto and one from Montréal, traveling east toward the Gaspé Peninsula, who thought they'd take the island tour.

By the time the frumpy grandmother from Saskatchewan began to claim her astrologer had sent her, Patrick had tuned them out. To the left, he saw an enormous cross atop a hill, overlooking the water. To the right, more of the structures, dating from mid–nineteenth to early twentieth century. The wooden buildings scattered amidst the coarse pines and cedars reminded him of summer camp in the Gatineau Hills, which he had always hated. Looking over the various 'sights,' he found feelings of loneliness, desolation and abandonment settling around his shoulders. Nonsense, he thought as he checked his watch—the next boat out was loading now. The next one in wouldn't be for three more hours. He sighed in frustration.

"What about you?" the cheery Francine asked. He glanced up to see the others waiting for his response, and cringed inwardly. He was not about to divulge why he had come here; telling them who he was would just have to suffice.

"My great grandfather took his fortune and left Ireland. He was clever enough to jump ship before it docked here, or I suppose he would have died of cholera."

"Oh, that would be Patrick Lynch," the guide said brightly.

"No, it would not be."

Francine looked confused and intimidated, which suited him just fine. His lineage was nobody's business. "Oh," she finally managed, "you're not related to Patrick Lynch? He's the man who jumped ship at the height of the cholera epidemic and swam to the mainland, where a French family took him in. He married one of their daughters. I think his descendants still live in the area. Isn't he your great grandfather?"

She must be a college student at Laval University, as her t-shirt claimed, and couldn't have been more than fifteen years younger than him, but Patrick didn't believe he had ever been so stupid. And although the circumstances were similar—his grandfather had married a French Canadian woman—that's where it stopped. "My great grand-father was Patrick O'Mallory. I was named for him."

"Really?"

"Yes, really. I think I know my own ancestor."

That gave her pause, but only for a split second. She blinked, then continued on, as though Patrick hadn't said anything at all, especially in a crisp tone. "We'll start with the autoclaves."

They walked a wide dirt road, passing buildings that she called the "first class hotel" and the "second class hotel." Apparently, most of the Irish who came to this Canadian version of Ellis Island were poor and had stayed in barracks or tents, but some immigrants had been well-heeled enough to pay for decent lodging. If his great grandfather had actually had the misfortune to land on this pathetic island, he would have stayed at the first class hotel, of that Patrick was convinced. The long line of money built on property investments that had come into Patrick's hands had been acquired through business savvy, not luck. From County Cork to his plush offices on St. Jacques Street, his great granddad had been a sharp man, taking advantage of opportunities, as was his grandfather, and his father until the dementia set in, and now Patrick. And if he ever had a son, the boy would be just as sharp. Privilege was in the genes.

Francine pointed out the bakery, the telegraph building, and eventually they arrived at what appeared to be iron boxcars, used to disinfect clothing by employing high–pressure steam. They were huge, rusted remains, stored inside a type of dark warehouse, and reminded him of photographs he'd seen of concentration camps, for some reason.

When the others had had their fill of snapping photos of the train cars, the small group moved along. Patrick, though, hung back for a moment. He walked to the open end of one of the cars and peered inside.

You promised me! You promised me!

Instant sweat stuck his shirt to his back. He glanced around nervously. The words were clear, and the voice—was it a woman's voice?—the same as he'd heard on the boat. But how could that be? He was alone.

"Oh! There you are!" Francine sounded wary, as if he might jump down her throat. "We're just up the road." She didn't seem to notice him jolt as she spoke.

She turned, paused to wait for him, then began to move slowly forward. Perhaps the sheer volume of sickness, disease and germs that had been annihilated here made him uneasy. And it was a very hot day. He loosened his shirt collar a bit more and joined her, stepping out into the sunlight.

They proceeded on, the tour guide rattling off facts about the island. Back then, it seems, the land had been divided into three sections, the gated west wall where the immigrants were brought on arrival, the east wall where the cholera victims were taken, and the center of the island, for staff. Patrick saw it all, much more than he cared to. He needed to get to his destination but leaving the tour at this point would obviously not work, not with the ever–vigilant Francine on guard. Besides, the next boat off the island wouldn't arrive for another two hours, and he might as well get his money's worth.

The island tour lasted far too long. Patrick saw churches—a Protestant and a Catholic version; the carriage that had done triple duty as a taxi, ambulance and hearse; the school and the children's cemetery; and the main graveyard with its Arlington Cemetery–like white crosses, precisely aligned, uninscribed, symbolic of the bones beneath the surface where the disease victims were buried in mass graves. The land of the graveyard rolled and dipped in wave after wave, untouched since the early plows had turned the bodies under. As he stared at the earth, it seemed to pitch like waves on water, making him slightly dizzy. The heat is really getting to me, he thought as he undid another button of his shirt. He wished he'd brought along a hat, and some water, but what the hell. This would be over soon and he'd cool off in the BMW's air conditioning.

Finally, and just at the point where he was almost ready to forget about the reason he had come here, they climbed the hill to the 63–foot Celtic cross.

The dirt path was awkwardly narrow, and as they winded their way up, they met one of the other tours hurrying back down. Finally they were at the base of the stone monument, woods surrounding it on three sides, a sheer cliff to the rocky water below on the fourth, which Patrick kept well away from.

The cross was impressive, he had to admit, and while the guide chattered on about how the Ancient Order of Hiberians had erected this cross in 1909 in memory of those who had died here, Patrick busied himself reading two of the three inscriptions on the base.

In English, the dedication was in memory of the Irish who had been victims of cholera. Another side, in French, said virtually the same thing, although it also thanked local priests for their work. The third inscription was in Gaelic, which Patrick did not understand, but which he assumed to be similar to the other two.

"I'll lead you to the cafeteria to wait for the boat," the guide said, "or you can wander around and take pictures. But don't miss the boat! It's the last one of the day."

Finally! Patrick thought as the others drifted, by ones and twos, back down the hill. He was alone.

He stood in the shadow of the cross, staring out across the water at the mainland. Absently, he reached into his pants pocket. The metal touching his skin felt cool on this hot day, a rounded shape against his sweaty fingers. He pulled it out and stared at the locket nestled in his palm. Burnished gold, hanging on a gold chain—wealth did not always presume taste, but in his great grandfather's case, it had.

He turned over the piece of jewelry, then turned it back again, and sighed. His father had gone completely nuts at the end, just like his grandfather and probably his great grandfather too. "Patrick," he said, "you must promise me! Promise me you'll go to Grosse île. Take the locket. Take it! Bury it there, beneath the cross!" His father had pleaded and begged, exacting a promise from Patrick, ranting the entire time about Celtic demons, and breaking curses. In truth, the intensity of his father's fit had unnerved him, and that's why he'd given his word. Now, he thought himself foolish. He should have just given the locket away, or better yet, sold it—after all, it was 24 carat gold. That he should travel so far, for such an irrational reason—

"Sure and it's a lovely piece."

Patrick spun around. Behind him, between him and the cross, stood a woman, barely five feet tall. She was attractive enough, red hair against a pale face waving down to her shoulders, green eyes liquid and lively. Her Irish accent was thick, though, and he had some trouble understanding her.

"Yes it is," he said, closing his hand, slightly annoyed. He wanted to just bury the locket and get off this island. And now he had this woman to contend with. From her clothing, she wasn't a tourist but must be a park guard, dressed in period costume. "Are you part of some...historical event?" he asked, for lack of anything else to say.

"Oh indeed," she said. "That's why I'm here, you know." And then she said nothing, just folded her hands together prayer fashion and stared at him, a look of rapture on her face, which made him think she was strange. How was he going to get rid of her?

"Look, Miss, I'd like a few minutes alone here. My ancestor..." He left it open ended, hoping she would fill in the blank, making a connection that didn't exist, that he felt some sort of emotion about someone or other who had died on this island, and that she'd respect that and get the hell out of here.

"Have you opened the locket, then?" she asked.

"No." He said it before he could stop himself.

"Ah, but you should. Here, give it to me."

She reached out for it, but he pulled his hand away instinctively.

A look crossed her face that he felt was hostile in some way. But maybe he'd imagined it. After all, he didn't know this woman, and her moods.

As if to negate that, she smiled at him, and looked him directly in the eye. It was a suggestive look, and he began to reassess her. A quick glance at his watch told him that if he could bury the damn locket quickly, he might have time for a private tour—

"I've waited for so long," she said softly.

"For?"

"I think you know." She took a step towards him.

The hairs at the back of his neck bristled, but he knew he was being ridiculous. What was there to fear? A small woman, coming on to him. It didn't happen every day, and maybe that's why the situation made him nervous. Despite the nervousness, he felt himself physically responding to her.

"I'm Patrick," he said.

Her smile broadened. "Of course you are!"

"And you?"

A look of complete surprise passed over her face, which shifted first to a pained look, then—again—an angry one. Her voice sharpened. "Sheleagh. Sheleagh McGuire." She said it as if they'd met before, and he had disappointed her by not remembering.

Something about this woman was very odd. Patrick decided that he could forego whatever pleasure might have been had with her.

But just when he thought that, she moved very close to him. The sunlight on her crimson strands mesmerized him for a moment, as if her hair was on fire. Those green eyes became mossy pools, soft, vulnerable, deep...Before he realized it, she was standing on her toes, pulling his head down so that his lips could press against hers.

The kiss pulled him in, sweeping aside all thoughts, overwhelming him with sensation, and awareness: of her, of him, of being enclosed together here, in the warmth of the day. He heard water below them. Time felt eternal—the kiss could go on forever...

In the distance, he heard a boat horn and a small voice in the back of his mind whispered he should pay heed, but he no longer possessed the desire to do so. And then he felt sharp coolness against his fingers, pressing in between them, like small icicles, wedging, trying to pry open the hand that held the locket.

He pulled back, barely able to break his mouth away from hers. Only then was he aware that he was short of breath, as if she had drawn all the air from his lungs.

Those eyes! Everchanging...hard jade one second, soft spring moss the next. As he gasped in air, he became aware of a smell. Soil freshly plowed. As when something that has been buried for a long time is brought to the surface!

Patrick shoved her away from him. She crashed back against the cross. He ran down the hill, tripping over fallen branches and rocks until he fell, then stumbling to his feet. Once he reached flat ground, he headed full steam to the dock. It was empty. The last tour boat of the day was halfway across the water, headed for the mainland. He had been left behind!

Patrick yelled and waved frantically, but they were obviously too far away to see him. A quick glance told him there were no rowboats or canoes tied to the shore. Panic set in. Surely he couldn't be alone on this island! They must have staff that stayed overnight! And telephones!

He turned and ran toward the buildings, the first and second class hotels, the bakery, pounding on locked doors, on windows, staring inside at rooms devoid of furniture, yelling, his voice growing louder as the panic deepened. How could they be empty? How could he be alone?

He raced along the path, hoping to encounter someone, anyone, and came to an abrupt halt at the graveyard. Now, in the twilight, the wavy soil appeared to be moving. It couldn't be an illusion from the heat: the sun was setting! One of the crosses piercing the earth began to push up out of the ground.

Patrick shook his head and rubbed his eyes. No! This couldn't be happening! Yet the wooden cross popped out of the ground and toppled. And what was coming from the hole it had left behind he did not want to see!

Instinctively, he took to high ground, and only knew he was back at the stone cross when he saw her, still there, as if waiting for him.

"I knew you'd come back," she said, opening her arms.

Terrified, he grabbed up a rock as a weapon. "Who are you?" he demanded. "What's going on?"

"Ah, but Patrick my love, you promised me."

The voice was the same he'd heard on the ship, and at the autoclaves. Some of the same words, said in the same way. He was sure of it now. But how could that be?

She reached out her hand. "You've what's mine, you know. And you swore to bring it back when you came for me."

"What are you talking about?" But even as he answered, Patrick knew she wanted the locket.

From below, down the hill, he heard sounds, like a thousand voices whispering. He glanced around. The forest on three sides, too dense; the cliff, plunging into the dark water below...

"Are you saying this is yours?" he said, holding up the locket.

"Why, Patrick, I gave it to you, don't you recall? When you left me on the boat, with the others. Left me to come down with the cholera. When you took my life's savings, and those of the others, and the deeds to our homeland, and swore to return one day with the profits you'd make. When you promised you would love me for all eternity, and come back for me. Don't you remember?"

She was insane! Or he was. Not that it mattered now. The whisperings had grown more intense. And closer. Animals moving through the grass and trees and bushes, scrambling, climbing the hill.

"Give it to me," she coaxed.

For some reason, he felt it was crucial that he hold onto the locket, and yet keeping it might spell his doom. Quickly, he snapped the latch, and the spring mechanism opened the jewelry. Inside were a dozen short strands of fiery hair. Hair the color of this Sheleagh's. And beneath that, an inscription: *"Ar ngradh is ar gcinniuint i gcomhar againn go deo deo!"*

"It means 'Sharing forever, our love and fate'. A blessing, or a curse. But you understand that, don't you Patrick?"

It was all clear to him now. His great grandfather had made a promise to this woman, to come back for her. He had avowed love and, as a token, she had given him the locket, with her hair inside.

And because the first Patrick O'Mallory had not fulfilled his promise, Patrick was standing here now—the last of his line?—facing what? The ghost of Sheleagh McGuire? A jilted lover, who had died of cholera? It sounded impossible to him. Utterly impossible! But what explanation could there be for the fact that he was seeing her, talking with her, believing her, just as she believed him to be his own great grandfather. Had the madness finally passed on to him? Was he as doomed as all the males in his family had been? Curses and spells didn't really exist! They were just things you made up when you were a child! No, she couldn't be a witch.

Now the whispering and shuffling were accompanied by other sounds: heavy breathing, wheezing, gasping. Sounds that were closer, much closer, crowding the top of the hill.

"If I give you back the locket, will you free me from the curse?"

Sheleagh stared at him for a long moment while his body trembled. He expected the worst: she'd want to get even, to exact from him the commitment made—broken—by his great grandfather. She would either kill him, or curse him with the same insanity.

Patrick felt immense relief wash over him when she said, "If you return that which belongs not to you, I'll release you from my love."

The light had dimmed and the darkness made him see things. The woods were alive with eyes. With flesh. And with a terrible odor that stabbed at his senses. He did not know whether or not to believe her, but there was no choice now.

"Here! Take it back!" he said, shoving the locket at her.

Sheleagh reached out for it. The moment the metal touched her hand, her face altered; deep sadness overwhelmed her features. The sounds in the woods stopped, as if a switch had been thrown.

Patrick stood quivering in the silence, hardly daring to believe that it was over. That he was free.

Sheleagh pressed the locket to her heart. In the darkness he saw now that she was not flesh and blood, but something ethereal, ephemeral, with no substance. He began to relax.

"Patrick O'Mallory," she said, her voice laced with sorrow, "I release you from our love." He breathed a sigh of relief; he was going to get out of this nightmare!

She turned from him and looked at the Gaelic inscribed into the enormous cross. "You know, Pat, though your heart and mind left me behind, you still should have remembered. You should have heeded these words in our mother tongue. They speak to your blood. They speak of our fate: 'Thousands of the children of the Gael were lost on this island while fleeing tyrannical landlords and the artificial famine they caused. God bless them. God save Ireland! And God bring them home.'"

She glanced back. "I can forgive you, Patrick, and release you. But they cannot."

From all around him, corpses emerged from the woods, their bodies torn, decayed. Was it possible that he recognized these skeletons? As if he had known these people when they were living? As if his great grandfather dwelled within him? As if the roots of every cent of his wealth could be traced to each one of them?

Terror permeated his body. He backed up towards the cliff. True to her word, Sheleagh made no move to stop him, or to intervene. But the others. The others! They were coming. Skeletal hands like claws, eye sockets devoid of compassion, jawbones grinding in fury.

At the edge of the cliff, Patrick's foot slipped, but he barely made the effort to catch himself. With gut wrenching certainty, he knew that the end was at hand, at their hands. The children of Gael would bring one of the lost ones home.

Killers

1 Animal Rites

Lauren stopped short as a dozen protesters swarmed the sidewalk in front of her. Motley, she thought—a cross between rebellious teenagers too young to know anything about the real world, and the retro–hip whining about one last cause before slouching towards geriatric–land.

"Hey, Lady!" A man about her age, mid–forties, leaped out of the crowd and stabbed a finger into the collar of her full–length silver fox coat. "Animals were *slaughtered* so you could wear that!" His mangy beard and pointed, quivering nose reminded her of a rodent. A lapel button read: STOP RAPING NATURE! The placard braced against his scrawny shoulder showed a crudely–drawn tree with the head of a man budding from one branch and the pointed snout of a fox emerging from another.

Lauren gathered the collar of the sensuous fur close to her face. *He's probably a meat eater,* she thought. *And that cheap–looking fat woman behind him—her boots are leather, that's certain, even if they are of poor quality. Besides,* she assured herself, *animals are dumb. They don't feel pain the way we do. They're bred for their skins, except for the wild ones, but trappers are always working on more humane traps.*

Lauren pulled the coat tighter and straightened her posture. *These people,* she thought, *have blown their synapses. It's survival of the fittest. Cream rises.* She concluded that they must be jealous. Of her. Of her coat. Well, she had her rights too.

She could have given these baboons an earful but Lauren was well–bred, and definitely too refined to be lured into tawdry public eruptions. She cut her way through the crowd then hurried away.

Just as she reached the corner, the scruffy man yelled, "That coat looked better on the original owner!"

Startled, Lauren lost her footing. Her ankle twisted off the curb and she stumbled. She turned in time to see the SPCA truck barreling down on her.

When Lauren came to, she was alone, lying in the street near the curb. There were no pedestrians in view, and even those awful protesters were gone. Around her, cars sat immobile in their parking spaces.

She felt dizzy but managed to stand. Nothing broken. Or bruised. No major damage to the coat.

She stepped onto the pavement and moved to the closest store to brace herself against the wall for a moment. When her head cleared further, she noticed the pet store was dark inside, and on the door hung a CLOSED sign. Every shop on the street was the same. What could have happened? Her watch told her it was after six PM, but still, there should have been *some* people around. *A natural disaster!* she thought.

Don't be silly, she chided herself. *There's always a rational explanation.*

Lauren decided to continue on to her dermatologist. His office was only a block away and she arrived within a minute. Not surprisingly, she found the door locked. No traffic meant no taxis. There was nothing to do but keep going until she came to a normal street, then she'd discover what was going on.

She walked through the growing twilight, heels tapping concrete the only sound. At first. Soon she heard vague noises. Until she paused. Then, nothing.

Eventually, the streets narrowed into canyons and looked unfamiliar. She glanced at a street sign—KARMIC ROAD. Lauren did not recall having been here before.

She kept walking because she couldn't think of anything else to do. The buildings began to remind her of concrete caves, the cars of metallic beetles. And underlying this alien landscape was the noise. A weird, low squeaking, as if hundreds of mice were being crushed in mousetraps at the same moment.

Suddenly, the squeaking intensified. She ran into the intersection, hoping that being out in the open meant safety.

Something sharp bit into her right ankle. At the same moment, she was jerked backwards off her feet, and screamed.

Lauren shoved her fur from her face and saw an inverted world. She had been caught in some kind of trap and hoisted off the ground. As she spun wildly upside down, the metal teeth continued to gnaw past flesh and chew bone.

She cried out, but no help came. As the sky darkened and powerful shadows overwhelmed the weak yellow street lights, someone did come. Or, some *things*.

They must have been stalking her all along. Hidden in crevices, down alleys between buildings, in garbage cans, under cars—now they scurried into the open and swarmed around her. Blood raced to Lauren's brain, blurring her vision, and at first she was not sure what she was seeing. Their features seemed grotesquely feral. Hair matted. Nails sharp, jagged claws. Soiled rags clung to flesh like skin. The air grew gamey, and she cringed.

"Cut 'er," a familiar voice said. Within seconds she lay curled at the feet of the repulsive protester.

Thank God, she thought, *at least he's human.* But before she could open her mouth, the seedy man ordered, "The fur!"

The bizarre thought came to her: *I was right! They wanted my fur all along.* Well, she wasn't insane. Outnumbered, alone, she was at a disadvantage. They could have it. Besides, the fox was insured.

Two of the creatures tore the fur from her body. She watched, startled and horrified, as they sniffed at it with disgust, then tossed it into the filthy gutter.

"Clothes!" the man said.

They stripped her naked.

"Look, have the coat! And my wallet. There's money. But don—" Shock quivered through her. The pleas spewing from her lips were like the cries of an animal, unintelligible.

The rat–like man extracted a crude bone–handled knife from a leather sheath. He stopped, ran a finger appreciatively along her shoulder, nodded approvingly, then grabbed her chin and held it steady. Precision steel pierced her jaw. The blade moved down, cutting her lengthwise, from throat to crotch, so quickly and expertly that, at first, she felt no pain.

But as the skinning intensified and skin separated from muscle and fascia, Lauren found no comfort in the fact that these hunters recognized her as a descendent of quality stock. She howled anyway, just like a dumb animal.

Base of a Triangle

You scan the empty subway platform, uneasy. A glance at your watch, then at the digital time overhead reveals the late hour. The trains do not run often this time of night. I can see you wondering why a man like yourself is standing here now when you could have been home earlier, safe in your bed. Wondering why do you do this so frequently. Why you feel so disconnected.

Your hands jam deep into your raincoat pockets. You jerk your head to the right and stare down the track into the black oblivion of the tunnel. In my direction. This sudden movement causes your body to weave. You do not see what you hope to and, as you turn away, I hear a prayer mumbled, *Please let the train arrive soon.*

I suspected you would come here again at night, alone. You're my age now, although I have been here five years already. It's nice to have company. I get lonely. It's as if I am one third of a triangle and cannot exist on my own. You must know how that feels.

I balance on one of the rails and lean into the platform—I can feel neither surface—and stare up at you. Because you're drunk, your perceptions are heightened but blurred, and your intuition soars; you look down, squinting, almost as if you can see me. I know, though, that you cannot. Few see beyond the concrete to the intangible, but many sense this nebulous realm. I am like a negative image, white on black, your opposite. All that is solid about you is ethereal in me. I emit no female scents. I can no longer be touched or caressed. And yet we are separated by only a crease in time.

You experience a mild air current pass over you as I edge along the track, closer; for a split second you imagine the train might be coming after all.

I see you often, you know. Here, during other hours, requisite brown briefcase in hand, reading a newspaper, your harried face mingled with thousands of other harried faces, looking hungry, not prepared to confront your fate. During the day you are gregarious and it feels abnormal to you now being here by yourself, except for the memories that have a life all their own. You glance around the long platform again, peering at the dark corners, trying to see through pillars, wrinkling your nose at an offensive odor, afraid you are not as alone as you believe.

All at once you sense me. The hairs on the back of your neck prickle. Fear makes your movements frenetic. You stagger past the newspaper box but the lurid headline—a fatal accident—cannot catch your eye. It is the tracks that draw you; as you near the platform's edge, caution becomes automatic. You wobble a foot from the rim, examining the cold steel in the pit below, and the dangerous third rail. You find the bleakness of the metal strangely uplifting. My dark world of base metals is so foreign to your own. There are no plastic cases here, pregnant with the latest micro–chips, already obsolete. All ties are finite connections, like a family with a long ancestry and the certainty of progeny. For a moment you long to meld the iron in your blood with the iron rails and become immortal. I cannot be replaced by the latest model.

Your ambivalence is touching. I know you so well I can almost empathize. You feel my struggle for emotional life ride the air and imbed itself into your lungs like a dense wet fog. Your eyes flash the horror you experience: I am a disease, digging in, becoming part of you as you will forever be a part of me. Panic claims you. You cannot breathe. You gasp for air.

In the distance, train wheels grind against the metal tracks. Their shriek causes you to reel back slightly from the platform's edge. Your hand claws at your throat. Your body, off kilter, threatens to catapult into my waiting arms.

I know what it is like to pitch forward, alone, crashing onto the icy steel rails only to be crushed and severed beneath the sharp wheels of an oncoming train, flesh singed beyond recognition when a hand touches the high voltage rail. I know the screech of metal against metal and bone. Human screams multiply. Faces blur. Warmth seeps from the flesh. Lack of oxygen strangles the fetus within, so dependent. And all the while aware that the clumsiness of a drunken stranger tore me from the living. Yes, I know this and more. That's why when you fall into my arms I will catch you. Believe me.

The powerful train barrels towards the station, too fast. You clutch your coat collar tight to your throat. Your muscles tense. Sweat streaks your forehead and trickles down your temples to your flushed cheeks. Tears gush from your wounded eyes.

You stare at me, pleading for forgiveness. I beckon you to join me, but you must hurry. You shake your head and at the same time lurch forward like a walking corpse.

The train whistle blasts a warning. The air rumbles. The concrete beneath your feet vibrates, or are you trembling? I grasp your ankle, forcing your foot to the edge again. You open your mouth to scream, but the sound is crushed by the whistle's extended shriek.

Only seconds remain. Take the step. Join me. Forever.

You teeter on the edge.

Leap into my world!

Now!

Wheels screech, but the brakes cannot quickly halt so many tons of steel. A pale face presses against the conductor's window of the lead car. The expression is haunted, fast frozen in déjà vu.

Metal passes through me. Devoid of a physical body, I cannot feel it, yet the lingering memory reminds me of the night our triangle formed, when, in an eternal moment, we three connected.

I examine your distorted features as you stumble onto the train. The doors slam closed. The conductor is rattled but manages to throw the correct switch and the train moves forward like a silver entity, at home in the bleak tunnels. Soon it abandons the station as you have both abandoned me.

It is always quiet here after the last train passes. I fall back onto the tracks, onto a familiar spot, although I cannot rest here, or anywhere. I know you will return to this station again and again at this time, because you must. For the same reason, the conductor drives through here nightly, always at this hour. I will wait for you. For both of you. I know some day you will join me.

I will make sure of that.

Creature Comforts

Only a year ago, plenty of club kids were calling the band Monster a bunch of British clones, cheap imitations of Nine Inch Nails. Until Monster flew the big ocean. Candy, though, had never seen them that way. She always knew Monster was brilliant, and Creature, their main man, a rock icon.

Tonight, from Dead Zone's small stage, the four band–boys pounded out heavy bass and garbled archaic lyrics from their latest CD. The sound that crunched through the amps and throbbed from the stack of oversized speakers said Monster was definitely headed for big time. Candy wasn't really listening, although her foot tapped automatically to all music. She was watching. Especially the lead.

Creature. Taller than tall. Lean. In his twenties. Long black hair, ear cuffs, trade–mark small–calibre bullet piercing his left ear lobe. Pasty skin, dead black lipstick, sexy eye makeup. Pale, wet–ice eyes that sliced right through you like chilled blades. Or at least that's how Candy felt whenever he glanced her way.

Fran leaned close, breathing hot, moist air into Candy's ear, and screamed above the music, "He's dangerously cooooool!"

Candy nodded, barely glancing at her friend. She couldn't take her eyes off Creature. She loved his scars.

This close to the stage she could see every one. They streaked his forehead, jaw and cheeks like red sutures, wounds from a battle. Tonight he wore black snake–skin pants, tight as flesh, matching kick–ass boots, and an open chain–mail vest. Signature black–skull bandanna wrapped around his head. Under the strobe, criss–crossing red marks flashed over most of his exposed body.

Something about those warrior stripes turned her on. She wondered what it would be like to run the tip of her tongue slowly over them, up the pink mountains, and down into the redder valleys. Would the skin be hard and smooth like a regular scar? Would they open and bleed? They looked so fresh, it was like he'd had surgery yesterday— but the doctor wasn't too good with a needle and thread.

She'd followed the band for a year, since they'd arrived from London, through underground clubs, never missing a gig. And now that they had a home club, she was here every night. Those scars had been the first thing she'd noticed about Creature. And from that moment, she'd been hooked.

Monster cranked it for the last song. At the end, the drummer slammed the cymbals and snares mercilessly, while his foot stomped the bass pedal to death. Creature and the two other axe players ran riffs that broke the sound barrier for sheer volume and speed. She was so close to the speakers, the low notes throbbed through her body, and the blast of sound ruffled her hair.

They had never played so well. The room exploded. Candy's eardrums vibrated, driving her to her feet, screaming and shoving with the rest. Man, if only she wasn't so shy, she could meet him. Those scars made her sweat sex!

But a dozen groupies clung to the band like mold. Even before Creature jumped down from the stage, adoring hands of both genders grabbed his legs, fondled his crotch. Reached for his scars.

Taped music replaced live.

"You have got to do it, and I mean now!" Fran yelled.

Candy sighed. Fran was right, but that didn't make it easy. Ground zero, nowhere to backstep to. If she didn't go in there and meet him now, she'd be crawling after him forever. And it didn't take a demon–brain to figure out that the competition was fierce.

She jammed her bag onto the seat, opened it, and pulled out a couple of things. "Watch me," she told Fran, then turned her back. The mosh–pit at the foot of the stage was packed with drinkers and dancers and she pushed between sweat–streaked bodies towards the corridor that led to the dressing rooms.

She hurried down a dead–black hallway, another strobe flashing, stills from *Night of the Living Dead* glued to the walls. The taped music behind her became muted. The floor sloped downward. She felt hot; her black velvet dress buttoned from the throat to the ankles.

Before she saw them, she heard them: the groupies clustered outside the dressing rooms, stage hands moving equipment, security controlling it all. She'd been back here once before, but lost her nerve. This time, she headed right for the door she'd avoided last time.

"Brake, babe! Nobody drives into the Lab." In front of her loomed a big guy with tattooed biceps, things with wings that flapped when his muscles flexed. His bulk blocked a door with a clean star mark in the center where that symbol had been ripped off. Over it, in blood red, 'The Laboratory' had been scrawled.

Man, what could she say? She wanted Creature's autograph? Lame. How the hell could she get past this guy? But being this close made her brave. Stick to the plan, she told herself. "I'm, like, here to interview Creature." She held up the notebook and pencil she'd brought along and waved them in his face. Stupid. Really stupid. He wouldn't fall for it.

"Right. And I'm here to fuck Madonna. Got any ID?"

She handed over the fake press pass Fran had created at the copy shop where she worked. Above her name, and next to the photo, it identified her as a writer with *Chaos*, one of the local entertainment mags.

"Creature don't do interviews. He don't talk to people."

"He'll talk to me," she said boldly. "Tell him I'm here."

He flicked the pass with his finger and gave her a hostile once-over. "Stay, baby sister." He rapped his knuckles on the door three times, then slipped inside.

What am I doing? Candy asked herself. *Now's the time to run, before he gets back and bars me from the club.* But she couldn't move, or maybe didn't want to. She might not get to meet Creature, but she just had to try.

The muscle came back without her press pass. She expected the worst and was boggled when he said, "Yeah, okay." He stepped aside and held the door open about an inch.

This guy's dumb, she thought, relieved. It made her braver. A little, anyway.

Heart jack-hammering, she pushed the door open. It was like staring into night space. The room stank of wet rot. The air felt dry electric. She touched the brass knob and got a shock.

In seconds her eyes adjusted. Two black candles had been wedged between the wall and the makeup mirror like torches. Ahead, shuffling in his seat, a dim shape. Remember, nowhere to step back to, she reminded herself. Candy picked up her Doc Martens and moved into the dressing room.

Silence pierced as bad as the music that had so recently punched her eardrums.

"Sit." A raspy voice. No mistaking it. Creature.

Nervous, excited, she looked around. It was hard to see. A kind of cot in the corner, and the chair he sat on. She perched on the edge of the hard cot, facing him. She'd never been this close to Creature. He sat at the makeup table with the candles behind him, the back of his head reflected in the glass, his face in shadow. Even sitting, he was bigger than she'd realized.

"I, uh…" she began, afraid to keep up the lie, but too scared to rely on the truth. "I know you don't do many interviews, but…You guys are great. You're great."

A kind of wheeze came out of him. He held up the press pass. "You are Elizabeth." His English accent was sexy.

"Candy." That sounded inane. "I mean, my real name's Elizabeth. Everybody calls me Candy."

Another sound. Maybe the word *appropriate?*

More nervous than ever, she fumbled with the pencil and notebook she'd brought with her, trying to look official, hoping to hell he wouldn't ask about the magazine she supposedly wrote for.

She tried to cover it by taking the initiative. "So, how long have you played music?"

"I began with the flute. Nearly two centuries ago."

"Right!" Candy giggled, but she was the only one laughing, so she stopped. "So, you're like, the real Frankenstein or something?" She'd heard this, the rumor in the clubs. What he'd said on MTV recently. His first interview. Great promo.

"No!"

The volume of his voice sliced down her backbone as if it were a scalpel cutting her open. Instinctively, she jumped to her feet.

"Sit. Elizabeth, please." His voice had dimmed to that fine rasp she found so appealing.

She sat, but glanced at the door.

"Victor Frankenstein was the man. I am his creation. Do you not recall his confession, as relayed to Robert Walton and recorded by Mary Shelley?"

What the hell was he talking about? "You mean the book? Frankenstein?"

Another snort.

"Well, we read it in school," she said hesitantly. Half true. The class read it. She'd skimmed the abridged version. "I saw the movie," she said hopefully.

"He created me, and yet his account was a lie! I am not driven by malice! Oh, of one thing, yes, he quoted me true. Immortal though it has been my misfortune to be, am I not as sensitive as any human being? Do I not feel cold and heat, pain and pleasure? Does not the sun blind my eyes, and the darkness of night stir fear in my heart? Am I not like you, beautiful Elizabeth?"

Wow! Was Creature coming on to her? She couldn't believe her luck. Alone in his dressing room, with the sexiest guy in the world! Fran will die, she thought.

His pause made her remember why she was supposed to be here. She jotted down the last thing he'd said, about her being beautiful. She looked up. "So, uh, what's the real story?"

Creature stood. She was startled by his height. On stage he was enormous, but here, two feet away, he was a giant. He must be eight feet tall! His head skimmed the ceiling as he paced, his hands scraped his knees, although his body seemed to be in proportion. He moved in that lanky, jerky way of his, as though his joints ached, or his legs had been badly broken. The candle glow created shadows in the valleys of the scars that lined his face, chest and arms. Her mother caught Creature on that tv interview and labeled him ugly, but Candy saw the beauty of being wounded.

"He did it for her," he finally said.

"Her? Who?"

He paused to look down at Candy, candlelight making his black hair shimmer, and the stitch marks on his face resemble war paint. He was so big! It was as though a warrior god peered down at her. "Elizabeth, of course. He made me for Elizabeth."

She wasn't sure what he was getting at. Then it clicked. He was like these guys who talk as if they're Lestat. Creature was trying to tell her about himself, and "Frankenstein" worked for him. It was a symbol. Of course. All the lyrics of all of Monster's songs had to do with being treated like a non-human. An outsider. They talked about being misunderstood and rejected.

Desperately she tried to remember details from the book. Even the different versions of the movie were vague. She couldn't recall anybody named Elizabeth. There was that other film, where the doctor made a female creature, with that great lightning bolt streaking up the sides of her hair. Maybe she was Elizabeth. Maybe not. Candy decided she'd better keep her mouth shut as much as possible.

"Say some more about it, okay?"

He had resumed pacing the small room, his steps heavy on the raw wood floor. His arms swung in a strange way, but it just made him more attractive to her eyes. He was different, not one of those pathetic clones on tv, pretty boys who spend all day flossing. Creature was flesh and blood. Human.

"He claimed to love her. Yet, can a man truly love a woman he cannot satisfy?" he said. "You see, Victor was impotent. The crude anatomical examinations of the day produced no physical cause. I would expect a diagnosis today would be the same. His problems lay in the realm of the mind. As you might put it, Victor Frankenstein felt inadequate. Inferior. Perhaps he feared women, or even despised them. Perhaps he despised all of humanity. In any event, he built a creature, me, one who would be what he was not."

"So, he wanted you to, like, be his stand-in with his girlfriend?"

"More. The lover of his soon-to-be bride."

Bits of the story of "Frankenstein" were catching up to her, but not enough that she could piece all this together. She started jotting down a few sentences, but then realized he wasn't really paying attention, so what was the point. She lay the notebook and pencil on the cot. "Look, that's crazy. I mean, she'd have to be crazy not to know it was somebody else in bed with her, right?"

Creature stopped. With one step he was at the cot, sitting next to her. His towering body was cool. Charged. He took her hand and Candy's heart thumped so hard she almost fainted. His nails were long and black, his scarred hand so large it engulfed hers. He was not just big, but strong. He made her feel protected. She looked into his moist eyes, taking in the gashes surrounding them, and breathed in intimacy.

"You so resemble her. More than in name. The same innocent blonde hair and blue eyes. The identical soft demeanor." His finger touched her cheek. A shock ran through her skin, all the way to her crotch. Suddenly, in the candlelight, a glint flashed through his eyes which she interpreted as torment. The moment she felt pity for him, he dropped his head and stared down at the floor.

Her heart reached out to him. She rubbed her palm over the chain mail vest covering his back. "Look, sometimes it helps to get it all out. I mean, this guy, Victor, he sounds like major corruption material. He used you. He was no friend."

Creature turned to her. His black lips twitched, as if they were struggling to smile but just couldn't cut it. "You are understanding, as was my Elizabeth. If only I had not loved her…"

Candy didn't like hearing about this old girlfriend, but maybe if he talked about it, he'd get over her. "So, how did she find out she was screwing the wrong guy?"

"On her wedding night. I am, as you have surely noticed, large even for this day. Then I was as another species, although my entire body is in proportion. Even in the darkness of the boudoir, she could not fail to detect a difference between the man with whom she had made her vows that morning, and the one who possessed her body and soul that warm Victorian night. And yet she was too sweet, too gentle to voice her concerns."

She didn't really want to hear the details of their sex life.

"Well, you must look different, too, right?"

"Alas, but no. Victor, as with all architects of abominations, had fashioned his creation in his own image. In my case, in every respect but stature. And, of course, these remnants of his inept hand."

Candy stared at the large scar running the length of his cheek. She wanted so much to touch it. To kiss it. To run her tongue along the red groove. Embarrassed, she looked away and said, "Wow! So she really didn't know for sure you weren't Victor until you two made it. 'Cause you were in the dark and all. Man, that's truly weird."

"Indeed."

"So what happened when she found out you weren't him?"

"At the moment our love was consummated, Elizabeth screamed. Frankenstein abandoned his voyeuristic pursuits and came upon us in a fit of jealous rage."

"He attacked you?"

"With all his might. In my haste to protect myself from his fatal blows, I fear that in the darkness and confusion the unthinkable occurred. Elizabeth was dead."

The silence was like dead air. Finally, Candy asked, "How?"

He raised his hands to his face and sobbed. Candy jumped to her feet. She stood before him, her legs straddling his, cradling him to her breasts. He didn't have to go on. She remembered now, everything. How Elizabeth had been murdered on her wedding night. And the book said Creature strangled her! And it was really that sick bastard Frankenstein! Something just like that story had happened to Creature and he'd been suffering all alone ever since. Not only was his girlfriend dead, but he was blamed. And he was innocent! Maybe that's why the band moved to North America! He must be so lonely.

While he sobbed, while she held him, stroking the flaky skin down the back of his neck, his arms circled her hips and he clung to her as if she were a life raft. He cried "Elizabeth!" over and over, pulling Candy down onto his lap, and she hugged him tighter.

Candy felt her body locked in his firm grip, as if he could not get enough of her. As if he would never let her go. He needed her. She could be his new Elizabeth, the one who wouldn't die on him.

His hands slid up under her velvet skirt while hers automatically slipped down inside the chain mail vest and found the scars on his back, on his arms, his chest. The hot gouges in his skin seemed to pump and throb beneath her fingers, calling for her to cool and comfort them. To offer them release. Her flesh fit the wounds as though she had been made to heal him.

She traced the scars that lined his forehead, his cheeks, sliding into the connecting grooves, links in his flesh that now joined the two of them together. Their lips met.

As he entered her, she felt pain and tried to shift into a new position to ease it. "You're hurting me. Let up, huh?"

He gripped her tighter. Her hands tried to pry his from her waist. She shoved at his chest, and struggled to twist out of his embrace, but Creature was too strong, his need too great. She yelled as her fists pounded his shoulders. The pain became excruciating, but he had locked onto her as if they were chained together.

All the while his face hovered before her own, so large, so forlornly sexy, so hopelessly scarred. She reached out a quivering finger to stroke the gash running up his cheek, searching for connection. But if she reached him, it was not in the way she intended; he jammed her body down onto his. Sharp, like a knife blade inside. He seemed to cut her in two. Candy screamed. Lightning exploded in her head.

One of his massive hands crawled up her body and encircled her throat in a stifling caress. She clawed at the steely grip, but it only made him squeeze harder. All the while tears seeped from his pale eyes. The scars in his cheeks and forehead rippled, and his face contorted. His black lips twisted; she did not want to believe he was smiling.

Candy gasped for air. For some reason it was important for her to choke out one final word. Saying it made it real.

"Monster!" But it wasn't the band she had in mind.

Horrorscope

Last Friday, Jerry had polished off the arms for lunch and roasted the rump for dinner. That left only the sweet liver; he'd saved the best for last. Sauteed with prunes in butter, he devoured it for breakfast Saturday. Saturn's day it didn't matter how much he ate. The dark planet, negative as opposed to positive, ruled his sun sign Scorpio, which ruled death, power, and sex. He could consume anything. It would all end up transformed anyway.

Jerry sat in his favorite chair beside the tank of scorpions. While gnawing at a humerus, he thumbed through the astrological alignment tables in the ephemeris. Fast–moving Mercury trined sultry Venus and angry Mars, same as when he was born. He could blow hot or cold. Love or hate. Female or male. And quickly. Of course, with Venus on the cusp between Aries and Taurus in his third house of relationships, he wouldn't be surprised if he met a lusty and unpredictable fire sign. That would be interesting. Especially a female. He hadn't savored fem flesh for over a month.

At seven AM the paperkid braked his mountain bike on the sidewalk and pitched *The Toronto Star* onto the porch. Jerry stood in the shade and turned to the horoscopes. He folded the paper back so it was manageable and ran a finger down the column of signs to Scorpio. "Excellent day to begin a diet. Don't be greedy. Restraint brings permanent changes."

Jerry made a kind of grumpy grunt and mumbled, "A cannibal on a diet! Restraint. *Right! Who the hell's this Lodestar who writes this crap,* he wondered, not for the first time. Obviously no astro pro. Misinfo gives the science a bad name. Why can't the dingbat line it up straight?

His sun and moon had been caught in Scorpio the day he was born, and boy, was he ever ruled by his dick. Even without the rest of his chart, any fool could tell that today's lineup meant it was a good time for arachnids to party.

He crushed the entire newspaper and chucked it into the trash can beside the driveway. He'd suffered one too many lame forecasts from *The Star*. He'd better have a chat with this Lodestar babe.

Downtown at One Yonge Street, The Toronto Star Building, a bag of bones stopped him cold. The newsroom's anorexically flashy receptionist with baby orbs and hungry lips folded her arms protectively across her ribs, tossed back her mane and said again, "Lodestar don't see her readers."

Jerry thought of turning on the charm but it would be wasted on this lean Leo. She wanted the spotlight all to herself. Instead he said, "I'll leave her a message."

"No prob."

Bright eyes passed a ballpoint and an inner office memo pad and Jerry wrote a terse, "Harvey's at five fifteen. Yonge and the Lakeshore. N.E. window. Red tie." He signed it, "An arthropod admirer," wrote "Lodestar" on the outside before sealing it with tape from the receptionist's dispenser.

"See she gets this *tout de suite*," he said, handing it over. "That's French for 'have a nice day while you still can.'"

He shelled out for the new Sidney Omarr paperback and stationed himself in the restaurant.

The newspaper building had been emptying for a while but even though it was a Saturday, by five the crowds thickened. He sat in the darkest corner; he could see everybody outside but the book made it look like he was reading. Plenty of females passed, mostly air signs. Few noticed anything below the second floor. Only one searched the northeast corner.

Surreptitiously he watched her root herself to the pavement, check out his tie then his face and, when recognition didn't dawn, move on. Jerry got up immediately and followed.

She crossed to the bus, and he was on her heels, which were high. Firm calves, a little thick. Sensible brown dress. Juicy ass that swayed a bit. Long blazing hair bounced as she ambled down the steps. She was big and he felt dwarfed by her.

They disembarked at Front and she boarded the subway, the northbound train, and he was right behind. She sat facing forward and he stood well away. She pulled papers out of her calf–skin briefcase. Probably her column for tomorrow, he thought. No wonder she gets it wrong. Lazy cow—it's all out of her head.

The train was packed. He felt claustrophobic and wished he could crawl under a seat, but being underground helped. At the last minute she jumped to her feet at Eglinton and ran out the door. He slid between the closing doors just as the chimes sounded before the rubber had a chance to slam together and crush him.

She was plump enough to be slow, which suited him, but it took too long to travel the six blocks to her highrise. Through the glass in the front door he watched her take the elevator. An old lady with a face like a goat admitted him to the building. He was just in time to watch the light on the master panel stop on six, then descend.

On six there were eight doors. He paced the corridor. A door at the end of the hallway with a brass stylized bull's head knocker made him smile. She was a Taurus, not the fire sign he'd imagined, but a terran planet. Ruled by Venus, the love sign, and the direct opposite of his sun sign Scorpio. This would be interesting.

He smashed the knocker down against the bull's muzzle and was amazed when she opened the door without the chain. Before he got a chance to sling any manure, she said, "Enter at your own risk," like she'd been expecting him.

The place was Upper Canada farmhouse, a wash of brown, beige and yellow. She showed him to a couch the color of a beef steer and sat next to him. "I saw you in Harvey's." Her voice was thick and moany. Without a doubt she had led him here; that put him on guard.

It was the first time he'd gotten a good look at her. Eyes big and brown and sadly liquid. Face square but pretty, in a country–fresh sort of way. Neck typically thickish for her sign, with the Taurus symbol hanging from it. Ample tits. But the red hair seemed artificial—distinctly un–Taurean. As if reading his mind, she said, "I'm on the cusp of Aries. Fire and Earth. A cross breed." Her smile was a tad melancholy. "You're a solid Scorpian," she said brightly.

He nodded, thinking, Not bad. But if she's so insightful, how come she makes such lousy predictions? Instead he asked, "How'd you guess?"

"The stinger. Scorpioid men out in the daylight can't hide them. Besides, Taureans know our natural enemies," and she giggled, but it sounded forlorn.

Jerry felt uncomfortable, like she'd cracked his shell and was examining his vulnerable innards. Instinct told him to do her right here, but then how would he get the meat to his place?

"Drink?" she asked. "Water signs are always thirsty."

"Mineral water, if you have it." He watched her slip off her shoes and plod into the kitchen, rear end swaying. He felt a bit overwhelmed; she was in control, he was not. He had to turn this tide now.

When she came back she was chewing on something green. "Chive?" She offered him one. "Good for the digestion."

He reached for the glass but waved a pass at the solid food.

"How long you been reading my column?"

He sipped the water before answering. "Too long. You're always off, Lodestar."

She looked at him with those bovine eyes, still masticating. "That's my pen name. Call me Bess. I guess I'm lazy by nature. But I try, you know. You can't ask for more."

Can't I? Jerry thought. But she grinned and one of her ears

twitched and that caught him off guard.

"Listen." She touched his knee with a hot and heavy hand. "Why don't you tell me what you see as wrong, and maybe I can make it better. Come on. We'll have some munchies while I start dinner. I'm a good cook."

He followed Bess into the country kitchen. One wall was covered in copper pots. A butcher's block sat in the corner. She hauled a huge skillet out of a cupboard, poured in oil and placed it covered on the old–fashioned stove. He sniffed the air and caught something sweet, like hay.

She looked sluggish as she pulled vegetables out of the crisper and began chopping up celery, snap beans, green onions and broccoli. She nibbled as she cut and then arranged a few pieces on a small plate that she placed in front of him. The bulk was tossed into the hot oil. "I'm basically a vegetarian," she said apologetically, sitting across from him. "Meat rarely. No dairy. You?"

"Carnivore all the way." He left the greens untouched.

"Well, there's a little meat in the house. So, tell me how to make the column better." She looked needy, like someone who can't be apart from the herd without suffering pangs of loneliness.

"What are you using for references?"

She reached over his head to a bookshelf, her large breasts mouth level, and he had an urge to bite. From amidst the cookbooks she pulled out a massive volume twice as thick as the yellow pages. He saw that it was a giant ephemeris; it made his paperback seem shabby and trite by comparison.

She plunked the book onto the table and he read the gold lettering on the spine. "It was mother's. She liked to cast charts and cook at the same time. She taught me." Bess caressed the smooth black leather with her fingertips.

He opened at random. Along with the numerical charts he found detailed interpretations, the language scholarly and arcane. Modernized, it boiled down to some of what he'd read in the paper today. At the bottom of each page recipes had been penned in, the ink fading.

As he closed the book she was looking at him with those sadly trusting eyes. He thought about killing her here, eating some, taking part with him and leaving the rest.

"Ever tune into 'Signs'?" she asked.

"My favorite show."

She glanced at the black and white cow clock. "It's on now. Want to watch? Dinner can wait."

She switched off the gas and they went back into the living room. Bess pressed the remote; the tv flickered on. Bailey Ferguson, the program's Libran host, was just introducing a couple. She was a Taurean from Pickering, he a Scorpian from Ajax, which got a lot of uh–ohs! from the audience. Bess glanced at Jerry and snorted; he felt poison surge through his veins.

The Taurus/Scorpio couple played the Astro Wheel. No matter what the question, their answers were at odds. There's no way for these two, he thought. Bess, however, said, "I think they'll make it."

"Why?" he asked gruffly.

She gave him that patient and soulful look. "Opposites attract."

The strain of being with her made his stomach churn. He decided quick and neat was the best way to go. He was about to grab her when a commercial came on and she blurted, "Want to see my bedroom?"

"Why not?"

Bess led him down the hallway. She left the overhead light off but opened the blind to let in moonlight. She sat on the edge of the bed and patted the space beside her. When he joined her, she turned to him with languid eyes and said in a throaty voice, "So, let's see that stinger."

Jerry thought, what the hell? She wasn't bad looking. He'd give it to her then he'd give it to her. It wasn't unheard of for a scorpion to sting a sex partner after the act. Besides, the exercise would sharpen his appetite. She'd taste just that much better.

He stripped off his pants and underwear and stood before her. Bess undressed slowly, the way she did everything. Her nipples were unusually long, hard red fingers.

Suddenly, Jerry flew backwards. He slammed against the floor and air whooshed from his lungs. Before he could reestablish control, her weight was on him, her hands holding his ankles, her legs pinning his arms. She began grazing at his crotch. He wondered idly about the symbol for Cancer—sixty–nine—and if she had much of that sign in her chart.

When she'd gotten him hot and bothered, she hauled herself to her feet and looked down. Thinking about what part he'd ingest first got him even more excited. The thighs and back would be gamey—he'd definitely take those home. Her white breasts made him drool. And he hadn't had female sweetbread in, God, how long?

The moonlight was faint but he thought he saw her nostrils flair and smoke curl up around her nose. Jerry was on the verge of striking when a heel stomped onto his genitals. Pain splayed his body. Tears erupted from his eyes. When he was able to make a sound, a cry lurched up his spine through his tailbone and he screamed. He tried to shield himself but she stomped again and again, a mad bull trampling him underfoot. By the time she finished and left the room, he was barely conscious but recognized he would never be the same.

Bess returned carrying two things: a meat cleaver and the ephemeris. She looked at him as if he'd just crawled out from under a rock. Excruciating pain curled Jerry's body. He barely felt the sharp blade sever his genitals. Her rage had faded; the phlegmatic eyes returned.

Blood gushed up over his stomach and wet his chest and face. Through crimson tears he saw her open the book. She took her time but finally found the page she was looking for. "Gee, you're right. I got Scorpio and Taurus mixed up today. Listen to yours: "Don't hold back now. Go ahead and indulge. You've earned it." She looked at him forlornly, chewing her lower lip.

Suddenly she brightened. "You've got a terrific recipe today for prairie oysters." She bent over and scooped up the dripping mass of red pulp from between his legs. "Don't worry, we'll make it together."

An Eye
for an Eye

Alexander Mifflin was stabbing my mother as my brother Bill and I walked in the back door. I dropped the Eatons shopping bags I carried and screamed. Last–minute gifts tumbled into the pools of bloody mince meat. Mifflin turned. He and Bill fought. Bill outweighed him; he had wrestled at college. I rushed to my mother's blood–soaked body. The knife was lodged in her eye and, desperate, I yanked it out. Mother died in my arms seconds before Bill brought her killer to the ground. Before I could dial 911. Before she could say goodbye.

I know what you're thinking, the same thing the media is saying—I'm a psychopath. What makes me believe I have the right to be judge, jury and executioner? Your silly questions have nothing to do with me. I have that right by virtue of the fact that I have fought to stay alive in the face of shattering despair. You know yourself, it's survival of the fittest. You've thought that, even if you can't bring yourself to admit such a politically incorrect idea. I was a woman with a mission. Mission accomplished. If you'll hear me out, I know you'll understand.

Four years after my mother's death I came to the conclusion that murder is not so terrible. We all die anyway so what's it matter when or how. That might seem a jaded statement, but you know in your heart you've thought the same thing. We all have. It follows then that if one murderer can get off virtually scott free, why not another? Why not me?

I used to believe in divine justice. Then I grew up. For a while I had faith in our man–made justice system. When that failed, when jurisprudence let a guilty man walk away with his freedom and my mother's blood on his hands, I grew up some more.

Who would avenge my mother? Who would stop that madman from repeating his crime against humanity? No one. No one but me.

Let me start closer to the beginning, the easiest place to try to make sense of me and my 'crime', although there's no sense to *his* senseless crime.

The evidence was tangible, not circumstantial: Alexander Mifflin, a thirty–five–year–old Caucasian male broke into our North Vancouver home on Christmas Eve, ostensibly to steal anything of value. My mother was preparing mince meat pies for the holiday dinner the next day. The lights were out in the rest of the house—apparently she had been working in the kitchen and when the sun set turned on only one light. He surprised her there. She fought him—she was a large, strongly built woman of Scandinavian ancestry who did not give herself over easily to being intimidated. No one would have ever called her a coward. Neither is her daughter.

It was apparent they struggled. Chairs were overturned, the floor was a sea of mince meat. A paring knife lay on the table, to trim crusts, but he reached to the white ash knife rack and pulled out a Henckel with a six inch blade. Mother always loved good knives and had the blades honed by the man with the knife–sharpening cart who came by weekly. The coroner commented on the sharpness of the blade, because the twenty–eight stab wounds were, for the most part, clean. There were seven in her chest, two in her stomach, one in her left leg. The knife penetrated her diaphragm. She was left–handed and that side received the worst treatment. But the majority of the stab wounds were to her back, puncturing both lungs, one kidney, and, because the blade was so long, her heart. The most gruesome sight was to her left eye, where I found the knife lodged. The blade had pierced her brain. As I withdrew it, pale matter seeped from the wound. I can still see the tissue, like wood pulp.

I lived in a state of numbed grief. At the funeral I couldn't cry. Later, when we sold the house, before I left for college, as Bill and I sorted through my mother's belongings and I asked for her knives, he stopped and advised me, "Connie, try to forget what happened and get on with your life." But how could I forget?

No fourteen year old should have to experience what I did. Unless you've seen death close up, you cannot know how shocking it is. When the body seems to sigh. When the light fades blue lace crystal eyes to flat dull agates. When a kind of gas—maybe it was her spirit—wafts from the open mouth and ascends, rippling the air. My mother was gone. Her murderer would pay.

But he did not pay. Four years passed before Alexander Mifflin came to trial. I waited patiently through the delays, the motions and counter motions. He opted for judge only, no jury, knowing that ordinary people would find his acts against my mother incomprehensible. Still, through my frozen grief, I had faith.

But he'd had a bad childhood, a therapist testified, and had paid in advance. A minister assured the court that Mifflin attended church, helped out in the community, would be missed. He was a father, out of work, with a lovely wife and children to support. Not a crazed dope fiend, but a decent man, just desperate, said his brother. A police officer reported he'd been a suspect in several crimes and charged with burglary once before, but those charges had been dropped for lack of evidence. The court ruled that information inadmissible. Mifflin testified he did not recall reaching for the knife. He did not realize he stabbed my mother. Twenty–eight times. When I pulled the knife from my mother's brain, effectively I destroyed his fingerprints.

All throughout the trial I felt nothing, just stared at Mifflin, memorizing how he looked, his mannerisms, and finally his cursory testimony. The entire process had been like mining a vein that turned out to be corrupted. And the further along we traveled, the worse it got. The delays only helped his case. And the deals. Not murder one for Mr. Mifflin, who pleaded guilty, but manslaughter. Twenty years. He had already served four, he would be eligible for parole after another six.

The system failed me. But I vowed not to fail my mother. How do you kill a murderer? It's not as easy as one might think. It takes a lot of planning. Alexander Mifflin was paranoid—he assumed everyone had an intent as evil as his own. I understand paranoia. I've lived with it since that Christmas Eve. I have not felt safe since because there are other Alexander Mifflins in the world and you never know when they will invade the privacy of your home and take control of your life and stab you or a loved one to death. You understand that, I know. You read the news. You have the same fears.

During those years of growing up without her, when I needed my mother most, I developed a plan. The day he entered that penitentiary as a convicted prisoner, legally I changed my name. I earned a BA, and then an MA in Social Work. All the while I was doing time too, waiting for Mifflin.

In anticipation of his release, I changed my hair color, even the color of my eyes—I needed contact lenses anyway, and blue to green was not much of a stretch. The business suit and crisp haircut that had become my disguise were a far cry from the sweater and skirt and shoulder length hair he would remember.

With my excellent grades at university, I could have taken a job anywhere, but I wanted to work for the province, in correctional services. Normally the so–called easy cases—like Mifflin—are the plums and newbies are assigned the junk no one else wants. I told my supervisor I needed extra work and begged for Mifflin's case—I wanted to research a case with a good prospect for rehab. She was happy to get rid of an extra file folder.

That Thursday morning of his release—Thor's Day—I phoned his wife and told her not to bother taking the six hundred kilometre bus ride to the prison. "I'll get him," I assured her. I left a message with the warden's office with instructions for Mifflin to meet me at the gate; I would drive him home. It was partially true—I did meet him at the gate.

The day was overcast, I remember, with steely clouds hanging low over the British Columbia mountains, determined to imprison the sun. The day suited my mood. It's inappropriate to feel jolly when a life is about to be extinguished. Even I know that.

I watched him walk out of the prison a free man. Mifflin reeked of guilt. But his guilt would not bring back my mother, and I wasn't about to forgive him. He would not make it home to his lovely wife and three children. He would not resume his good works in the community. He wouldn't make it past the parking lot.

Mifflin hadn't seen me in six years—since the case finally came to trial. My testimony had been brief. Over that week as the travesty of justice unfolded, he faced front and didn't look at me, although my eyes were drawn to him like iron filings to a magnet. I will never forget his left profile.

He looked the same, although his muscles were more developed—presumably from working out in the prison gym—and his cheeks more gaunt.

"Mr. Mifflin," I said, removing my glove and extending a hand. I wanted to feel the skin of this killer, the flesh that held the knife that had ended my mother's life. Is the flesh of a killer different from normal flesh? Would I feel the slippery blood of my mother that had seeped into his pores ten years before, blood that could never be washed away?

He shook my hand. His grip was not as firm nor as cool as I'd anticipated, but mine made up for it. He looked at me skeptically. "Sheleagh McNeil," I said, "your new case worker."

Mifflin ran a hand through his greying hair; his brown eyes reflected confusion—he didn't know what to do with me. Maybe it was hard for him to be in the presence of a woman without a weapon of destruction.

"I have a car," I said. "This way."

I slid behind the wheel of the tan Datsun and he got in on the passenger side. I sat without turning the key, staring at his left profile.

He fidgeted, punched his thigh in nervousness, looked out the window. "Mind if I smoke?" he asked, pulling out a pack of Rothmans.

"Yes I do," I said.

He slid the pack back inside his jacket submissively. The silence was getting to him.

Finally he turned. "Do you need my address?"

"I know your address."

He scratched his head. "Can we get going? My wife's waiting. Christmas, you know. The kids and all."

"I know everything I need to know about you, Mr. Mifflin. All but one thing."

He waited, expectant.

"How did you feel as you murdered Mrs. Brautigam."

"How did I feel?" Now he was really uncomfortable. "Look, I talked to a shrink about all this, inside." He shifted and turned away from me. "Can't we talk about this later?"

"That's not possible, Mr. Mifflin."

He turned back. His eyes narrowed. He struggled to make a connection but there wasn't enough left of the girl who had watched her mother die. And it wasn't just the physical changes. I was no longer vulnerable, but he was.

He put his hand on the door handle. "Look, I'll catch the bus."

"The last bus is gone," I told him, "and I believe your parole stipulates that you are required to meet certain conditions, including working with your social worker. I simply want to know how you felt, that's all. When you stabbed Mrs. Brautigam twenty–eight times, and her blood gushed out, splattering you with red gore, and her screams filled your ears. And her son and daughter watched their mother die. How did you feel?"

He turned away. In a small voice he said, "I don't remember."

"I need to know how it feels," I said, slipping a hand into my briefcase, "because I don't remember feelings either." I hit the automatic door lock.

His head snapped back.

I used both hands to plunge the knife into his left eye. I had sharpened the Henckel daily after the police returned it.

Most of the six inches slid in as easily as if it were pie dough I was cutting. I felt the finely–honed steel pass the eyeball and enter the pale brain tissue. He clamped his hands around my wrists; I couldn't tell if he was trying to pull the blade out or helping me push it in as far as it would go, but I held tight.

Mifflin went rigid. He stared at me for a moment, his face creased with uncomprehending horror, his pierced brain struggled to make the awful connection. His hand clutched the handle and he yanked the blade out. Blood spurted into my face, across the windshield, over his brand new prison–release shirt. He was shocked. Before he could react, I grabbed the knife and stabbed him twenty–seven more times, counting aloud. He didn't struggle, like my mother. He did not possess her character. The same character her daughter possesses.

The media would be surprised to know how passionate I felt as I stabbed him. My feelings, the first after so many years, were surely different from whatever Mifflin must have felt as he murdered my mother, although I'll never be certain. Pressure lifted from my heart when I pierced his. My mind cleared of thoughts as blood and brain tissue gushed from his mutilated left eye. His body cooled and I defrosted. I watched his life dwindle much as I had watched my mother's life fade, and now I feel released. Finally I've reached the end of the corrupted vein and moved beyond that constricting tunnel into a world of complete and utter freedom. I have arrived back where I began, into a state of innocence. Justice has been accomplished. Don't you agree?

Many questions have been asked about me, but I have questions of my own and I hope you'll consider them calmly and rationally now that you've heard how it was. Do I deserve a worse fate than Mr. Mifflin's? Is my crime more heinous than his? I'm charged with murder one. The papers say I'll get life in prison unless I plead insanity, but I can't do that. He killed my mother. I killed him. What act could be more rational? An eye for an eye. Isn't that the purest form of justice? You decide.

Generation Why

"I'm not 'menacing'!"

"Rand, I'm sure he didn't mean to upset you. I think he just meant that, well, under the circumstances—" The Psychiatrist turns her palms up, and scans the prison's interview room. "Your statement about being a sensitive male is odd." The Psychiatrist crosses her short legs and leans forward, resting both forearms on her thigh, clasping her hands together as if she is pleading.

Rand likes the shape of her thigh, the way the pastel silk skirt clings to the taut skin and just lies there, passive, resting, waiting for fingers to reach out and separate fabric from flesh.

"Can you elaborate?" The Psychiatrist asks. "How do you see yourself as a sensitive young man?"

"There's lots of guys like me. Regular guys. Sensitive. Decent," Rand says.

"Yeah. A regular, sensitive, decent serial killer!" The Reporter's remarks are aggressive. Hostile. Violent.

Rand focuses on The Reporter. "A lot of guys are serial killers. More and more every day. You see it on tv. In the news. Guys like you write about guys like me. Guys who are trying to help."

"Help? Right!" The Reporter stabs symbols into his notebook, barely glancing down. The carved lines of his face deepen under the glare of brilliant tv lights.

"You created me."

The Reporter looks disgusted. His skin is tight, but with no appealing insulation beneath his cheeks. Just bone, nothing but bone. Hard, not subtle. Holding up a face with limited flexibility. He starts to say, "Look, you little sh—"

"Rand, I think what you're trying to get at," The Psychiatrist interrupts, "is that the media portrays violence and that in turn encourages violence in young people like yourself, with a predisposition."

"Fuck!" The Reporter mutters under his breath, low enough that the microphone will not pick it up. Rand watches him glance at The

Guard by the door, whose eyes are non–committal, but whose mouth—the one that spits saliva when he talks, that opens and closes like the jaws of a vice, that utters sound bytes that Rand breaks into chunks and swallows whole—whose mouth twitches at the left corner. Nice touch, Rand thinks. But too far in the background to be effective.

"Well, Rand?" The Psychiatrist says. "Do you see yourself as a victim of media violence?"

"Oh, come on!" The Reporter says. "Tell us why you mutilated all those—"

"Let him answer the question," The Psychiatrist interrupts again.

The Reporter crashes back against the chair. Rand knows The Reporter would love to jump to his feet and punch The Prisoner in the face. The Reporter is violent by nature, that's clear. His turn to ask the questions is coming. They are supposed to take turns. Politely. That's the way it's supposed to go.

"I love television," Rand says. His voice is not as sincere as he wants it to sound, so he concentrates on lowering his eyes, dropping his head down a fraction. He looks up through his long lashes at The Psychiatrist. The dark eyelid hairs cut her body into strips. "And newspapers. It's important to know what's going on in the world around you."

Her face softens. She reminds him of The Teacher, and The Minister's Wife. The Others in the room wouldn't notice that her face has changed, but Rand does. She understands.

"Tell us about your childhood," The Psychiatrist says gently.

This script is familiar. He has repeated these lines many times and knows them by heart. He wants to sigh, but that would not be the right thing to do. In a moment of inspiration, he tilts his head and looks away. If only his hands were free, but the chain keeps them six inches apart, which means he cannot rely on his hands to speak for him, and they speak eloquently.

"I had a very normal life," he says matter–of–factly, repeating by rote what he has said so often. Why won't they believe him? "My parents were divorced, but that wasn't a problem. Mom was great. She took real good care of me."

"How so?" asks The Psychiatrist.

"From when I was a baby. She had a monitor in the nursery and everything. So nothing bad would happen."

He remembers the monitor, even when he got old enough to go to school. His mother hovered just in the next room, always listening, waiting, as if for a sign.

"And there were home movies, then videos," he adds. Many. Endless tapes. She recorded them from before he could walk: Rand strapped into his cradle, the television set on—he still remembers his favorite show, the cartoon with the blood–red lion that chomped off the heads of its enemies; moving images of Rand eating meatloaf with his hands in front of the tv in a highchair; wandering the mall in his toddler harness, so he wouldn't get lost, or be stolen or be violated by some sick man. "She liked to shoot me. She said I was a natural on tape."

The Psychiatrist smiles.

The Reporter scribbles more notes.

The Guard shifts his weight to his other leg.

This room is small, like the set at a television station Rand saw once on a school tour. They had been broadcasting the news. The set, the size of a bathroom, consisted mainly of a plywood desk, the front veneered so it looked like real wood on tape. Two cameras. A control room with a bank of monitors before The Reporters. The Class visited the control room. The Technicians sat at the panels of switches and buttons and levers, wearing headsets, sending and receiving instructions as directed, zeroing in on The Female Reporter, then The Male Reporter. Back and forth, back and forth. Then The Weatherperson. The Technical Director controlled how everyone looked, what they said and how they said it. It was just like a movie.

"I'm sorry," he says when he realizes The Psychiatrist has asked a question.

"I asked if you would try to explain your motivation. Why you did what you did, to all those people...You must have felt very angry—"

"I never feel angry."

The Reporter leans forward.

The Psychiatrist sits back.

"Who's the first person you killed?" The Reporter demands.

"I never killed a person."

"Your DNA matches the DNA found at the scene of six murders. Six mutilations. And the jury found you guilty of—"

"They were wrong. I'm innocent. DNA can be wrong, you know. I saw a show on *60 Minutes*—"

"Yeah, kid, I know the stats. If you're not an identical twin, it's one in a million—"

"Two million. One in two million, depending on the tests used. But two million and one could be a match—"

"How did it feel to just tear off—"

"Please!" The Psychiatrist grips The Reporter's arm, tempering him. Reluctantly, he moves back in his chair. His face tightens. The Psychiatrist moves forward. This is her territory.

"Rand, I read the reports and evaluations. What you told the court. What you told the other doctors. You said you never felt the slightest bit of anger toward anyone."

"That's right," Rand agrees. "I don't believe in getting angry. That's how Mom raised me."

"But you must have been angry at your mother now and again. And your father—"

"Nope." He knows he's answered too quickly. It sounds like he is trying to hide something, but he isn't. Not at all. There's nothing to hide. "My father wasn't around, so why would I get angry at him?"

"He was around until you were ten."

"I didn't notice. He was always at work."

"Rand, there's a history of domestic violence, your father assaulting your mother, and—"

"Yeah, well, she divorced him. Besides, she protected me. I didn't know about it until later. I was busy."

"You played a lot of video games," The Reporter says, struggling to get with the program at last.

"Sure. Some D&D stuff, then Nintendo when I got older. Doesn't everybody?"

"Yeah, but everybody doesn't—"

"I mean, doesn't everybody like video games? All the kids at my school did."

"Rand…" The Psychiatrist searches for another avenue, as though if she keeps probing he'll split apart, spill what's inside him. Bleed for the camera. But there is nothing to say that he hasn't said before. "Some of those games get pretty violent, don't they?"

"I guess."

"After you played them, you went out and played them in real life, didn't you?" The Reporter interjects, blurring the picture again.

"No."

"Sure you did!"

"Why should I? I had the games."

"And the urges—"

"Nope."

Rand looks up, presenting the face of The Innocent to The Videographer, a slim–bodied young woman with the head of a camera. *How many hundreds of thousands, maybe millions of people will watch this drama unfold?* he wonders. Most, he is certain, will understand. Most are against violence.

The Lawyer sits beside him, prepared to nip any compromising questions or answers in the bud. So far she has said nothing. Now she does. "My client's answers to these questions are a matter of record. It's all in the trial transcripts."

"What's the basis of your final appeal?" The Reporter asks. The Videographer shifts the camera to the left, to capture The Reporter's profile.

"Evidence that should never have been admissible," The Lawyer says.

"The video tapes?"

"Yes, the tapes."

A flash–fire races through Rand—The Reporter isn't supposed to steal the limelight! Rand is The Prisoner. The–Juvenile–Sentenced–To–Death. The one who has agreed to this three–way exclusive. The only one the camera should be focused on!

Rand knows he should say nothing but he needs to regain control. "The only urges I have are to get rid of The Evil."

The Lawyer jumps in. "Don't say another word—"

"What is The Evil?" the Psychiatrist asks, leaning far forward, until Rand can smell her perfume.

"You mean evil, like you?" The Reporter says sharply.

The Videographer turns the lens back to stare at Rand. Rand smiles slightly and gazes seductively into the impassive camera eye. For effect, he fingers the white ribbon he always wears on his prison shirt, over his name. "I just mean, the world is full of violence. I wish it wasn't, but it is."

"That's enough, Rand! My client is—"

"Men are the violent ones. Everybody says so. The tv, the newspapers. So men have got to stop the violence. 'A man's gotta do what a man's got to do.' John Wayne said that, you know. My mother used to quote him."

"Rand, have you heard of the psychiatric term 'projection'? It's—"

"If men don't do it, who will? The good guys have to stop the bad guys, or there's gonna be violence."

"Listen, kid, I've been a reporter for twenty years, and I know BS when I smell it—"

"My mother didn't raise me to be violent. She didn't want me to be like my father."

"As your counsel, Rand, I must advise you—"

"Most men are violent, don't you think so doctor? You're a woman."

"Rand, people can project feelings they have onto someone else—the way a camera projects an image. Angry feelings, or feelings of wanting to harm someone we fear will harm us—"

But Rand tunes her out. He directs his remarks exclusively toward The Videographer, to her cold, precise eye, studying him, controlling him, never letting him slide out of her objective sight.

"If there were no men in the world, there wouldn't be any violence. Isn't that right?"

Silence cuts the air for barely a second.

"I'm sorry, people, but as Rand's attorney, I must protect my client's interests. This interview is—"

"Deny it! Go ahead and deny it!" Rand shouts at the retreating camera, using emotional charge to lure it back. "You say it all the time, all of you. How can you say something different now? You're phonies!"

"Rand, do you feel attacked? No one here is attacking you—"

"All of you! You want all males dead!"

"Turn off the camera, or I'll file a civil action—"

"So do I! Then there won't be any more violence."

"Listen, you little shithead, you're the violent male!"

Rand lunges. He is aware of the camera zooming in on his hands. The chain from the wrist cuffs is hooked to a waist chain and his reach stops inches from his grasp.

Silence clutches the air. The Videographer has captured all. The shocked looks. The gasp from The Lawyer. The cry of "No!" from The Psychiatrist. The Guard drawing his gun. The Reporter, struggling to protect his genitals, what would have been seconds too late, but for The Prisoner's restraints.

Rand stares down at his hands. They are bony and thin, 'sensitive', his mother always said. The fingers stretch like talons, ready to claw The Evil from its roots. Ready to deposit it into his hungry mouth, where powerful jaws can pulverize and razor teeth rend. Where what should not exist, by being devoured, can be eliminated forever.

That would have made a great shot. His mom would have loved it. Rand sits back and smiles into the camera's eye. He just hopes that The Videographer had the lens in sharp focus when she captured him.

O...*And Thou!*

Over at the color copier some guy's playing around with the paper trays, trying to shove in the top tray backwards, pulling it out, doing the same with the middle tray. He doesn't have a clue. I'm just handing over a box to a customer—copies of a photo of her missing daughter—so by the time I get to the color copier the guy's amusing himself by trying to jam the 11 by 17 paper into the 8–1/2 by 11 tray.

"I'll do that," I say, taking everything out of his hands. I've been on night shift for six months, but never run across a dude as weird as him. He's got on these round sunglasses that just cover his eyes. The lenses are iridescent, making him look like a bug. Otherwise, he's a study in black and white—chalky polyester pants my grandfather would wear golfing, and an inky silk shirt buttoned to the neck with a big 'disco' collar. His legs and arms are skinny but his trunk is thick. I wonder if he's got some disease—his skin is almost paper white.

As I fill a tray with the larger paper and slide it into the right slot, he's stuffing something smelly into his mouth.

"What do you want to copy?" I ask him.

Whatever he's chewing dribbles down his chin. It's the color of bread mold and stinks. He scratches the top of his head with his little finger, real fast, then stabs the finger towards the machine. I notice his nails are long and filed to a point. The back of his pale hand is a field of spiky black hairs.

I lift the cover. Lying on the platen, face down, is a photograph. "You want it enlarged?" I ask, because of the 11 by 17 paper.

He nods.

I set the paper size, color codes, contrast, then ask, "How many?"

He holds up his little finger.

I press START. We wait. A single sheet of paper slides out. Before I get a good look at it, he snatches it away, lifts the lid and grabs the photograph too, like it's a shot of some guy's dick. He jerks his way to the cashier, hands in his plug, and pays his dollar plus tax. On the way to the door he checks out the black and white photocopy tacked to the bulletin board of the girl who's been missing for a week. The description says her name is Jean. She's eighteen, 5'4", has auburn hair and green eyes. A student, like me, but a freshman.

His head quivers. I hear a noise like air being let out of a tire. The minute he's out the door he reaches into another pocket, pulls out more food and munches his way down the street.

The same guy just came into the store again. I'm alone and tired. It's closing time and I'm just about to lock up. He snatches a plug and zeros in on the same copier.

I lock the door and turn the sign so CLOSED faces the street. On my way back to the counter I hear an angry hissing noise.

Over at the Xerox, he's lost it. He's got the front panel open, exposing the developer and toner bottles. His hands grip the top of the machine at the front corners. His feet are wide apart, toes touching the copier. His ass sticks out into the air and it's jerking in every direction. From where I stand, he looks attached to the Xerox the way an insect attaches to a wall.

I grit my teeth and go over. Being near him isn't fun. He smells like he's been sleeping in somebody's basement and eating dead rats.

"Got a problem?"

He hobbles backwards and points to the panel on the top. The copier path is jammed, which has nothing to do with the developer and toner. I press RESET, shut the front panel and open the side panel. A piece of paper is caught between the rollers and I ease it out. It's stained blue, almost black. I toss it into the trash, but not before spotting a faint image of lines in one corner, like a parabola design. "That should do it," I say.

The guy is eating again. Something greasy and the smell turns my stomach. I wait while he makes his enlargement. The second it slides out of the machine he grabs it and the photograph. I catch a glimpse of red.

He thrusts sticky change, a crumpled buck and the plug at me, then lurches towards the door. On the way he stops at the missing girl's picture again, like he's obsessed with it.

It's ten after nine and I'm not about to stay longer than I have to. I've already cashed out and made the night deposit so I toss the money into the register and grab the baseball jacket I keep under the counter.

The guy's at the door, which is locked, but he keeps yanking it towards him anyway. "Hang on," I yell, but he doesn't seem to hear me.

Out on the sidewalk, cool air snaps me awake. I'm flat mentally but not physically, and want to clear my brain before I go home and read a chapter of textbook Martin Buber so I'll know what the hell the Urban Philosophy prof's talking about tomorrow when we get into 'I and Thou.' Somebody passes eating a falafel and the smell of parsley and sesame wakes my stomach. I haven't eaten since breakfast, and there's a place I go after work sometimes and I think I'll stop in for a beer and some food. The last time I was there a foxy redhead with green eyes and slim hips served me and I feel like seeing her again. Who knows, maybe I'll even ask...

A block ahead, skittering in the shadows between street lights, is the weird guy. Something about him being so repulsive fascinates me. He's twisted enough that I think he might be an artist, but he's no trendoid. I start wondering about where he lives, what his life is like. What the hell he's enlarging.

I follow him about six blocks, into a warehouse district that's deserted this time of night. I'm just about to turn west and head for the cafe when he enters a building. I get to the glass front door in time to see the number over the elevator stop on six, the top floor.

Maybe I'm bored, maybe I don't feel good about the way he keeps staring at that missing girl's picture. Maybe I've seen too many movies. Suddenly I'm in the lobby and scanning the register. This is the kind of pastel deco decor that needs the marble cleaned and the brass polished.

I take the elevator, which is loud—the doors clank together behind me when I get off. The sixth floor is lit with bulbs in the high ceiling spaced about ten feet apart. I pass doors: a fur manufacturer's workroom, a ribbon company, two theater spaces, something called Baba–Cooper. No artist's digs. Around one corner are washrooms with a ladder between them that leads nowhere. The N in MEN is missing. I look inside: the urinal's crusty and the toilet's clogged; I change my mind about using either one.

Being here is a waste of time so I push the elevator button and wait. Something must be wrong with the damn thing because it doesn't come. After a few minutes I decide on the stairs, but the push bar tells me if I go in the door will lock behind me and I'll be trapped in the stairwell.

The only other thing on this floor is a freight elevator. Big, battleship grey. The metal doors close vertically; there's a dirty glass–and–chicken–wire window. I peer inside. At the back of the shaft I see a window, probably one on each floor. Inches of decade–old dust clog the corners of the lead between the small panes. Light, but not much, filters through from the street lights on that side of the building. Above, the shaft is swallowed by shadow.

What's in front of me is a maze of cables and pulleys black with grease and dirt. I wonder if the elevator still works. I'm thinking about that when suddenly the gears grind to life. One cord rises as another drops, then my view is blocked for a moment.

The elevator stops. I step back. My heart's pounding, but the doors don't open. I look through the little window. I shove the top part of the door up and the bottom goes down automatically. Inside: dirty wooden floor boards. Flat iron bars for walls. Rotting plywood slats for a roof. One dim bulb. It's empty.

I get in. The metal doors are the only doors and I pull them together. The elevator's like a cage, open at the front. There's a corroded brass lever, the numbers worn away. I press it forward and the cage descends. I pass five. Then four. A quick look through the small glass convinces me every floor is the same. Dance studios. A lace wholesaler. At one I pull the lever back, but the elevator continues to descend. I wonder if I should panic but it jerks to a stop.

The metal doors here have no window; when I open them, blackness invades. Down the corridor I see some kind of light, but it's too dim to be useful. The air is hot and moist and there's not much of it. I want out.

But the lever doesn't do anything, no matter which way I move it. It's like the power's gone. "Great," I say to nobody, trying to pump myself up so I feel as brave as I sound. I have to find the exit. I'll even take a chance with the stairs. But the door marked STAIRS is locked. I have to go into that blackness.

The light ahead is a beacon and I grope my way towards it. I don't want to touch the slimy walls but I'm afraid I'll miss the stairs. The further in I go, the hotter it gets. It turns out the light is at the dead end of the corridor. There's a door, though, and I push it open.

Earthy–smelling air wafts out. The light shows me that the stairs lead down only. It's black as videotape down there. Maybe, I tell myself, they lead outside, but I don't believe it. Too many of the movies I've seen have been horror. Still, there's nothing I can do but go down. Unless...

I head back to the elevator with a plan. One last try with the lever. Nothing. There's enough space between the cage and the shaft and the bars are wide enough and me slim enough that I just get through. I haul myself up the bars, ripping the back of my jacket, making a mental note to get back into bench–pressing.

Finally I'm standing on the plywood on top of the cage. My idea is to climb the cables to the first floor, which isn't far, pry open the door and get the hell out. That's my plan, until the elevator groans into life.

"Shit!" I yell, struggling for balance. The lever must have been stuck and my jumping on the cage probably loosened it, but none of that matters now. The windows let me know when I pass the first floor, then the second, the third. I grab a greasy cable for balance and slam the plywood with my boot heel. It begins to shatter. As I pass five I'm praying there's space between six and the roof. One rotting plywood slat falls to the elevator floor.

Six goes by. I hunker down and protect my head with my arms. I plunge to the chest into a mass of stickiness. The elevator jerks to a stop. Whatever I'm caught in feels thick and slippery but sticky, like

Crazy Glue; the more I struggle, the more locked in I am. I don't want to guess what this stuff is.

My upper body's stuck but my legs are free and I stomp on another slat. I'm suffocating with the heavy dirty air plus this stuff that's trapping me; I'm having trouble holding back the panic. The elevator light barely lets me see what I'm tangled in. Pale, smooth, fine strands. Webbed.

I hear something. A wheeze. Above, a shuffle in the darkness. I feel a tremor. It's like something's sliding down the strands on all sides of me.

A loud hiss out of the blackness, then another, shoots a chill up the back of my spine. I notice the stink. Mildewy fabric. Decaying meat.

I kick frantically at the plywood, my leg pumping faster than I thought it could. Two more planks fall through. The opening's wide enough for me, if I can just untangle myself. I tense my sweaty hands and use them like knives to slice upward then down. The tough strands don't cut and they tighten like a cat's cradle but give in places when the pressure's right.

I manage to free my head a bit and ease the sticky webbing from my chest. I slip and make adjustments. I drop a bit further, the snare catching me; from the waist down I'm in the elevator. Not much more. Easy does it.

Dry spiky hairs brush up my cheek and across my forehead. An inhuman caress. I scream and jerk and shoot a tangled arm up karate–style to knock it away. The movement breaks another slat and more light springs into the shaft. It also frees me. Just before I crash onto the elevator floor, for one split second I glimpse things I don't want to believe exist. Enlarged color copies tacked like paintings to a living room wall. A human arm dangling in the pale strands. A livid mask so hideous it will haunt me forever.

If I'm injured, I don't know it. The metal door smashes open as if I'm Hercules. I'm through the sixth floor, down the stairwell and breaking the glass in the door that leads to the lobby. I'm out of the building, running, running, and I don't stop until I'm at the copy shop.

I lock the door and lean against it gasping. As my breath comes back, so does my sanity. I can't believe how much I panicked. What a hallucination! Maybe my blood–sugar level plunged, or the adrenaline surged, who knows?

As I glance around the room, my eyes focus first on the poster of the missing girl, then to the color copier in the corner. On impulse, I head there, and look in the waste–paper basket beside the machine. Inside is one crumpled sheet of paper, 11" x 17". I pick it out and take it to the magnifier.

The sheet's badly smudged and creased. Except one corner. Inter-secting pale web–like lines. Imbedded in them are faded images and I'm not sure: the lobe of a flesh–colored ear? Strands of red hair? Half of a green eye, wide in terror? Most of a pink mouth frozen in a death scream? Just before the blue–black ink swallows everything, the clarity of the last image suddenly imprints itself into my mind: a fragment. The edge of an iridescent lens, round, glowing. An alien eye.

The paper slips from my grasp. I feel trapped in invisible strands of horror. This unnatural pause lets part of my brain click into a cool philosophical mode and one question expands to gobble up everything that might hinder pure reason: I am human, but who or what are 'thou'?

Rural Legend

At twilight, Old Mother Rainey's cypress cane stabbed the dry earth, then her dust–covered sandals shuffled forward down the dirt road. She'd travelled this route her long life, the highway to the left, the Okeefenokee Swamp on the right. The swamp bred life, all kinds, and death. Of course, so did the highway. The swamp had always been here, but the highway hadn't; now that it was, things were easier.

As she reached the curve in the road, her stomach growled. The bog in the swamp came into view. She sighed, squinted her aged eyes to focus better and ran a skinny hand through her hair as if she still had a lush head of it.

Nearer the bog's edge, the air changed. Hot and humid to chilly. Insects stopped scuttling. A fake coral paused, suddenly comatose on the road. Others might be put off. And she was hungry. She knocked the snake into the slimy water with her cane.

The fallen log stretched out into the green water. A terrible stench rose up through the static air. Old Mother Rainey gingerly stepped onto the wobbly log.

Once she'd gotten her balance, she poised there, stock still, cane in one hand wedged into the bark, nearby cypress branch clutched in the other.

Good thing it wasn't long before a car pulled onto the shoulder. Something about how the light hit this curve and bounced off the trees blinded the driver. And then, of course, they'd caught a glimpse of her…

Pennsylvania plates. Figures.

The driver got out, young fella, city type. The woman stayed inside. "Hi!" he called.

Old Mother Rainey just stared at him.

The woman, still seated, said something, then got out of the car, as women do. "You alright?" she called.

The sky darkened suddenly; often did this time of day. It took the glint off the curve, which was fine. Wasn't needed now.

The old woman was as feeble as Janice's grandmother, as her

mother was becoming, as she herself would be one day. As her daughter would end up. The dismal thought caused her to lay a protective hand onto her swollen stomach.

Bill was too suspicious. If people couldn't help one another, well, they weren't worth much.

Janice walked to the dirt path, Bill following. "We just stopped to make sure you're okay," she smiled. "Do you...live around here?"

"I am from Cthulhu," the old woman said. Her voice creaked, like the boughs of a tree bending in the wind.

"Ca...who loo?" Bill asked?

Janice ignored him.

The old lady didn't answer.

In the eerie gloom, the old lady seemed to blend with the cypress trees. Each time a car passed, both she and the trees glowed silver. It was as though she was not flesh, not even bone...

"Come on, Janice—" Bill began.

"It's okay," she told him. Just an optical illusion. What else could it be?

Suddenly the old woman's arm moved, the one holding onto the branch. She lowered it and pointed to her stomach as another set of headlights flashed. In that moment, Janice saw a hollow cavity. Within the emptiness, something moved, like a fetus...

Before she could stop herself, Janice hurried forward.

"Don't!" Bill yelled, but it was too late.

"Why, it's a..." Janice said, reaching inside that eternal womb.

The cord slithered up her arm. Around her body. Strangling her, and behind her Bill's body, and finally reaching the living fetus within her belly...

"Nothing mysterious at all," the stocky cop hiking up her slacks said to her new partner as they got out of the cruiser. "Light draws 'em. They step onto that log, and wham! Weight sinks 'em. Then the gators come."

"What about her?" the skinny one said.

"Who?"

"That old woman..."

The chunky cop laughed. "Old Mother Rainey. The old woman who eats babies before they're born. My ma told me, and her mamma told her, and I tell my kid. Don't make her real."

"Well, she was there."

"Still is." The cop walked out onto the wobbly log and pointed to a cypress directly across the bog. The tree did resemble a skinny old woman, balding on top, stick arms, and a big gap with a knot in the middle, where her stomach or her womb might be.

Youth
Not Wasted

Tummy rumble. This is dicey, Reta thought.

"Stretch it and meltdown!" The aerobics goddess out–grated the ghetto blaster. Reta crushed her eyelids together and hoisted a lumpy calf. The amplifiers belched bass. Muscles hungered for deliverance.

Shake.

Pound.

Squeeze.

Chop.

Famished, Reta thought half an hour later. She elbowed past a limp twenty–something stuffed into silver–blue spandex then blasted through the swinging door, nearly creaming a dishy Madonna–clone with thighs the size of Reta's humerus. Youth, she sighed. What a waste.

She crawled into the sauna and, thank God, it was empty for once. The top bench sizzled her butt. Reta forced herself to chill. Waves of heat from electrically cooked rocks pulsed toward the ceiling, microwaving her sinuses. She stripped off the corn–colored leotard, lemon wrist–and–head bands and lay back. What the hell, she thought. No pain, lotsa gain. At her age beauty was a ravenous bitch.

Before she fried, Reta treated her cellulite to a knife–point shower. She bandaged her torso in terry cloth until she resembled a turkey wrapped in cheesecloth then dragged her blow dryer and makeup bag out to the communal vanity. Only one stool was left—way at the end where the glass had spiderwebbed. The girl who'd been wearing teal spandex perched on Reta's right chatting to the sun–ripened Madonna look–alike on her right.

"So I bought it anyway," the one two seats away said. "But I can lose a few, ya know? Color's dynamite. Matches." She raised a tube of lipstick.

"What shade?"

"Candy Apple Red."

Meat red, Reta thought, and glanced at herself. Three hairs the color of shiny cow's brains glinted among strawberry strands and she plucked them out. The new contacts, fabulous—chestnut—contrasted with her hair. She'd need another lash extension soon, though, and she'd better book electrolysis fast for those brows. Shit! That fat mole on her chin had just been chopped six months ago and already it was sprouting again. At least the face–lift held. Taut miracle. Evaporated laugh lines. Melted crow's feet. She caught the shadow of a double chin in a pie slice of mirror and her spirits fizzled. Time for a major overhaul.

The one two seats down giggled. She had the dark, sultry looks of the girl pictured on cans of tomato paste. Lush, pouty lips. Naturally crimson. Reta watched her outline those tomato lips in creamy Candy Apple Red. The fine brush slowly rounded the edge where firm flesh kissed the lip line.

Famished, Reta thought, and turned away.

When she had coiffed and colored, she struggled into skin–sticker cow–hide pants. It was like they had been shrunk by the steam instead of her flab.

She abandoned the gym by the alley exit. Night air cold enough to freeze mineral water slapped her cheeks until they burned but she refused to cover the skin. She wanted the get–it–while–you–can look.

Once on the street she avoided The Doe–Nut Shoppe, Costa's Souvlaki Den and Hamburger Shangri–la. A taxi with neon tubing whipped past: Deep and Dangerous Pizza. Reta's three–inch spike heels speared candy wrappers and fast food cartons as she hurried away.

The trendoid eatery was jammed. She cut toward the stand–up bar, en route sizing up a scrumptious dude fingering his chocolate brown tie. Reta grinned his way.

"…no chicken!" he mumbled, looking past her to scan the room.

Chicken.

Dark meat.

Famished.

The black leather crowd packed the window, undyed suede owned the opposite wall. Like the middle shelf of a refrigerator, the center of the room was crammed with a nauseating mix of goods; fruity–colored tie–dies, rough Tibetan lamb's wool and gobs of shot silk the color of uncooked rice noodles. The air reeked of sour grapes. Thank God the lighting was deco and dim but it was hot as a barbecue and she felt like a sow roasting on a spit.

She reached the bar and checked out the far end. Chubby spandex was squished into an armed bar stool, gnawing the fat with a loser in an eggplant jacket. Tomato mouth clutched the brass rail while chocolate tie zeroed in to leave his order in her ear. The cherub's cherry tomato lips compressed into a delicious little pout. When she escaped to the can, Reta followed.

The ladies' was cramped and mildewy. It stank of urine and half digested food stuffs, but what could you do? The Mediterranean princess took one stall, the other john was occupied by somebody puking up dinner.

Reta slipped the sign from her bag—a stick figure in a skirt, encircled, red line carved through the body—and stuck it on the outside of the door over Women.

A toilet flushed then a pasty–faced girl staggered out and rinsed her mouth. As she exited, Reta's eyes brushed up her fashionably–ripped jeans to a broccoli designer top that exposed ribs.

Ribs.

Ummmm.

Reta shoved the tangerine trash can against the door and waited. Her stomach churned.

She caught gaunt features in the glass.

When the Madonna replica swirled out, she seemed rattled to see Reta. The black–haired angel ran her fingertips delicately under the faucet, took the lipstick and a brush from her pigskin purse and made repairs.

"Nice color." Reta's tummy growled.

The girl's honeydew eyes skipped from the tube to Reta's stomach to Reta's face. Her expression proclaimed Reta overdone.

"Thanks," she mumbled, turning back to the glass.

"Pretty enough to eat."

The tomato shriveled. Reta caught sight of her own potato–skin orbs.

Fodder.

Feeder.

Famished.

Items were jammed back into the purse and the tidbit was already slicing by when Reta wrung her neck. The sweet treat dropped like a slab of mutton hitting a butcher's floor.

Poor starving bambino, Reta thought, meaning herself. She licked those delicious ripe beefsteak lips. Hard. Harder. Juice dribbled and gushed. She nibbled for a few seconds, then indulged. The breast was divine. The dark meat heavenly. By the time she had devoured the rump and moist organs and was left with only bones to chomp on, Rita felt ecstatic. Youth was never hard to swallow.

She tidied up, tore the sign from the door and dabbed Candy Apple Red onto her freshly washed tomato lips. Then she headed back to the bar, a new woman.

"So, how about dinner?" chocolate tie slurred in her new ear. "My place."

"Just ate."

"Dessert?" Creme de cacao breath braised her cheek. "Not too much, not too little. Tasty, know what I mean?" Through two sets of clothing, firm flesh nudged her stomach.

Digestive gas lurched from her tummy and blasted out. She managed an embarrassed grin and checked her bulging gut then his bulging pants. Yeah, she was stuffed. Even a bit was bound to show. But, what the hell. You're only young and hot and female for so long.

"Maybe just a bite." Reta licked her chops. Youth is irresistible, in any flavor. No sense wasting it.

Lunatics

The Power of One

Mira counted the checkered squares that made up the deep pile on Dr. Rosen's waiting room floor. A row of sixty black and sixty white lined the cardiologist's broadloom from the door to the window. Seventy of each across. Sixteen thousand eight hundred. She felt sure the space taken up by the desk held twenty and twenty. Those plus the three blacks and three whites under every one of the six chairs meant the floor should contain, altogether, sixteen thousand eight hundred seventy–six. Only base numbers from one to nine held meaning. She had to reduce that large total.

Quickly she added the individual digits that made up that number horizontally. One plus six plus eight plus seven plus six. The muscles of her chest tensed. She thought about using the calculator her dad had given her but felt guilty, as though that would be cheating. After all, she thought, he wouldn't use it, although the gift implied that she would.

Twenty–eight. Two plus eight equals ten. One and zero. Uh–oh. One. A paralyzingly unlucky number. The number of sacrifice. Her chest constricted further.

Dr. Rosen's nurse stood and walked down the hall. Mira watched her, twisting a Kleenex into a corkscrew, more of a nervous wreck than usual. The test results would seal her fate, the predestination that she had been struggling to avoid since birth.

The three other patients waiting and Mira made four, a stable, balanced number, but not good enough. There had to be a way to annihilate that one.

She signed and glanced around the room. A Wandering Jew hung in a macrame hanger near the window. The first vine had thirteen leaves. One and three makes four again. She took a deep, relaxing breath. Her chest muscles eased some. The second vine had ten. One plus zero. One again. Her pulse escalated as neck muscles cramped. If she added the four and one she'd have a five. Even numbers were safer but this was midway. Adventurous yet solid. She felt a dull ache beneath her rib cage. If only she could stop now. But she'd have to count the other vines; she knew she took after her dad in that way: compelled, as always, to finish what was begun.

She multiplied the fifty leaves by the number of vines, twenty. One thousand. One plus three zeros. The horror of one was just slicing into her mind when the nurse said, "Ms. Jacyk? Doctor will see you now."

Mira stumbled across the room and down the crisp white hallway with the chain of mini Monet prints—ten of them, or one—clinging to the walls. The ache in her chest had increased to a steady throb. The nurse led her to the examination room at the end of the hall. Still unsteady, Mira sat in the white chair next to the small desk.

Dr. Rosen followed her in. He carried a red file folder with her name typed across the flap. She already knew that by assigning the letters of the alphabet numbers from one to twenty six, the letters of her name added up to one. And she'd been the only child of a single parent. She'd been trying to pay off that solitary karma all her life.

"Mira." He smiled, a bit crookedly, and she counted seven upper teeth. She wondered if he had all thirty–two, like her father. Three and two. Five. "We've received the results from your EKG." His mouth was tight but not nearly as severe as her dad's. Her heartbeat accelerated and the ache intensified. "I don't want to frighten you, but it looks as though you've suffered a myocardial infarction. A mild heart attack."

He paused. The silence made her aware that she was shaking. To keep from falling apart completely, Mira concentrated on counting the pencils and pens in his tray. Six pencils, five pens, plus the ballpoint in his hand. One plus two. Three. The number of change. Amidst the fear she felt a glimmer of elation.

"I think we should look on the positive side," he said. "Take this as an early warning. Now's the time to make lifestyle changes. I've reviewed the results of your cholesterol test and the cardio–vascular evaluation. There's room for improvement in both areas. Here's a diet that's worked very well in cases like yours." He handed her one sheet of paper of daily menus. Three per day for seven days. Twenty–one. Two plus one. Three. "High in fiber and carbohydrates, low in fatty foods. We'll also get you on an exercise plan, walking, swimming, easy at first and gradually we'll have your pulmonary status to where it should be."

Mira had stopped listening. She'd been studying the numbers on his large day planner attached to the wall. One plus two plus three plus four, all the way to thirty–one. Adding each of the digits together produced four hundred and ninet–six. Adding four, nine and six gave her nineteen. One and nine equaled ten. One. It would be unfair to add in the number values of the word December to try to dilute that one. Her father always said what goes around, comes around. He'd never blamed her for her mother, never said a word. Not one word.

"…but the main difficulty I see," Dr. Rosen was saying, "is that you've got to learn to relax. Are you worried about anything in particular, Mira, because if you are—"

"No. Nothing. I'm fine."

She counted the value of each letter of his name. Hal Z. Rosen. One. She felt her left eyelid spasm uncontrollably.

"Tomorrow is the first day of a new year," he reminded her.

Day one. The first. The last. The beginning of one life, the end of another. She was born on January 1st, the day her mother died of heart failure.

"Many people make New Year's resolutions. Why don't we think of this as a time for you to make some healthy changes in your life? It wouldn't hurt to study a relaxation technique. Yoga might be helpful…"

Mira stared out the window. One car went by. A 1990 Chevrolet. Everywhere she looked the message blared, indelibly imprinting itself on her soul. All her life she'd known things would have been different if only her mother hadn't died giving her life. Her father had said that often enough. If only she could reverse this perverse fate. But again her dad's words rang true—"Nobody cheats God."

"…we only have one heart. We have to take care of it. Even when a weakness of the heart runs in a family, there's a lot one can do to reverse what seems inevitable. Make another appointment—say three weeks—we'll see how you check out then."

By the time Mira reached home she had convinced herself that the universe was sending her a message. Dr. Rosen was the medium. Atonement was possible, despite the dismal view of life her father had drummed into her head. Change was in store. She began in the kitchen.

Mira cut off the broom handle to add a fifth leg to her kitchen table. Four chairs with four legs each made sixteen, plus the five table legs. Twenty–one. Two plus one equaled the fortuitous three. Next she cleaned out the cupboards, chucking a tin of tuna so that the cans numbered nine. There were nineteen leaves left on the Boston lettuce. One went into the garbage chute in the hallway. Glasses, dishes, her mother's good silverware that she'd begged her dad for when she'd been old enough to appreciate it, were counted. The number of napkins left in the package. The pages of each cookbook.

Moving to the living room she panicked and shredded a throw cushion then, realizing she had miscounted, frantically shredded another. The middle of her chest still ached but she knew she had to finish or there would be no peace. Forty minutes later eight flower pots were left, a dozen magazines, forty–seven compact discs and just two coasters, but the last didn't matter because only her father visited, when he was in town.

The bedroom was easy. Long ago Mira had made a tally of the pink tea roses on the curtains and matching bedspread. She counted under-wear, socks, hangers in the closet. She checked the bathroom, adding up Stimudent picks, assessing how many ounces of vaginal douche were left in the bottle, checking her weight on the scale in both pounds and kilograms. The model number on the blow dryer totaled six. The shower curtain rod held nine rings.

By the time Mira finished it was midnight. One and two. The eve of a new year. Change was underway, she could feel it. She called her father and left a "Happy New Year" message on his machine, secretly relieved that she didn't have to talk to him. Especially tonight. Now that she had taken control of her future, she didn't need any negative influences jinxing her efforts.

Despite the ache in her chest that had turned into a dull pain, she celebrated by brewing herself two cups of Earl Grey tea, using two bags, and bringing them into the bedroom so she could lie down and listen to the radio.

She sipped from one cup, then from the other, and closed her eyes. The broadcast from Times Square was lively. Normally she hated New Year's Eve and spent the evening alone, except when her father was around. For once she felt in tune with such exuberance. There was a feeling of transformation in the air. Out with the old, in with the new. Dr. Rosen was right. Relaxation was the key. Her fate was, after all, in her own hands, not some crazy numerology system. She'd been push-ing herself. The pain in her chest was becoming sharp.

She took in a deep breath. Air filled the pockets of her lungs and she expelled it in two easy breaths. The chest pain dulled a bit. Her arms and legs felt heavy. Her neck and chest began to lighten. Tension floated away.

Her eyes snapped open and her heart slammed hard against her chest wall. How could she be so stupid? She raced to the tool box for the tape measure. The floor. Ten by nineteen. One hundred ninety. One and nine. A small cry burst from her. Double that for the ceiling, but the height of the walls had to be counted as well. She climbed a chair with two phone books on the seat. The room's dimensions totaled a number that, when the digits were added together, produced three. But Mira knew she had to count the dimensions of all the rooms or it would be cheating. The living room, the kitchen. She totaled them on her calculator. Only the bathroom was left.

Pain stabbed her chest every few seconds. She placed the chair with the phone books in the tub for a little extra height. Her breath came in shallow warning gasps. This last set of numbers, she thought, will be final. She added the bathroom numbers in with the dimensions of the other rooms. The total of everything added together eventually broke down to the number three. She was in physical pain but emotional relief.

As her foot felt for the tub rim, Mira glanced at her digital watch. One AM. The phone books slid apart and she toppled sideways, twisting, grasping, finding nothing concrete to grab on to. Her face smashed against the sink. She heard a crack at the base of her neck. The side of her head slammed onto hard floor tiles.

Consciousness returned slowly. Time blurred. Images floated by, dragging her body to the phone. Ambulance attendants in deathly white, police officers in mourner's black. The invasive odor of antiseptic. A light dazzling enough to usher in those being born, or to draw out the dying.

She tried to cry out for mercy but a clear plastic mask over her mouth and nose silenced her. "Count backwards from ten," a voice commanded. Ten to one.

Later, another voice. And her father's face, smiling. "A shame. One vertebra, damaged irrevocably. Paralyzed for life."

Mira could not see her useless body. At least she was no longer aware of the splitting of her heart. She sensed her cells beginning the long, torturous process of decomposition. They would break down first in large groups then individually until finally the last would dissolve. A fitting offering to the god of one. The stern god of sacrifice. A demanding god who had finally been paid off.

Or had he?

She needed to know for sure. A sign. A number would indicate whether or not he had been appeased once and for all. But Mira's head was locked in place. Now. Forever. Her field of vision limited to the ceiling. Blank, empty whiteness. Cold terror burned through her stomach and up her chest and stabbed the back of her throat, ready to spew from her mouth. There was nothing to count! No way of ever being certain.

She squeezed her eyes and mouth shut to contain the dry ice wail. Frost on the inside of her eyelids condensed into a face. Her father's face. It swirled and shifted and became someone else's face and that one melted into someone else...This was the sign!

Mira counted her four co-workers at the office—Mary, Lucy, Jason, Betty—and the twelve tenants in her apartment building—the Fairwells, Mrs. Owen—wait! She'd better count that woman who only worked one week then quit...what was her name?...and the couple who sub-let the Andrews' apartment...that made nineteen...one and nine...one!—her two cousins and three aunts and one uncle and two grandparents still living, her father's friends—twenty-three...yes, there were plenty to count—five people at the laundry—what about the woman walking out the door as she walked in?—twenty-seven worshippers the last time she'd attended church, or was it twenty-eight?—

The total was fifty-six...no!...fifty-seven...five plus seven...twelve...

one plus two...three...the faces changed so fast!—the supermarket, the subway, Christmas shopping—she was on the up escalator, how many were coming down?—four customers in line at the corner grocery, two at the dry cleaners—did she get them all?—the three men who collect the trash cans every Thursday—no, six shoppers at the corner store...that totalled what?—the people who read the news on television—

Eventually she would reach the final number—the hair stylist and shampoo girl at the salon—why couldn't she keep track?...she'd have to start over—her father, Mary, Lucy, Jason—four—Doctor Rosen's three patients and her dentist's patients—

And when she saw that final, conclusive number—a snapshot of her girl scout troop—she forgot the total again!...if only she could use the calculator...she'd have to start all over—her father, Mary, Lucy—

That final number would—the boys on the high school football team—faces sped by—her father, Mary—where was she now?—the thirty–three hundred seventy–two students pictured in her graduating class photo—

Would seal—her college roommate Virginia and her parents—her head was about to explode—and Virginia's brother's girlfriend—

Her fate—the paperboy and her father and—

She'd better go back—her father...

Truth

The old woman seemed to materialize out of the fog. Gaye braked hard. Her body lurched forward. Her head slammed against the top of the steering wheel before her neck whiplashed back to crash against the headrest. She rubbed her forehead, wishing she'd buckled up.

The old woman leaned against the hood, stared straight through the windshield at her. The edges of the car's headlights carved sinister shadows as they crawled up the cadaverous face.

Gaye admitted to herself that she had been upset, was still upset, barely paying any more attention now than the instant the Ford had almost crushed the woman. Pain tangled in emotions. The divorce papers had arrived before breakfast, and already Bill was busy trying to sell the house out from under her. Only quick thinking slowed the process when she'd lied that she'd lost the deed. And Puzzio broke his chain and had been missing from the backyard since last night and she'd better think of something to tell Puzzio's owner when Peg got back from Cancun on Monday. And yes, her mother's chiding voice—preserved and ever present thanks to answering machine technology—kept ringing through her head. All of it created an undercurrent of blame that floated about the level of Gaye's shoulders.

The old woman moved to the side window. Before Gaye knew what she was doing, she pressed the button and the glass between them disappeared. She caught herself in time to stop it halfway. "I'm sorry. I didn't see you," she blurted, knowing the truth sounded false.

While she babbled further excuses, the crone–like creature said nothing. Her disheveled hair imbedded with muck reminded Gaye of her mother's iron gray. They were the same height, too, the same towering build. Suddenly Gaye realized she was doing all the talking and stopped.

The traffic light changed; a green the color of new mold flickered in the woman's dark eyes and reflected off pale, almost translucent skin. Gaye had an urge to roll the window up but that would be rude. She'd almost killed her.

She glanced around at the deserted intersection. Rain had slicked the asphalt. Boarded up buildings outnumbered grated storefronts. The air felt dense with ozone and stank of things rotting. Nothing warm–blooded in sight, not even an alley cat. Except for the old woman.

Guiltily, Gaye looked up into the puckered face and saw a familiar expression.

"Liar!" the old woman shrieked.

The light turned yellow, not sun yellow but the discolor of aging. It reflected in those eyes and dripped down sagging cheeks. In a flash, blood bounced off her, violent crimson rage. The thought came to Gaye: she's a chameleon.

"Look, are you okay?" she asked.

The old woman stared down at her, staring her down. She must have been attractive once, Gaye thought, and then felt sick. The threadbare coat matted with dried God–knows–what. A ragged mildewy scarf wrapped haphazardly around the throat.

The crone had kept her hands in her coat pockets. Until now. One hand began to lift. It glittered scaly and twitched like a fish being pulled from the bay. Gaye blinked hard, wondering if she'd suffered a concussion when she braked. Dread crept up her spine, as if a door had opened into a realm that should never be exposed to the light of day. But there was no light of day, just the darkness of night. The time when what lay hidden finally, finally surfaced, and…

The hand moved level with her face. A finger separated from the others to point at her. The four inch stained fingernail was more crooked than any she had seen on a human being. Her skin crawled. The jagged claw pivoted, as if taking aim at her left eye.

Gaye jabbed the window button. Painfully slowly the glass climbed. Not fast enough. The single claw jammed between the glass and the frame. By instinct, Gaye shoved the stick shift into drive and stomped on the gas pedal. The car screamed into the night. Heart slamming, she glanced at the window on her left and breathed a sigh of relief: the woman was not hanging onto the car. The side mirror. The rearview. Not on the street either.

But panic swallowed relief. Gaye skidded a corner. Tires shrieked. The odor of gas clogged her nostrils.

For comfort, she switched on the radio. Sound blasted from the speakers, eerie music that stabbed at her soul. Acid words, gnawed at her brain:

> *Strange is the night when black stars rise,*
> *And strange moons circle through the skies,*
> *But stranger still is*
> *Lost Carcosa…*

She punched the OFF button, trembling. The night felt like an enormous black leech that offered no predictions, no protections.

It wasn't until she reached her own street, far across town, that both the car and her pulse slowed. She pulled into her driveway and stopped, not quite ready to reach for the control to open the garage door. Her hand still shook as she flipped down the sun visor. Instead of her face in the mirror a plaster mask of terror met her brown–circled eyes. The stylish Guatemalan cap lay askew over mahogany hair that had tried to escape in all directions. Fear lines gouged the normally smooth skin of her face.

Too much stress lately, she told herself. It's taking a toll. Maybe I'm losing it.

Finally, she pulled herself together, raised the garage door and parked. She switched the ignition off and opened the door. As she stepped from the car, something dropped from her lap and pinged onto the concrete. She looked down. A severed claw lay like a gnarled opaque insect about to fly up and attack. Under the dim garage bulb it sparkled and glowed as if possessed by an otherworldly light. Gaye not only couldn't stop screaming, she didn't want to.

"Why are you lying?"

Her mother's voice vibrated through the phone at high pitch, as always. Gaye moved the receiver a couple of inches from her ear and pulled a kitchen counter stool close to the wall phone. Last night left her exhausted and she slept late. Her eyes would hardly open, she felt drugged, and wondered why she'd bothered getting up to answer the ringing phone when she knew who would be on the other end. "I'm not lying, Mother, I didn't call you back because I was busy."

"What were you doing at midnight?"

"None of your business."

"How dare you speak to me like that? Now that you let a perfectly charming husband walk out on you, naturally I'm worried, you living in that big house all alone. Any mother would be—"

"I won't be living here much longer."

"You're not letting him sell it? I hope that doesn't mean you're planning on moving back home because—"

"No to both questions, Mother." One lie, one truth.

While her mother rattled on, Gaye shook her head, trying to clear it. Once again her mother had caught her vulnerable and she'd revealed more than she'd wanted to. But Gaye was not in the mood for a fight.

The night had sucked her energy. When she stopped screaming, and she stopped suddenly, as if crashing into a verbal glass wall, she'd used the dustpan and brush to scoop up that hideous claw.

Not only did she toss it in the trash can, but she threw away the pan and brush as well. At least she thought she did. The whole event felt gauzy, distant. In a state like sleep–walking, she'd wheeled the can to the curb.

Gaye only vaguely remembered entering the house, locking the door, scrubbing her hands. She stripped and tossed everything she'd been wearing into the hamper, showered, and crawled into bed. And lay shaking beneath the covers. She left the night table lamp on but closed her eyes, thinking, it's over. I'm free.

She must have drifted into a sweat–soaked, comatose sleep until the phone rang and she'd staggered into the kitchen where her mother bulldozed into her mind.

"Look, Mother, I'm sorry I snapped at you. I had trouble sleeping."

"You're not taking anything, are you? You know what I mean. And don't lie to me the way you did before."

"For God's sake, if you're referring to marijuana, I haven't smoked grass for a dozen years, since college, as you know perfectly well."

"If your brother said that, I'd believe him. What, in God's name, were you doing that you couldn't sleep?"

Gaye sighed. "Thinking. Just thinking."

Last night she'd shared the bedroom with terror. Had there always been shadows in the darkness? And sounds, even in the light? Why should a new house groan as if in pain? She heard a sharp tapping sound, but couldn't locate the source. And the words to that stupid song she just happened to tune into on the car radio: "*…But stranger still is Lost Carcosa.*" Carcosa. What was that? Some poetic license thing, an Atlantis?

"What?" she said, unsure what her mother had just asked. In the warm kitchen, even with the remnants of late afternoon sun streaming through the window, she shivered. Fear crawled up the back of her thighs and prompted her to walk to the window and glance out. The rain had washed most of the fog back out to sea. The trash can sat at the curb, as solid as her mother's voice.

"I asked you why?"

"Why what, Mother?"

"Why were you thinking in the middle of the night?"

"Look, I had work to do."

"Since when do you work on Saturday nights, or is this another one of your little fibs? Gaye, when will you learn to tell the truth. The truth will set you free, you know—"

Gaye felt the poison clawing its way through her brain. The left side of her face felt hot.

Gaye knew she had lied. The kind of fib all children tell. She stole her mother's fingernail polish. And used it. And said she hadn't. Her mother forced a confession.

"The truth will set you free, Gaye." An open palm cracked against her cheek. One blood red fingernail sliced flesh and gouged her eyeball. Shards of color stabbed her brain...

As her mother rambled on, Gaye thought, *I'll never win. Why can't I remember that and stop trying?*

She flipped on the coffee maker and turned to the fruit bowl on the counter. And froze. Three Granny Smith apples. Two oranges. Two tangerines. A spotted banana with a rotting claw jammed into a seam. The sharp tip of the grotesque thing pointed at Gaye.

She fell back, knocking over the stool.

"You were always so dishonest. God knows, I tried to correct—"

"Mom, gotta go."

Gaye slammed the receiver into the cradle.

Sun beams penetrated the glass in the window and stroked the talon. It glittered multi–colored. Mesmerized, Gaye overcame her revulsion and stepped closer. She balled her trembling fists and massaged her sore eyes. The thing was still there, pointing at her. Accusing her.

She closed her eyes and shook her head. When she reopened her eyes, the claw was not in the banana. But the decomposing skin bore a long gash where it had been.

Gaye looked around, shaking. It was in the house. With her. Waiting to dig into her eye, past the iris and into the pupil and imbed itself right smack into her vulnerable mind forever.

Fear coagulated into two–dimensional reality and Gaye felt her mind slip, like a transmission shifting to another gear, another time. Terror accentuated hard edges and brightened colors, investing inanimate objects with the potential for movement.

When the fruit bowl skidded across the table and the table hopped along the floor, Gaye screamed and grabbed onto the edge of the sink. It rattled angrily beneath her grip. She let go and the force of the tremor threw her across the room.

She fell. The floor beneath her rumbled. She crawled to the door frame and curled into a semi–fetal position, covering her head with her arms. The room and everything in it pitched. Her body felt small, filled with panic at being shaken by a large and threatening force.

The tremors stopped. Gaye opened her eyes. The talon lay inches from her left eye. It had sucked in the color of the tiles but mutated the blue to the ghastly color of a corpse.

One thought surfaced: if she returned the claw to the old woman and admitted that she tried to kill her, the retribution would stop.

She picked the thing up with tweezers and wrapped it carefully in a tissue, which she folded and stuffed into a side pocket of her purse. The sun had set and light faded from the sky as she drove back into the dark heart of the city.

The sun finally set and the sky faded. Gaye had been driving for hours near the wharfs, searching for the intersection.

Searching for the woman.

Her brain cried out that she was acting irrationally, but Gaye heard that warning as a faint whisper and paid no attention. She was too busy battling the shrieking dread that threatened to overwhelm her.

By nine she'd found the intersection. She resigned herself; she needed to ask the locals for help.

Makeshift housing littered the sidewalks. Cardboard flattened and propped up, plastic garbage bag tents, plywood structures for the lucky ones.

Gaye climbed out of the car and approached an old man lying half inside a ripped sleeping bag. A rancid smell stopped her cold. "Excuse me."

Rheumy eyes plugged into a bobbing skull stared at her. Gaye saw something out of the corner of her eye skitter under his leg. She wanted to run.

"I'm looking for a woman. Old. Big. Gray hair. Dark eyes. Dressed in an overcoat with a scarf. Really long nails. Do you know her?"

The milky eyes stared unfocused.

"Our Cass. She gone." The voice boomed from behind Gaye. She jumped and gasped and turned all at once. When she'd calmed enough to speak, she said, "Gone? Where?" to the black woman perched on the edge of the curb behind her. Her skin and clothing were so dark she seemed to blend into the night.

"Inland."

"Inland?" Gaye repeated dumbly.

"Last night. Out the middle." She pointed to the intersection. "Hit by Satan's jalopy."

After a moment Gaye said uneasily, "The driver of the car, did he take Cass to the hospital?"

"Nobody see that driver but G.O.D." The woman stepped closer and Gaye stepped back. "Our Cass, she don't need no infirmary in inland."

"Where is inland?"

"In land of the dead." She grinned like a corpse returning to life.

Gaye bolted. The moment she switched on the ignition, the same song as last night crashed her eardrums, but tonight the words were different:

Songs that the Hyades shall sing,
Where flap the tatters of the King,
Must die unheard in
Dim Carcosa.

When Gaye arrived home, the rotting corpse of the old woman was standing in her kitchen.

A putrefying arm lifted and a finger without a fingernail pointed accusingly.

"How did you get in?" Gaye asked.

"Anybody can get in an unlocked door. You know what I want."

Gaye dropped her purse onto the table. Even dead, this woman resembled her mother. Iron hair. Iron will.

She'd come back for the claw. Well, there was nothing to do but give it to her.

"The truth will set you free," the woman laughed.

"I'm sure you're right." Gaye took the tissue from her purse. "I lied. I tried to kill you. I stole what's yours. Maybe the truth will free me." She handed over the soft tissue.

Without missing a beat, the woman unraveled the paper. When she reached the claw, color pierced the room.

Gaye tried to hide her eyes from the harsh colors but pain seared through her brain and she cried out, "The truth hurts. It always hurts me."

She snatched up the luminous talon before the woman could say anything more and plunged it deep into her dead left eye.

The rigid claw slid easily into the boiled–egg–like flesh. The eyeball held the talon for a moment. Then, in a heartbeat, the pupil swallowed it completely.

The woman's face drained of color. The livid mask expressed confusion then betrayal. The claw must have reached something soft and vulnerable because Gaye noticed an emotion she was familiar with— the feeling of being misunderstood.

A scream. Body convulsing as it fell.

When the coffee finished dripping into the pot, Gaye poured herself a cup. The radio played music that she'd grown to love, and she sang along with the lyrics of Cassilda's song:

Song of my soul, my voice is dead,
Die though, unsung, as tears unshed
Shall dry and die in
Lost Carcosa.

She pulled a stool up to the phone and dialed her mother's number.

The phone rang and rang until the answering machine came on. The voice offered neither prediction nor protection, but it was familiar, and Gaye found herself laughing until tears streamed down her cheeks. "Mother, I'm so sorry. You were right all along. Truth does set you free. But first it makes you awfully miserable."

Inspiriter

Paul spotted her the Saturday after he arrived at the farm. Unrelenting sunshine had bleached her quaint straw hat titanium, as white as her waist–length hair. Under the cloud–studded cerulean sky, hair and hat glowed brilliant as white gold. Pale arms at her sides, she headed north at an easy pace through the corn fields toward what he'd learned was "the Jacobs place."

Paul opened the screen door and called out, "Hi there!" imitating the locals.

She should have heard him. A crow protecting raspberry bushes across the road screeched. The warning vibrated through the fresh air, startling him, but she didn't seem to notice.

He inhaled. Sweet hay. Sweet and sour manure. Rich earth. Basic scents untainted by the worship of product. He was sick of the city, the twisted values that substituted racing into the future for life in the present, annihilating process en route. More, he was sick of himself. Life no longer reverberated with passionate mystery, constantly unfolding. His days had become predictable hysteria, people busy stereotypes, and worse—he concretized that frantic banality in highly commercial art that sold so well in Toronto, Montreal and Vancouver. The horror of his empty existence had driven him out here for the summer, to Odessa, small–town Ontario. Maybe, if he could just slow down, catch the moment, he could unearth his *anima*. What the classical artist had called soul.

Her slim body, in loose purple nightshade pants and a daffodil shirt, glided easily through the young corn. She stopped to pick and husk an ear and eat the raw kernels straight from the cob.

When she started walking again, her movements struck him as animal grace imprisoned in human form. Primitive within socialized. He wondered what she was seeing. And thinking. Although he had abandoned the bulk of his materials in Toronto, he fantasized about painting her and absently reached for the sketchbook and charcoal on the porch swing. If he had his acrylics, he would layer thin washes to create shading and capture that repressed wildness. Or better yet air–brushing, although he had not brought that equipment with him either. As the fields of corn engulfed her, an outline formed unconsciously on the page.

Snap out of it! he told himself. He was helping form devour content. Fantasy annihilate reality. The medium suck the life out of the message. He threw the sketchbook onto the swing and ran across the lawn to the dirt road. She was already out of sight but he jogged after her, determined to make human contact.

As he rounded the curve, a startlingly modern farmhouse came into view. It was at the dead end of the road and Paul noticed the stainless–steel mailbox with JACOBS precisely stenciled on the side.

On his first shopping trip in the town, the man at the hardware store had mentioned Jacobs. "Moved up here some five years ago," he'd said. "Claims he's from down in the Caribbean. White man from the Caribbean. Imagine that."

Paul learned more about Jacobs than he wanted to know—produced a super yield insect–resistant corn that he refused to sell locally—the entire crop exported back to where he came from.... The store owner warned that Jacobs wasn't friendly; he had also confided, "Pays cash for everything, and has plenty of it."

The girl was nowhere in sight. A large man, mid–fifties, with ruddy cheeks and midnight hair that trapped sunlight carried an aluminum pan toward lethargic hens inside a wired yard. He wore crisp overalls, and the requisite Wellingtons, all of which were spotless.

As Paul passed between the shiny viridian pickup—even the tires were clean—and the pristine house, he peered through a window and saw an empty kitchen. No sign of her. Near the chicken coop lay a neat vegetable patch, mature plants meticulously staked and tied, not a weed in sight. Five corn cribs loaded with the early crop stood at the edge of the closest field; beyond, the fields sparkled, dense with emerald stalks.

The man scattered a meager amount of corn meal through the chicken wire. Seven hens jerked toward the grain like animated puppets. The man turned on a hose and aimed it at a water dish.

"Hi there." Paul spoke louder. "Mr. Jacobs?"

Before the hens could get to the food, water flailed them, chasing them into the coop, soaking the grain and the ground. The man then carefully rewound the hose and returned it to its hook. When he turned, Paul was shocked by the pocked skin, gouged with down–turned lines and dabbed with white scars. His thin lips seemed incapable of either offering or taking. From this hideous mask, hooded obsidian eyes glared into Paul's—vulture assessing potential carrion.

Paul stuck out his hand reluctantly. "Hi. I'm Paul Williams. I'm renting the old Knowlton place. Next door." His hand was ignored so he lowered it. "I was just out for a walk. Thought I'd meet my neighbors.

I saw your daughter, or a young lady wearing a straw hat coming this way, and—"

"I own this property, and everything on it. Get off it while you still can." The man turned his back on Paul, crossed the clipped yard and walked up the back steps and into the house, his movements as efficient and economic as his words. The screen door slammed behind him.

Once Paul got out of sight of Jacobs' place, he realized his shoulders were tense. He knew men like Jacobs in the city. Gallery owners. Masters at the game of control. The end rationalized the means. Product was the god that granted money, power and prestige. Paul rotated his head slowly, feeling the calcium deposits between the vertebra in his neck crack. The anger loosened its grip.

Split–rail fences ran along both sides of the road. Every fifty feet Jacobs had posted TRESPASSERS WILL BE PROSECUTED signs. *Master of all the corn he surveys*, Paul thought. The idea of Jacobs staking out territory infuriated him again. He climbed over a fence and fearlessly walked between the stalks planted north–south. Blue cornflowers lined the path. The air smelled verdant and sun kneaded his back muscles, but he still felt irritated. Jacobs reeked of death and power. And barely controlled sadism. Paul wondered if the girl was a relative, or a friend, not that he could imagine Jacobs having any of the latter. Maybe she didn't even live there. But that was the last farm on the road before the lake. A woman so delicate, sensitive, yet earthy—she couldn't be with a gargoyle like Jacobs by choice....

White glinted ahead. Two rows over. He saw her reach out and pluck an ear from a stalk. She didn't seem to hear him approach from behind and he was afraid he'd frighten her. He rustled leaves and cleared his throat twice, then said "Hi!" but she still didn't turn. Maybe she's deaf, he thought, or, like Jacobs—doesn't want to hear.

He stepped around to face her. She had stripped the cob, exposing kernels even whiter than her hair. He wondered if this was a hybrid Jacobs had brought with him from the Caribbean. The only corn Paul remembered seeing even remotely like it was the starchy 'white corn' his dad fed the pigs back in Brandon, but that was yellow compared to what this girl held.

She dug out one kernel, put it in her mouth and swallowed without chewing. He watched her eat two more. When she still didn't look up, he tapped her arm; the heat of the day had not penetrated her skin. Her eyes followed his hand, as though waiting for signals. *She is deaf*, he realized. He moved his hand to his face, and smiled to reassure her.

Her eyes reminded him of Jessie's, the depressed life–drawing model at art school who most of the time had been drugged to the hilt on heavy–duty anti–depressants. The irises were ash. Matte. No luster at all, as though the liquid had dried up leaving circles of powdery gray tempera behind. He knew this girl wasn't blind, because she'd followed his hand, but she stared blankly, unseeing.

He pointed at his chest. "Paul. Your new neighbor."

Her skin was calcimine, smooth, lineless flesh that the big hat did an extraordinary job of protecting. Set against it were brows as black as her widow's–peek was white—India ink on bleached paper. Where her generous lips didn't quite meet in the center, the space between them formed a tiny 'o', as if caught in perpetual surprise. His energy galvanized. The aesthetics of perfection enthralled the artist; her bizarrely controlled wildness taunted the man. The thought crossed his mind: *she might be the most repressed woman I've ever seen, but, God help me, what's under that?*

She had not blinked once. In fact, she seemed to be barely breathing. He considered that she might be mentally impaired, and that what he was about to do could be construed as politically incorrect, to say the least. But the urge to draw her was overwhelming. Now. And there was more. He didn't understand it, but he needed to be near her. To smell her. To touch her skin.

"Hot day. Come over for a cool drink. We'll get to know each other." When she didn't answer, he took her hand and she followed obediently.

What am I doing? he asked himself, leading her up the porch steps. But the sensation of the small cool hand within his merged with the penetration of the sun, the clarity of the air and the unpretentious perfume of the soil.

He placed a glass of lemonade on the table and sat next to her on the porch swing. She picked at the corn cob she still held, continuing to eat the chalk–white kernels. Paul put one in his mouth and bit down. Sour mold coated his tongue. He spat the kernel out. As she ate, she watched without really seeing him. For some reason he could accept that.

He picked up the charcoal and sketchbook and drew her heart–shaped face, then the maize yellow shirt, open at the throat, exposing her delicate collarbone. Hands damaged from rough work had collapsed around the cob in her lap and he smudged the coal lines to capture them. It had been years since he'd drawn a human being and her eyes challenged him. Behind the gray flatness were sparks. Pain. Terror. Anger. And something ephemeral. It called to him, awakening a feeling crushed by the weight of passionless glass and chrome. He heard the whisper of life buried in burnt umber soil. Writhing. Undulating. Hot.

His hand moved faster—he felt driven to recreate that primitiveness, to possess it, to bring her darkness into the light.

Hours passed in silence. She had not moved. He could not remember a model as patient as his 'muse.'

Paul filled two sketchbooks, one with black charcoal, the other using oil pastels, cursing himself for the lack of better materials. Gradually he geared down to her stillness. He felt his heart beat and touched the inside of her cool wrist, hoping they were in sync, but couldn't find a pulse. Her essence was near, though, within reach. He longed to stroke the unknown lingering behind the fortress, to meld with the concealed.

A noise jarred him.

Jacobs' half ton plowed the lawn and screeched to a stop feet from the bottom step. He jumped out, leaving the door open, and in two steps reached the porch.

The girl only noticed him when he yanked her to her feet. Her face remained expressionless.

Jacobs glared first at her, then Paul. His eyes bulged like a bird–of–prey on the attack.

"Look," Paul stood, "she just came over for a lemonade—"

"Come near her again and I'll kill you!"

Jacobs dragged her down the steps and shoved her into the pickup before Paul could stop him. The vehicle door slammed. The truck reversed, then barreled across the lawn. It accelerated. Paul raced to the road, using his body as a roadblock. Jacobs bore down on him. In a split second Paul hurtled himself into a ditch, gasping in pain as his ankle twisted. The truck missed hitting him. Just.

He crawled to his feet, ankle smarting, and stared down the dust-enshrouded road. Twilight and silence pressed into the empty space within him where she had lived. That emptiness ached but behind that feeling loomed blind fury.

It wasn't until he stood peering through the side window of Jacobs' farmhouse that Paul realized what he was doing.

The girl, emotionless, ladled thick white liquid from a pot into a porcelain bowl. She carried the bowl to the table where Jacobs was tearing into roast chicken and mashed potatoes. The girl sat quietly, facing Paul. If she saw him, she didn't let on. Blank–eyed, she brought a steaming spoonful of soup to her lips and swallowed it, disregarding the temperature. Despite himself, he saw an Alex Colville painting: window split into four panes; beautiful, silent farm girl eating soup; hurricane lantern on sideboard. Jacobs was the flaw on this canvas.

Paul stood at the window until the sky turned raven and crickets screeched. He watched her waiting on Jacobs, hand–and–foot. Jacobs had her paralyzed with fear, that was obvious; Paul's blood seared his veins.

After dinner—after she had washed the dishes, thoroughly cleaned the already spotless kitchen and taken him a beer—Jacobs went into another room, out of sight. He yelled, 'Mira.'

Immediately, as if she were mechanical and a switch had been turned on, she stopped what she was doing and lighted the hurricane lamp. She carried it with her out of the room. Paul moved to the back of the house.

A small part of his brain flashed a warning: this is not your business. But when Jacobs pulled her roughly onto the bed and tore open the buttons of the yellow blouse....

Her eyes got to Paul. A helpless animal. Trapped by a manipulative power. An animal that had given up struggling. As Paul burst into the bedroom, he was vaguely aware that the irrationality of his act did not matter to him.

Before Jacobs could get up, Paul's hands clamped around his throat. "You treat her like a slave! Your own personal whore!"

Jacobs' fist smashed against his ribs. Paul gripped the windpipe tighter. Strong hands grabbed his wrists, nearly crushing them.

"She's not your wife or your daughter, is she?" Paul screamed.

Jacobs gasped, "You don't know what she is."

"I know what you are!" Suddenly Paul saw his thumbs crushing the vulnerable air passage. Jacobs face had become a hideous crimson bust.

Paul pulled away. Mira, the front of her shirt torn open, stood beside the bed like a marble statue. The plea for freedom in those dimmed eyes tore open his heart. "She's not happy. Not with you." He took her hand and turned toward the door.

He heard a sound behind him and let go of Mira for a second. Only a second. Too many things happened at once. Glass shattered near his head and hot lamp oil scalded his cheek. Darkness overwhelmed light. Something slammed into Paul's stomach. He struggled with it and then, inexplicably, it was gone. Jacobs' scream split the black air. The curtains ignited and at the same instant, flames licked the sheets. Jacobs became human fire. Paul couldn't find Mira. Smoke forced him out of the blazing bedroom. He shouted her name and searched the house, but the fire had already spread to other rooms.

He staggered outside coughing and finally found her at the edge of a field, as if protecting the corn. The full moon illuminated her face, her naked breasts, her hair, giving her a silver, other–worldly hue. For a moment her dull eyes appeared to shine like white light, the absence of all color. But Paul had no time to study them. He grabbed her and ran.

They swayed together on the porch swing, as they did each day and night, through sunrise and sunset, munching raw corn. Corn that before—how long ago was it?—had tasted bitter to him, and been impossible to swallow. The last moon of the harvest reflected off her ghostly face, as pale as his limp hands. Her cold ash eyes rested too easily on his. The sketchbook lay abandoned on the table.

His longing to capture her had evaporated, dispersing like the image in a cloud. He felt no need to touch her. Or even to speak with her. And why should he? Her essence wove through him now, a single memory eternally forming, decomposing, reforming. Undying. Undiminishing. Forever.

Punkins

Old Faris ruined it. He really did. Even up until last night, Mischief Night, I felt okay about pumpkins. Now I'm spooked.

"Punkins scare back them tries to return," Faris told me and my brother Jack last month, the night before they found the old guy dead in his upstairs bedroom.

Right! I thought, but didn't say anything. Maybe I was afraid even then and didn't want to know about it.

Jack's twenty–five years older than me. I'm his little sister and he's always on my case, trying to protect me, especially from guys. Anyway, later that night he said, "The old fart's early. When I was a kid, Faris waited until Halloween to shoot the same shit. He's lost it. Only a geek would take him seriously."

Jack had finished raking his leaves just as I delivered the newspaper. Faris handed us cans of Coke so we couldn't just walk away. He was really old, bald, with a face badly puckered, the way a pumpkin gets about two weeks after Halloween. And he was so skinny that when he walked up the street, I got the feeling his bones were about to fold at the hinges. I always thought he was from here because he'd lived next door forever, but that night he said he was born in Ireland and that's how he knew about the Celts.

"Them days folks was wise. Respected the spirits. Knew if they's given half a chance they'll return." Faris lit his pipe and leaned forward in the wicker rocker. I sat on the edge of the porch, Jack sat on a step close to the ground. As I watched the light drain from the sky, I only half listened.

"'Round harvest," Faris continued, "people'd offer up crops, squashes and punkins and the like, to the old ones, those the church men said ain't real. But them clergy couldn't wedge no doubts in a real farmer's mind so's they got tricky. Swore the new power was just like the old. Took the harvest holiday, Samhain, and said t'was the same as All Saints' Day and had 'em give up the grains and such to every saint and pagan alike. Did it to Christmas—that was winter solstice. And

Valentine's was your Lupercalia, but that was back in Rome's heyday. See where changes has got us?"

I didn't see where changes had gotten us and I don't think Jack could either. My brother finished his drink in a quick swallow and crushed the can in his fist. Me, I felt like getting out of there but didn't want to insult old Faris. Besides, I had to collect for the paper the next day. If I could get it now, I wouldn't have to come back.

Faris always made me feel funny. His eyes were weird—two kernels of dried corn. And when he got excited, they lit up as if he'd turned on a yellow light bulb behind them. I hated those eyes but wanted to look, too, if you know what I mean. That night as the sun went down, it flickered in his eyes like a candle flame.

Old Faris stared at me a long time then pointed his pipe at my nose and said, "Dress up Allhallows' Eve. When the seam cracks. They'll try'n slip back."

"Why'd you dress up?" I asked, missing the point. I wasn't sure if I wanted to know but felt I should be polite.

"If'n you walk the streets and appear a vampire or a witch or goblin or such, or even a shadmock or banshee, maybe, just maybe, they won't feel the warm breath comin' outta your lungs and smell the fresh blood pumpin' through veins."

Jack stood and stretched. He nodded at me. I got up too, glad to leave, but old Faris grabbed my wrist. His fingers felt hard, icy bones, the way a corpse must feel. He pulled me close. I had to turn my head because his breath stank like he'd forgotten to brush his teeth for a couple of months. I looked for my brother. He was already on our lawn. Faris sounded like a dog growling when he said, "T'wer punkins warned lovelies like you."

"Come on, Fran!" Jack yelled from our porch.

"That's yer sign. They're comin' back."

"I gotta go." I eased down a step, but Faris held tight. "No pretty faces!" he warned, his breath wet against my ear. "Make 'em fierce. And keep a fire glowin' within. Won't get but half a chance."

I heard our front door slam and nobody had to tell me Jack was inside. Maybe I was rude, but I yanked myself from Old Faris' grip. I took his steps in one leap, hit the ground and flew the four feet across the lawn to our steps, yelling, "See ya, Mr. Faris. Thanks for the Coke." I forgot all about the paper money. Never did collect it.

The clock on the VCR said 11:45. I was still having fun and didn't want to go. Lindsay throws a great Halloween party. The decorations we made together hung around her basement. They looked pretty cool, especially the ghost rising out of its grave. The music was the best—she kept playing the Guns 'n Roses video. There was orange pop and pizza and Andy Toplac said he liked my costume and asked me to dance four songs. I was Jon Bon Jovi again, same as last year, partly because I couldn't think of anything else. The other reason is I'm saving for a new Walkman and didn't want to spend the money on unimportant stuff. Anyway, this year I used silver glitter makeup and a white wig and must have looked more like a girl because everybody thought I was Annie Lennox.

My brother was supposed to pick me up at 11:30. Mom says I have to be home by twelve school nights and keeps warning me about weird guys out there looking for girls my age. I called Jack at the restaurant downtown where he works part–time to help pay his tuition but they told me he was busy and couldn't come to the phone. I decided I better go home by myself or I wouldn't be allowed out on the weekend.

Lindsay's house is thirteen blocks from mine. Usually I wouldn't even think about walking that far, but the buses don't run often at night. I started out going from stop to stop, but the bus never came.

There were a few people out, mostly older, dressed like werewolves, robots, pirates—and one belly dancer—but the kids were finished trick–or–treating. Lots of doors had cardboard witches, Indian corn, and skeletons and there were carved pumpkins in windows and on porches. I didn't like seeing the pumpkins; they made me think about what old Faris said the night before he died. I didn't want to be scared but I guess I was because I kept glancing over my shoulder all the way and shivering. It wasn't exactly cold; wind whistled through the bare trees like in a horror movie. I walked pretty fast and got home about an hour ago, around midnight. Just as I came up our walk I noticed something spooky. There were pumpkins in Faris's windows.

His house has been empty since he died in September. Mom said Mr. Morrison, our neighbor on the other side who sells real estate, told her Faris has a twin brother somewhere out west who wants to put the house up for sale when they finish with the will and stuff. Nobody's supposed to be there now.

Mom was in bed, struggling to wait up for me, and I went in to let her know I was home. She said, "That's good, honey," kissed me and closed her eyes. She works hard and I knew she was tired; I decided not to tell her about the pumpkins.

I came here to my room but haven't taken off my costume yet. I'm too scared to move.

The lights are off. I'm sitting at my window—thank God it's closed. I can see a wedge of Faris's front porch. Empty. Just dead leaves the wind's sweeping across the boards. The three windows on this side of his house are open. The rooms are all black inside. It's what's outside that's got me spooked.

Sitting on each window sill is a pumpkin. All of them are grotesque.

Our houses are so close I can see right through the chunks cut out for eyes and mouths and noses to the other side where different ugly faces are carved at the back. This is too weird.

The pumpkin on the left looks pissed off. The one on the right is so twisted out of shape it looks psychotic. But it's the third pumpkin, in the window directly across from mine, that's making me sweat. I don't know why, but the face reminds me of old Faris. Something about the slit of a mouth, narrow downturned eyes, and the fact that it's not fat but tall and skinny with thin, puckered skin.

Jack just pulled into the driveway. I hear the front door close and him walking up the steps. He opens my door.

"I told you to wait for me." He looks exhausted. "Somebody was sick and I had to work overtime."

"Come'ere," I whisper.

"Holy shit!" he says when he sees them.

"Look at that one." I point at the Faris–like face.

I can tell Jack sees the resemblance, but all he says is, "Sick."

"Looks like old Faris, doesn't it?"

Jack gives me a serious adult stare, one he's been practicing lately. "It looks like a pumpkin. Everybody knows the house is empty. A couple of kids snuck in. It's just a Halloween prank." Then, "I'm beat. See you in the morning." He tries to rumple my silver wig but I duck before too much damage is done.

I don't know why I'm sitting here or what I expect to see. I keep thinking of other things Faris said that last night before they found him.

"Orange is hell fire, the black that's ready to eat you is the evil. Gotta keep the flame inside alive so's the face'll scare 'em back to the other side. Then again, if you're dressed for the occasion, you might try convincin' them you're one of 'em. Failin' that, my lovely, you're doomed."

The candle just went out in the pumpkin that I keep thinking of as Faris. My heart nearly stops. I should get Mom, or Jack, but I'm afraid to move.

The window across the way is opening. It's black in there, dark in here. The fingers lifting the window glint silver in the moonlight. Bony. There's part of an arm, the wrist bone jutting out at a funny angle.

I feel for the candle on my desk and I light it, trying not to think about what I'm thinking about. I can't believe I'm doing this, but I hook my feet under the baseboard heater, open my window and lean out. The ground looks pretty far down. The window across the way is half open and something's materializing from out of that darkness—a face, one I recognize, one I don't want to be seeing.

The wind picks up as I try to bridge the space. I have to keep my hand around the flame so it doesn't blow out and it makes me nervous not holding on. My heart pounds so hard it shakes my body; I'm afraid I'll fall. All the while that window is being raised higher, higher, and inch by inch I'm getting closer to that dark pumpkin. And that skeletal limb. There's a bad smell in the air. Rot.

I lean out just a little further, stretching my body across the gulf that separates us. I can slip the candle inside the pumpkin, I know I can. Just as I start to ease it down into the hollow cavern, the wind kills the flame. My feet come unhooked and I'm off balance, falling. Icy fingers lock around my wrist like a frozen handcuff, just the way Faris grabbed me the night before he died. The air stinks of death.

I scream, first just noise, then "Mama!", then words that sound phony, but I can't stop myself—"Don't hurt me! I'm just like you! Really!"

The skull that was once a face that looks so much like a pumpkin laughs. "Will be, my lovely," I hear an ancient voice promise. "Will be."

i Vermiculture

It stank. Rotting broccoli leaves and tomato ends. Rancid orange peel. Sickeningly–sweet overripe banana. Harsh and bitter coffee grounds. Francis picked through the reeking garbage with the blade of a paring knife. He'd been proven right again. Like most new ideas, this one wasn't working. The worms weren't doing their job.

He dug under the remains of a week's worth of meals, down past the newly formed rich topsoil. They should have been there. Ten starter worms. Dull red–brown. Four–inchers. Squiggling up through the dirt to gobble the putrid mess through one indistinguishable end and excreting something that leads to new earth through the other.

The knife blade flipped over a lemon half. Three fat–bellied creatures slithered along the edge of the yellow–brown citrus fruit, slinking away from the kitchen light. Francis felt his stomach churn. One burrowed under a discarded romaine leaf that wasn't quite long enough to hide it. An end of the worm lifted up into the air slightly as if that were the head and it was looking at Francis. The thing gave him the creeps.

Why was Monica always changing things? After forty years of marriage, he should be used to it, but he wasn't. If she hadn't been such a nut on recycling, they'd still be tossing food scraps in with the rest of the trash like normal people. But oh no, she'd wanted a composter— the latest toy on the market. He thought they were a waste of money. Besides, they needed to be kept outdoors, and the condo had no yard or lawn, only a small deck. One of those cone–shaped plastic bins would have used up a quarter of it; Francis had put his foot down. Kitchen composting was the answer, Monica assured him. Earth worms. In the cabinet. Under the sink. Clean. Out of sight. But not out of mind.

Francis hated creatures that not only failed to resemble human beings but might actively be involved in their decomposition. Insects and reptiles in general. Any kind of worm in particular. Earth worms especially. Blind, dumb, soft–bodied creepers. Driven by instinct. They'd swallow anything, the worst garbage, even rotting flesh. The plumper they were, the more elongated the body, the more detestable.

It was only Monica's promise to be responsible for the whole enterprise that swayed him. All he had to do was empty food scraps into the bin occasionally, instead of into the trash can. The worms would do the rest.

"Eat up," Francis ordered harshly, "or you're fired."

The exposed end of the worm seemed to quiver and Francis blinked. Just looking at it made him nauseated. He had an urge to attack it with the knife but then remembered that when you slice a worm in half you end up with two. He slammed the composter lid shut as well as the cabinet door and started dinner.

"Fabulous meal." Monica dabbed her lips with the napkin, stood and carried only her own plate away from the table. He sighed at her laziness. Through the doorway he watched her open the grey cabinet door and dump the remains from the plate into the compost. "They're doing a great job," she called.

Francis got up and went to have a look. The mound of rotting food that had been sitting near the top of the bin not two hours before had turned into fertile silt. "Impossible!" He could hardly believe his eyes.

"You old curmudgeon. You didn't think it would work." Monica nipped him on the ear lobe gently and at the same time tried to close the cupboard door with her knee, and failed—Francis had to do it. She turned to rinse one glass under the faucet and place it in the dishwasher. "Why can't you do all of them, or none of them?" he said, rinsing the rest of the china and cutlery, but she'd already left the room.

They watched a little tv, crawled into bed early, watched a bit more television and, after an aborted attempt at lovemaking, Monica was snoring. Francis, though, lay wide awake. He should have been reviewing the figures for tomorrow's meeting but instead his brain was busy trying to comprehend how the worms had processed so much waste in so short a time. Eventually it got the better of him.

The kitchen tiles felt cool against his bare soles. He flipped the light switch but the bulb chose that moment to blow. "Wonderful," he mumbled, thinking he really should be asleep. Tomorrow was the big meeting, first thing, and he had to report on the company's profits for the quarter. They were down and it would be tricky and he'd need to be wide awake to use the most conservative wording or be eaten alive by the ravenous up–and–comers, who were pushing for change.

There were no spare bulbs in the storage closet—Monica had forgotten to buy them. He wrote LIGHT BULBS in large letters and underlined the words on the shopping list attached to the refrigerator with a magnet shaped like a briefcase. The light from the dining room would have to be enough. A quick peek, his curiosity might or might not be satisfied, but he'd be off to bed getting the sleep he needed.

The moment he opened the cabinet door he thought he heard a

low rumble, and held his breath. Nothing. The building had been constructed the year he was born; things creaked. He lifted the lid of the compost bin.

Francis had to rub his eyes. The scraps from dinner—quiche, carrot tops and skin, bits of fettuccini, Earl Grey tea leaves, whole wheat pie crust—all of it had vanished. He got the flashlight from the tool drawer. The added light just confirmed reality. The clock on the stove read eleven. The nightcrawlers had devoured everything in what? Three hours?

He was confused, upset in a way he couldn't explain, about to turn away and try to repress awareness of the whole thing, when a sudden movement caught his eye. From the rich new earth a glistening pale dot surfaced. The head, or the tail, of an albino worm. It lurched up and plopped itself onto the topsoil in jerky movements. Francis had no idea a worm could move so fast and it rattled him. Once the worm was still, it lifted one end straight up in the air. There was something abject in its position, as if it were the leader appealing on behalf of the others. Francis knew he was thinking irrationally, but he couldn't help feeling stared at. And he sensed that the worm was waiting. "You get a reprieve. But it's temporary. Until your performance can be reassessed," he said nervously, wondering what on earth kept prompting him to talk to these disgusting invertebrates.

The plump pasty nib facing him seemed to relax. Its body went flaccid. Francis gagged and reached the bathroom in time to throw up dinner in shades of orange, tan and brown.

The meeting did not go well. Francis, half asleep, stumbled verbally. The newest, youngest vice president was on his case the whole time. He left work early, claiming to be exhausted—which he was. All the way home he berated himself. Two new factors that had gouged into profits—the recycling program the local government had forced the company by law to set up, and the union's demands for changes in the working conditions—had eluded him completely during the meeting. No wonder the CEO and the other vice presidents had looked at him as though he were incompetent. The loss didn't make sense because he hadn't fully explained the unorthodox expenses. And now it was too late. Given the current cost–cutting agenda, he'd be lucky if the Board didn't dismiss him. Of course, he could float a memo to each of the brass; in other words, grovel. Might get him off the hook. He'd have to come up with a legitimate–sounding reason as to why he hadn't mentioned the anomalies responsible for such major disbursements.

Damn those worms! If it wasn't for their insatiable hunger, he'd have slept the night before and been wide awake for the meeting.

As Francis pulled into the driveway, anger severed rational thought.

He made a decision. Like a man possessed, he tore open the cupboard doors and lifted the bin out. He snapped a jumbo extra–strength Glad Bag open and deposited the entire recycling bin inside. After he double tied the bag shut, he took it to the trash disposal room and dropped it down the chute.

As he re–entered the apartment, Francis brushed invisible dirt off his hands and sighed in relief. Monica would just have to adapt; they would do what they did before—bag the garbage with the rest of the trash. He poured himself a glass of Chivas and toasted to the adage, "The old ways are the best way."

"You did what?" Monica stood in the kitchen, arms crossed over her chest, lips downturned.

"Calm down. We'll get one of those cone things you wanted in the first place and put it on the deck, all right?" He kept his voice even, his tone rational.

"No, it's not all right. What was wrong with the worms? They were doing the job."

He didn't know how to tell her. And, since having a nap and a decent meal, his earlier actions seemed a bit ill–considered, not that he'd admit it to Monica. "Worms aren't meant to live under kitchen sinks. It's unnatural. They should be outside, in the ground, where they belong. You didn't want a dog for that reason."

Monica stared at him with suspicion. "I don't believe this," she said, shaking her head. "You're afraid of them."

"Don't be ridiculous." Francis picked up his cup of Columbian and headed for the living room, but she was on his heels.

"You're afraid of a few earth worms. That's it, isn't it? They scare the pants off you because they're something new and therefore terrifying."

"I refuse to indulge in this inane argument. They don't scare me at all. It's simply a matter of a humane approach to another life form."

"Bullshit!" Monica stalked from the room. He heard the apartment door open.

"What are you doing?" he called. There was no answer. A few minutes later, the door closed. He heard plastic being rustled, and hurried to the kitchen.

She had retrieved the bag he'd disposed of and was reinstalling the bin under the sink. "Since it's just a question of humane treatment," she said, scraping leftover salad onto the dirt, "it seems reasonable to keep the worms another day or so, until we get the new recycler. Then we can release them into the park, which is much more compassionate than suffocating them in a non–porous garbage bag while they starve to death, don't you think."

Monica left Francis staring at the closed cupboard door. She'd beaten him at his own game. His temples throbbed. He touched one with a shaking hand; the skin felt clammy.

First thing the next morning, Francis was at the local hardware store. The cones were popular—the store had sold out. The clerk said they expected more next week. It was the same at the other three smaller stores he stopped at on his way to work, and at the two department stores, which he had his secretary phone later.

Damn, he thought, pulling into his driveway that night. He'd been so preoccupied all day that he completely forgot about sending the memo. Now he was stuck in a circular train of thought: he had to find a compost bin; the entire city of Toronto had gone crazy for the latest fad; maybe he should instruct his broker to buy stock in one of the companies—obviously a blue chip of the future. But beneath that track bubbled fear—the worms were under his sink. Waiting.

As Francis walked into the kitchen, he saw a note on the table: call the CEO at home, and a reminder from Monica that tonight was her first pottery class—she'd be in late. He hated changes in their routine.

Although Monica detested cooking, she'd prepared a seafood casserole before she left for work that morning to placate him. It was in the freezer. And there was an amaretto cheesecake—his long–time favorite "…to keep you from eating garbage while I'm away," she wrote. The worms will like that, Francis caught himself thinking, and shuddered.

He picked up the phone, about to dial his boss at home, anxious about what could be important enough to warrant a call on a Friday night, when out of the corner of his eye he noticed the cupboard door beneath the sink open a crack. He hung up and hurried over to close it.

That same rumbling sound came from inside the cupboard, like a trash compactor, grinding. A machine that just won't quit processing. He shook his head, trying to clear it of nonsense.

Francis opened the door slowly. The lid of the bin was ajar. Just like Monica to leave it that way; she did everything half–assed.

He reached in and gripped the lid to straighten it. The churning became a physical sensation. The plastic hummed in his hand. The vibration crawled up his arm. Francis shoved the lid away from him. It clattered to the floor, leaving the interior of the bin exposed.

"Oh my God," he whispered. The remains of breakfast had vanished. There were no scraps from the preparation of the casserole in sight. Rich black soil nearly overflowed the bin. Soil that writhed and undulated from some force just below the surface.

Francis stepped back. He couldn't believe his eyes. Whatever was happening here was abnormal. Perhaps he should get help. But logic intercepted that thought. He hadn't read up on the process, Monica had. Maybe this was part of the composting. It stood to reason there'd be more soil. *But this soon, and this much?* a little voice in his brain warned. And the movement. What about the rumbling?

While Francis struggled as to what to do or not do, a hole spiraled downward into the dark earth. He stared, transfixed, as a white fleshy form nudged its way to the surface. The legless elongated body slithered across the black dirt. Francis was repulsed but relieved. It was still a worm, disgusting to be sure, half the length of a pencil, but thicker. Reality was intact. But tension prompted him to be sterner than he felt. "Don't overproduce," he warned. "You'll flood the market." The worm seemed to shrink back.

The bizarre thought flashed into Francis's mind that the thing was ashamed. He was about to castigate himself for personifying a non-human creature when awareness hit: *the damn thing's pissed at me!* he thought. *It wants praise for its efforts.*

But Francis felt too stubborn to give any. It was enough that he was even talking to a sub–species, talking reasonably, as one intelligent form to another, but to acquiesce to cheap emotional ploys, real or imagined? He had to draw the line somewhere and this was the line.

"Shape up or ship out!" He grabbed the lid and smashed it down onto the bin, slammed the cupboard door shut, then raced from the room. He ripped the clothing from his body, crawled into bed naked, burrowing under the covers, shivering, hiding his head beneath the pillow.

He woke in a cold sweat. Groggy. Not himself. The clock radio read eleven.

Francis's eyes felt glued shut, his stomach an empty pouch. He staggered blindly into the kitchen and to the freezer, instinctively drawn toward nourishment.

The casserole was at the top, the lid of the Corningware frosted from condensation. He lifted the dish out and slid it into the microwave, setting the dial to defrost. While waiting for his meal, Francis rubbed his eyes open then located the course catalogue for the art college. Claywork, Advanced, ran from 7:30 to 10:30. Monica should be in soon. It was too late to call the CEO.

When the timer rang, he yanked out the serving dish. The food was still cold on the surface but he couldn't wait any longer. He took a large slotted spoon from the cooking utensils rack, about to scoop casserole onto a plate, but changed his mind. Instead he used the spoon to eat right from the dish. Chunks of frozen tuna, icy shrimp hardly warm at the center, broccoli imbedded with frost, teeth–chilling noodles; he gnawed through it all.

Everything tasted the same, but Francis was starving. When he looked down he was surprised to see that the serving dish was empty, but for a few onion bits and half a slice of carrot.

He shoved the Corningware away and went to the refrigerator for the cheesecake, then to the flatware tray for a fork. The plate he had been going to use for the casserole was still on the table. But when he sat down and opened the baker's box, the sight of the familiar swirling brown and creamy texture triggered an unforeseen instinct that overwhelmed him. The next thing he knew he was licking cheesecake coated hands and staring at a circular cardboard tray littered with crumbs.

He sat for a few moments feeling blank mentally and bloated physically. Then he took the few bits of food that remained to the composter. The lid had fallen off. Earth overflowed the bin and was piled at least an inch deep on the cupboard floor. The soil pulsed and raged hungrily. Within moments the white worm surfaced. "Contemptible glutton! Overconsuming. Underproducing. Well, you'll get nothing more!" Francis snapped. He felt savage.

The worm reared like a cobra about to spit venom and Francis ducked. He grabbed the slotted spoon and used the convex side to bash its head–tail in. But the hole swallowed up the worm.

Francis dumped the bin's contents onto the kitchen floor. Down on all fours, he grabbed handfuls of dirt and frantically sifted through the soft clods, using his feet to etch trenches in the soil. Finally he found it.

The gross form squiggled in his grip, but not for long. Francis tore it to pieces. At least half a dozen. Then he used the edge of the spoon to chop the warm chunks of flesh as fine as chopped garlic. "Try to recoup those losses!" he shouted.

Fists on hips and breathing heavily, Francis paused. He surveyed the destruction at his feet like a man who'd put in a distasteful but productive day's work. He was just about to congratulate himself when he heard the rumbling. The silt began to move. Fast.

He couldn't believe what he was seeing and rubbed grimy fists into his eyes. Suddenly he became aware of earth packing itself tightly between his toes, spreading them wide, then along his arches, circling his heels and sliding up his ankles. By the time he reacted, his calves were confined by the dense, hard soil. He struggled to shake his legs free but couldn't budge them. Arms flailing, he dug at the dirt cast that now imprisoned his thighs and groin. The frenetic motion resulted in only outer particles falling to the floor; the dirt had hardened like baked clay.

As the earth pack reached his chest and constricted his rib cage, Francis feared he was being buried alive. The putrid stench of decay lit into his olfactory nerve. "There are options!" he screamed. Humid dirt crawled along his shoulders and up his neck. "You've proven an asset. Invaluable. You've still got a bright future ahead—"

Compost squished between his compressed lips. Warm wet life slithered over his tongue, along the roof of his mouth and down Francis's throat. Simultaneously, he gagged on and eagerly swallowed that life. And when the soil blinded him, his heart outpaced itself.

Time stopped.

In the metamorphosis of that eternal moment, old, dead matter transmuted into fertile new life. Although he hated to do it, Francis had to accept the change.

The Middle of Nowhere

The subway train screeched to a halt at the mid–town station. Doors swooshed open. Passengers struggled to get out while those waiting impatiently on the platform fought their way in.

"Why don't they move to one side or the other and let people get on or off?" Ann shook her head in disgust. She turned to Cynthia, seated beside her.

"Nobody wants to budge."

"We're lucky anyway," Cynthia said cheerfully.

"Lucky?" Ann was astonished, then annoyed. She shoved a wayward strand of brown hair back from what she knew was an inoffensive face. She could not seem to keep the bitterness from her voice. "How's getting caught every day in rush hour lucky?"

"Because we usually get a seat."

"Oh." Right! It's the little things. Ann had no illusions that she had ever possessed anything close to Cynthia's optimism; didn't want it. In her opinion, the ride was long, noisy and unpleasantly crowded. On hot, muggy days, like today, getting stuck in one of the old cars without benefit of air conditioning tried her patience. She struggled to not take it out on Cynthia.

When the car was packed with as many people as it would hold, the doors slid closed. The train didn't move immediately so Ann gazed out the window, watching another crowd fill the platform, an endless tide of people. Gradually she focused on her dim reflection in the glass, and her thoughts drifted to familiar territory.

It had been six months since Jerry died. Long enough to grieve. She should be getting on with her life.

Every so often, when honesty crept into her consciousness—usually just before sleep, or when she awoke in the morning, or at moments like this, when nothing was happening that engaged her—she had to admit that life weighed her down.

She felt as trapped by existence as Jerry's plane had been trapped underwater. Every waking moment she was not occupied with work or some other mundane activity she felt tormented by a pall that hung over her, a darkness so insidious she could barely breathe.

Despite a stern warning from her logical mind, her thoughts drifted back, as they always seemed to do, to the phone call. The word *expire,* what the foreign–sounding NYPD blue used, stuck with her. It was such an odd way to put it. A plane had crashed. Everybody was lost. The man paused, then said Jerry's name, then, "I am sorry to inform you that he has expired."

Remembering the phone call started the grim thoughts that traveled a prescribed route to a predictable end. The shock of all the events even now sat under the invisible weight she carried. That blanket of emotionlessness made the thoughts bearable.

The second she had hung up, the word "expired" reverberated through her mind.

Then, a cold realization hit—she felt nothing. Acknowledging to herself the strangeness of that state did not alter it. Her lover had died. Suddenly. Violently. Unexpectedly. Her soulmate was gone. All their plans for the future nipped like the bud of a rose that now had no hope of flowering. The past relegated to only memories, devoid of emotion.

The train slowed. It ground to a halt in the tunnel, between stations. The lights flickered, off, on, off, then back on, but only the auxiliary lighting. She and Cynthia glanced at one another. "Still feeling lucky?" Oh, why did she have to be so nasty to her friend?

Cynthia grinned sheepishly.

Ann could not bring herself to make even a remotely conciliatory comment. This was not right. What was wrong with her?

They waited for the inevitable announcement, which came with a tinny voice, about delay, and patience, and how every effort was being made. As if the passengers didn't know they were delayed, and needed patience! And service would be restored…whenever.

The days blurred in her mind. The heliport on the East River. The memorial service, so cold and objective, at least to her mind. She couldn't associate any of it with Jerry. The trip home in the freezing rain, and then going to his apartment. She selected a number of items as a remembrance, and then decided at the last minute to toss all but one into the pile for The Salvation Army. She kept only the pocket watch she'd given him, that had belonged to her Grandfather. At the back of the watch, in the secret compartment, she had placed strands of her hair next to those of her grandmother's. "You'll be safe if you always carry this with you," she'd told Jerry last Valentine's Day. "My gram told my grandad that, and it's true. They died a week apart, of old age, in their beds, healthy until the end."

Jerry laughed. And kissed her, his generous lips parting hers as he pulled her to him. "I'll wear it always," he said. But he forgot it on the trip to LA, and phoned from the plane to tell her he missed her already, and mentioned the watch, and... And more than six months had passed, and she was still alive. He was not.

"We apologize for the inconvenience."

"Inconvenience! It's been a long time!" Ann snapped. The lack of air conditioning combined with the staleness of the tunnel to make the air feel close. Everyone in their car look wilted. Ann searched in her bag, found a barrette, pulled her hair back and clipped it. The one degree of difference helped for only a few moments.

"Shouldn't be much longer," Cynthia said to the man standing near them, and smiled.

How could she know that? How could anybody know anything? Life was completely unpredictable. No one knew if they would still be breathing in a few moments!

Jerry's death left her cynical. She went through the motions—work, food, tv, sleep. And on weekends—laundry, shopping, etc. Socializing had been cut drastically—what was there to say to anyone now?

At times she wondered how long she could live like this, an emotionless zombie. Friends suggested grief counseling. But no amount of counseling would bring Jerry back. And without him, life felt meaningless.

Before they met, she had given up. That was clear to her. Thirty–five years old, childless, a career pharmacist at a downtown drug store, a small circle of girlfriends she went to movies and the theater with, met for drinks. She had dated, been married briefly to a man she didn't know and then realized she didn't want to know, and had gotten rid of the idea that there is such a thing as love.

Or so she thought.

Then Jerry appeared. Out of nowhere. Quiet. Unassuming. More gentle than she believed a man could be, and still be straight. They met on a park bench, it would be two years ago next month. Each had bought a hot dog and a Coke. They ate, made eye contact, talked about the squirrels, and then both appeared at the same place the next day, not by coincidence each admitted, and that was the beginning of an openness and honestly that bred an intimacy she had not dreamed existed in this world of isolated beings. That such a love could also be filled with physical passion astonished her. It seemed too good to be true. Too good to last. But then, it hadn't, had it? Nothing of value lasts!

The car was unbearably hot. A stench of decay wafted in from the tunnel. So much so that people had progressed to the nasty comment stage.

"This is what we pay for?" one man asked rhetorically.

"Let them try to raise the fares again!" another snarled.

"For goodness sakes, can't we open all the windows?" a woman said, her voice a desperate whine.

"They are open. Maybe we should pry open the door."

And on and on. People impatient to get out, as if they were engulfed. Out of nowhere, it struck her, as if she had lived it, what Jerry must have gone through. The plane, dropping into the river, plunging, the cabin filling with water, everyone panicking, knowing what had happened, not knowing what—if anything—they could do about it. Sensing their own demise.

The experience became vivid, embedded with traumatic emotion. Cold sweat sprouted on Ann's forehead. Her heart pounded quick and loud in her chest. She could not fill her lungs, as if the space was occupied by something else that kept her from sucking in air. She trembled, then convulsed. Voices around her expanded.

Visually, everything appeared too bright, objects and people hard–edged. I'm dying, she thought, a simple thought, and then she heard Jerry's voice. Crystal clear in her head. "I'm dying!"

"No!" Her scream crashed into the air. Oblivious to those around her, Ann kept screaming. "Let me out! Let me live! I want to live!"

Somehow, she reached her feet, shoving through the crowd, clawing at the door, desperate to open it, knocking back the hands reaching for her, blocking the voices of reason surrounding her. Gasping as she suffocated. No one understood. She was drowning. As Jerry had drowned. Alone!

It did not matter to her that the train began to move. That Cynthia had reached her side. That the officers in their dark uniforms and the others in white uniforms converged on her, and forced her into a waiting ambulance. None of it mattered now. Because in that instant when past and present collided, when her emotions burst through the door to touch her soul like a powerful river obliterating all in its wake, then she knew she would always be alone, stuck here, in this life, not alive, not dead, a ghost, trapped in the middle of nowhere. Alone, until she could join him.

i Cold Comfort

James felt caught by the frozen tension of a Montréal winter. He lingered in the hotel dining room over a late meal, but still did not feel sleepy. After dessert, he decided on a walk along boulevard de Maisonneuve before heading to bed.

As James left the hotel, icy air wounded him. He adjusted the collar of his gray wool coat. Head bowed, he moved west towards rue Crescent, into the wind. Snow drifts lining the gutter had frozen into dirty mounds that would be difficult but not impossible to scale. He hoped the full force of the storm would hold off until after his departure.

Few cars moved along the street and Maisonneuve was empty of pedestrians. While walking, James focused on an enormous machine noisily eating its way through the impacted ice. As the slow–moving monster consumed solids, it excreted only a dribble of liquid from its opposite end. Transformation took place deep within its gargantuan belly, hidden, and it surprised James, who prided himself on rarely indulging in idle speculation, that he was questioning the process.

His thoughts shifted to demographics and target markets. Glancing at his watch, he pictured Millie and the boys skating at the community rink. He hoped she'd remembered to take the car in for winterizing.

Sharp wind demanded awareness of his surroundings. He heard what sounded like a hinge squeaking and turned his head. Amid the glow of imaginative displays in brightly–lit shop windows, a darkened doorway stood out. He suspected this was where the noise originated. When Arctic air slashed his cheek, interest in the noise faded. Tomorrow's a busy day, he thought. I'd better head back.

Again the squeak, and his impulse to look. He heard other sounds, emitted from the blackness, reminiscent of a primitive language. He thought he could make out the words, *"Le change?"*

"Le change?" he echoed, insecure about his French. He glanced behind, afraid to be discovered talking to himself.

"Change," a voice said in English. "You know."

A tremor of stupidity passed through James. Gusts of snow eroded that feeling, buffeting him until he could barely keep balanced. When the current shifted, he faced the doorway, eyes narrowed. "You mean you want money."

The wind stilled and another sound reached his ears: bark crackling in fire, a scalp being scratched, raspy laughter. Through swirling snow, he watched a hand emerge from the darkness, palm up. Each finger of the split glove revealed soiled flesh. The hand withdrew so quickly it was as though it had never existed.

James knew that at home he would not be exposed in this way. Street people, he had convinced himself, are a city phenomenon, relegated to the downtown core, where life congeals. On the rare occasions when he encountered them—business trips and vacations—he usually crossed the street, avoiding contact. He felt as much responsibility as anyone. But there were places for the unfortunate, organizations to help. He contributed to charities. Once his wife drove an hour into the city, taking a bag of canned goods to a food bank after hearing a plea on the radio. I'm not cold–hearted, he reassured himself, but you have to draw the line somewhere.

"I suppose you want it for coffee, or a sandwich," he said, feeling uncomfortable.

A rumble attracted him. Another machine turned the corner, bulky, oddly tentacled, tires large and deep–threaded. Methodically it sprayed salt crystals along the ice–slicked asphalt. He watched as the awkward vehicle lumbered, struggling to reestablish traction.

"Coffee? Don't touch the stuff."

James shivered and stamped his feet. His gut constricted. Trapped between instincts, he endured paralysis for several moments until he heard, "Not food neither."

"You want it for alcohol!" Paralysis gave way to savagery. Quickly James glanced left then right. Maisonneuve was still empty.

"Nope, not booze."

A long–forgotten feeling surfaced: fury at being toyed with. Madness brushed him. There's still work to do, he reminded himself. Tomorrow's going to be hectic. Sleep beckoned.

He began walking east but before snow had crunched under both of his feet he heard, "It's this book I gotta read."

Incredulous, James turned. He stared at the blackened building entrance but still could discern nothing.

A bus drove close to the curb. Distracted, he peered into eight passing windows, eight rectangular eyes inviting him to view a contained world. Two pale, heavily–bundled figures, resigned to the elements, sat at opposite ends of the vehicle. When the bus was gone and silence restored, James glanced down. He was annoyed to find the bottom of his coat stained.

"Costs twelve ninety–five new," came the scratchy words, "but it's an old story."

"You're a derelict. Why am I talking to you?" His voice boomed in his ears. As James restrained himself, again the cold seeped in.

"Andrea 'round the block's got it used for five fifty."

The unwanted explanation had an odd effect; a glacial force threatened to engulf him. A small groan slipped from between his chilled lips.

"I'm done *L'Etranger*."

"What...?" *The Stranger*? By Camus? James was afraid to hear more. Quickly he pulled off one glove and reached into his coat pocket. "I won't give you all of it." He had intended to present the words as controlled, justifiably gruff, but they hung in the air like plastic icicles, cheap and silly. "Why should I subsidize your reading?" he grumbled. "Go to the library if you want a book." He opened his wallet and sorted through the bills, finding a five and a ten, plucking out the former. With his vulnerable hand he extended the bill, aware his skin was freezing.

The hand reached out again from darkness into illumination. It was followed by an arm, only to the elbow, and James fell back. Rotted coat sleeve. Matted fabric adhering to wrist and palm. Ancient gnarled fingers, three bare to the knuckles, quivering. Gritty, jagged nails.

The fingers snatched the money. Although that flesh had barely touched his own, James was grateful for the temporary loss of feeling.

He watched the arm, the hand and finally the bill vanish into the shadows.

Quickly he shoved his own numbed hand back into the leather glove, then under his armpit, hugging himself. Alarmed by the reviving sensation, he wanted comfort. Maybe he would hail a taxi back to the hotel. The street was deserted.

He felt foolish. Gullible. Allowing himself to become upset. What possessed me? he wondered, shaking his head.

Quickly James turned from the doorway muttering, "That will have to do," and hurried away, unaccountably relieved that no gratitude had been shown.

Even before daybreak, the storm ended. Montréal's snowy streets glistened in the blinding sun. Cars and pedestrians crowded the downtown, reinjecting vitality into the city.

With a good night's sleep to carry him through, James was off early to meetings that lasted the morning and much of the busy afternoon.

Twice during the day he astonished himself by idly speculating about the book. Of course, he had read *The Outsider*, when he was at university, but he could not recall what it was about.

He checked out of the hotel and ate a hurried late lunch at a coffee bar because he wanted to catch the five o'clock flight. He could be home by eight.

That night, safe in his own bed, Millie snuggled close, the boys asleep down the hall, James jolted awake. Hot sweat burned his flesh. His heart rammed his chest wall. Layers of sweltering shadow wrapped his world in unfamiliarity. He did not recognize this woman lying beside him. He did not recognize himself. Yet he knew two things to be true: he longed for the numbing cold. And he understood with crystal clarity that the future would not be like the past; he would never again feel that comfort.

Whitelight

The massive door clanged shut behind Anna. Sound reverberated through her skull. Tight metal shriek.

The cell was sparse—bed, chair, night table—but that didn't bother her. The colors did. Chipped pink and dirty green paint. Faded pastel sheets. Gray granite walls, a crack in one. High up in the ceiling a round skylight. Whitelight. She studied the magnetic beam for a long time, lost in its purity. Suddenly she noticed the air. Flat. Stale. Yesterday's oxygen. Somebody else's carbon dioxide. She sipped in thin breaths.

The waste can had a used tissue lying on the bottom. Anna wondered how long ago the last occupant had been here. Where was she now? Had she been carried out? Carried out the way Anna's mother had been? The way Anna probably would be.

Staring at the crisp sheets weakened her. Hospital corners. Military creases. Not like her own bed, with it's snowy down comforter and lacy pillow cases. Where the air was crystalline, the water transparent.

Anna refused to touch or be touched by anything in this room. That was their plan. She knew it well. Her mother had explained everything she needed to know: "Their food, even their thoughts will contaminate you, my precious Anna, binding you to a harsh reality. Take care."

All the cells must look alike, yet the thought that maybe her mother had been here, or next door, or at the end of the corridor. She closed her eyes and tried to feel any of her mother's emanations. Disinfectant stung Anna's sinuses. The ruthless chemicals had eroded all traces. Besides, it had been too long ago.

She still missed her mother. "Anna comes from Hannah—I named you after me," she remembered her mother saying in her wispy voice. "We're so much alike." Anna wanted nothing more than to be like her mother. To be with her mother. Always.

She stepped into the cylinder of brilliant sunlight. Standing without moving was difficult but long ago she had disciplined herself to accept stillness and pain. Not to inhale deeply. Not to participate. The light from the sky cleansed the circle of concrete floor where she stood. Dust motes filtered down like insignificant organisms floating aimlessly through water. Anna panicked with the sudden knowledge that if enough of them landed on her arms, her shoulders, on top of her head, they would gather there, layer upon layer, dirtying her skin, building in intensity and weight, pressing her fragile body down in their attempt to merge with the black soil.

She stepped out of the corrupted light, back into a corner, careful not to touch the gray walls. And waited.

They came when the room darkened. A square within the massive silver rectangle in the wall opened. Fingers with green plastic skin slid a stainless steel slab onto a little platform. Hideous lumps of manure and mold and a jaundiced colored mound. And a cylinder of metal. She did not want to know its contents.

Fetid odors infiltrated the air molecules like a virus penetrating a cell. Fear shriveled the skin stretched over her backbone. Scents like floral perfume seeping into a virgin handkerchief. Her mother had had many cotton handkerchiefs with delicate crocheted trim and her initial—H—embroidered with ivory silk thread in one corner. In Anna's mind her mother's tiny hand gracefully lifted the glass stopper from the milky bottle and touched the narrow tip to the initial. Flowers blossomed and Anna inhaled deeply white hibiscus and gardenia.

Rankness clotted her nostrils. Sour. Putrefying matter. Rancid flesh.

Sharp pain chewed at her gut. She gagged and flung herself to the corner farthest from the invasive stench and retched, knowing she was on the right path. Dry and clean within. Undefiled as her mother's immaculate handkerchiefs. Perfect as dustless sunlight. Whitelight that had now abandoned her.

Even when the plastic fingers snatched back the reeking things, the foul stench lingered. Outside the window crickets chirped. Wheels creaking. A gurney squeaking along a raw gray corridor as it carried an empty shell to the fires.

Anna shivered. She was glad the liquids had finally dried up for good. When they took her she would not give them tears. She resented having to leave even this imperfect shell behind. If she could, she would leave them nothing.

She wondered how her mother had felt when bones burst through her skin. When flesh turned the color of silt and pores sprouted wiry hairs. When clumps of hair fell from her scalp and the gums shrank and bled and teeth cracked. When the huge skull defined the head. Anna suspected her mother had not minded those things and she did not mind them either, except for the skull. The rest she hardly noticed. The body was, after all, defective. A receptacle of impurities. Impurities generated by a poisonous and flawed world. At least the body was temporary. Escape possible. She only regretted that they would have that much.

Daylight brought nightmares. Massive greasy creatures with different colored skins. Loud. Rough. Thin–lipped and fierce–eyed. Stinking of things rotting, remnants of which were trapped between their sharp fangs.

While they did things to her trembling body, she retreated to the land of glaciers, whitecaps, colorless air and water, and daydreamed of melding with clear light. When they left she vomited furiously until she was again purged. Clean inside. She hated these repulsive, polluted monsters. She would never submit to them again. Never. If only she could destroy it all. Leave nothing behind.

Anna stared at the wall to the outside. Oyster with a crack in the shell. Was there a pearl within? Long before they took her mother away, she remembered her mother wearing strands of seed pearls around her slender throat, her lean frame draped in a magnolia dress. The spring air carried white lilac through the gleaming French doors, open just a crack. Light and pure. Innocent. Untainted by the entropy surrounding her now.

They wanted to poison her body with their grisly sustenance, contaminate her mind with their heavy ideas. Infect her spotless soul.

Anna pressed her lips to the crack in the wall. "Mother?"

Air rushed from the hairline. Anna's heartbeat became erratic. She wedged her fingertips into the line until they burned. The pressure stretched the crack. Crisp light seeped through and cooled her cells one by one.

Are you lonely, Anna? I'm lonely.

"Mother, help me!" She shoved one hand in, bending the thumb back until she heard but did not feel the joint pop. One bony arm slid in to the elbow. She panted and struggled. Her right foot edged in. The hip was a problem. If only she were thinner. She wiggled and contorted. Her hipbone snapped; hot pain electrified her skeleton.

Murmurs. Dull thuds in the distance. They were coming to take her to the fires.

Goodbye, Anna.

"Don't leave me alone with them. Momma!"

Her head spun and her vision blurred. Anna exhaled and stuffed crushed ribs through the opening. The second leg scrapped in. The fractured hip bone became a shattered pelvic bone. The crack swallowed all but her skull.

Crisp light beckoned. If she could just get her bulbous head through.

Metal screeched at metal. They were about to enter. They would pull her back, steal her right to whitelight and punish her with sweltering darkness, making her dense and corrupt. Then she would be just like them.

The cooler air from the other side was warming. With the temperature shift pain vibrated through her torso. She had to do something. Now. While there was still time.

Anna stretched her neck out and jerked it back, again and again smashing her head against the wall. First one side, then the other. Bone splintered. Gray matter squished. Her vision narrowed to a strip.

Door and wall separating. Creatures belched into the room. With a final burst of hard energy, Anna yanked her entire body backwards in one convulsive movement. The mashed gray pulp and shattered cranium swooshed into the cool crack.

Two ugly ones glared at the wall, eyes bugging, ravenous mouths gaping. Monstrous talons scraped granite. It was too late.

Anna closed her eyes as the blindingly familiar whitelight penetrated her. Finally she was invisible. This time they would go hungry.

Projections

Anne parted the sheer curtains. She watched the nearly colorless sky being forced aside by a chilling grey. All the while the snow increased. At first the flakes fell large and wet, melting on contact with the cement walk in front of the house. But too quickly the white piled on top of itself, suffocating the lawn, walkway and steps under an opaque crystal blanket that glittered eerily in the preternatural light, like a scene from a child's fantasy world.

Remember, she reminded herself, *Dr. Fuchs said not to worry.* When Anne thought about the psychiatrist, his reassuring smile, the comforting habit of tugging at his neatly–clipped silver beard, his eyes, warm as old pewter, she relaxed. But with her brother Larry out of town on business, and Grandad vacationing in Florida until tomorrow, the weekend had been hard.

Finally she released the curtain and returned to the couch. She sat down with a sigh. *I'm not in the best shape these days,* she thought. Being alone so long wasn't the greatest idea, but she didn't know what she could have done about it.

Both nights Anne had phoned her friend Sue. She refused to make a pest of herself by calling again. And on top of everything, today she woke with the sniffles and couldn't shake off an achy, sick–to–the–stomach feeling. Her head felt stuffed with gauze and over the hours reality had assumed a tinted, off–kilter quality. All day she stayed indoors and now felt not only sick but bored and restless too.

Absently she picked up her brother's copy of *Playboy*. She automatically flipped to the centerfold, but did not really look at the photograph. A different picture came to mind, the first in a series of bizarre drawings.

"Look at this," Dr. Fuchs instructed.

The crude sketch showed a closed door, a girl on one side, and a crooked stick–figure on the other.

"Sometimes," he continued, "when we're afraid, we can actually project our fears outside ourselves. What we see with our eyes is symbolic."

"Project? Like a movie?" she asked.

"Exactly! What we need to do when faced with such projections is bring them back inside our own skin; reclaim them." He sat back in his chair and steepled his fingers. "Suppose, like you, I'm afraid of supernatural creatures that feed off the living."

As Dr. Fuchs described her greatest terrors, Anne began feeling foolish. The psychiatrist looked as wise as her grandfather, as charming as her brother, and she was inclined to trust him.

"But what I'm afraid of, doesn't it seem weird?"

"Not really. Our culture is riddled with phobias and yours isn't uncommon. For example," he continued, "I remember being thrown off balance by the movie *Night of the Living Dead*. Films like that tap into our collective psyche, unearthing powerful, universal images. The media has that effect on most of us, so you're not alone there."

Anne sighed, continuing to realize just how silly her fears sounded, especially coming from someone else's lips.

"I'd say, Anne, from what I know of your life, growing up in a roughhouse of males—your grandfather, brother, and your father before he died, without a strong mother figure—well, as much as you feel loved, I'd bet there's a certain amount of repressed fear, too. For you, those feelings get in the way of intimacy."

She felt her cheeks color.

About eleven PM, the phone rang.

When Anne answered, a blast of static cut across the wire, probably caused by the snowstorm playing havoc with the lines. She thought she heard a voice say, "Anne?" but couldn't be certain because her ears were blocked.

"Is that you, Grandad? Larry? Speak up. This is a terrible connection."

More static crackled, interspersed with a couple of words that might have been 'delay' and 'arrive later'.

"You sound so far away. Where are you? What time will you be home?"

Before any reply came, the line went dead, then the dial tone buzzed.

The clock struck midnight. Anne didn't feel sleepy, just sick and tense. Larry wasn't in yet. The storm was bad for driving and she worried that something had happened to him.

To distract herself, she browsed through her grandfather's library of paperbacks. He was a big collector of horror books, which meant that, for Anne, there wasn't much of a choice. Still, she selected Stephen King's latest novel. *I'm too nervous for this,* she told herself. But she had read every magazine in the house, and television had become boring. She forced herself to read the first page, but her thoughts kept drifting back to that last session with Dr. Fuchs.

"Anne, look at the second drawing."

In this one, the door stood ajar and the distorted stick–figure was striding through the opening towards the girl.

"What do you suppose happens now?" Dr. Fuchs asked.

Anne realized that her heart was beating too quick. She heard herself stutter, "I...don't know," but really believed the stick–figure would devour the girl.

As if intuiting what she felt, Dr. Fuchs reached across the coffee table and patted her shoulder. "Anne, I can see you're very frightened and expect the worst. Think of the ghoulish figure as part of yourself, what you're afraid to face. He's only a projection."

"So..." Anne managed to stammer, "the ghoul is a projection? Of my fear of men?"

"Absolutely."

When the doorbell chimed, she jolted. *It must be Larry,* she thought.

Quickly Anne unwound the blanket she had encased herself in and hurried to the front window. She pulled the curtain aside and looked out. No one stood at the door. Clean white snow shrouded the walkway, the steps, and the landing, all unmarked by footprints. Anne stared in disbelief, stunned by what she did not see. Desperately she scanned the lawn, the street and the driveway. Only the blizzard moved, raging in uninhibited fury through the quiet empty streets.

As she dropped the curtain and returned to the couch, the house struck her as too quiet. A faint hiss of wind outside blended with the click/clack of her grandfather's clock as it relentlessly ticked off each second.

It's the book, she thought. *I'm scaring myself.* She turned on the television. All the regular channels were off the air for the night so she switched to the pay station. An image jumped out of the screen, the full–color face of a vampire. Blazing red eyes and jagged, dagger–sharp incisors caused Anne to fall back from the set, horrified. She switched the tv off and the radio on, fine–tuning to an all–night easy–listening station. *If only Larry was here,* she thought. *Or Grandad would call.* Moments later, when the lights flickered, she decided that a Valium couldn't possibly hurt. She went to the medicine cabinet and took one.

As Anne came back into the living room, the disembodied voice of the radio announcer accentuated the emptiness. "It's *crazy* out there tonight! But don't worry. The Sandman's here, and he's gonna take real good care of *you.*"

She turned towards the couch and froze. Her heart slammed against her chest as if eager to escape. A silver–faced demon glared up at her from the sofa! Hollow cheeks, fiery pin–prick eyes. Teeth primed for biting, for tearing...Anne flipped the book over. That didn't feel secure enough so she shoved the paperback into a desk drawer where she wouldn't have to see it.

Hands shaking, she gathered up the blanket and enfolded herself in it again. As she leaned back, her eyelids grew heavy. The grandfather clock, click/clack, soft music, the wind...

"Let me show you what actually happens," Dr. Fuchs said. Quickly he drew a third picture.

Anne saw a wide–open door and only one figure, a bizarre unpleasant image that, on closer inspection, seemed to be a blend of the girl and the stick–figure. To Anne, the combination looked half dead and half alive. It frightened her.

"You see," Dr. Fuchs said, "she lets him join with her. She owns him and, by doing that, the two become one."

It sounded simple, but Anne was far from convinced. "But...how do you *know* he won't hurt her? How can you be certain?"

Dr. Fuchs lay his pad and pencil on the table and sat back. He stretched out his long legs and crossed them at the ankles. "During the half dozen times you've been to see me, do you feel I've said or done anything that's harmed you?"

She shook her head.

"Have I introduced ideas that have not been in your best interest?"

"No," she answered weakly, avoiding his eyes, too aware of what he was getting at. She was being childish, letting her fears run wild.

"Look at the third drawing."

Anne picked up the paper by the edges and felt her body tense. She couldn't bring herself to like what she saw, and was afraid of offending him. But when she glanced up, Dr. Fuchs smiled openly, and his smoky eyes glowed.

"You know, Anne, many men, including your grandfather and Larry no doubt, find it difficult to acknowledge hostility towards women. Of course, some women naturally sense such feelings and become afraid. Unlike more primitive societies, in ours, anger is largely viewed as unacceptable behavior. If I'm mad at you and you're afraid to face that, it's probably a lot easier for both of us if we label me inhuman and you a helpless victim."

Anne totally focused on the psychiatrist's words. He was the most patient man. And what he said made more sense than anything she had ever heard.

"Can't you see, Anne? Your fear of men, projected outward, *must* be seen as something horrible. It's *yourself* you're afraid of." Dr. Fuchs checked his watch. Her time was up.

The moment she noticed the tapping, Anne's eyes flashed open and she said aloud in a particularly reassuring tone that struck her as false, "It must be the branch of a tree against the window." Even as she spoke, part of her brain reminded her there were no trees close to that side of the house. "I'm not going to look," she said, her voice still strangely confident. But before she finished the sentence, Anne was on her feet and walking through the dining room. Soon she stood before the vertical blinds.

She found herself pulling the silver chain, causing the panels to swivel. A sheet of frost clung to the bottom half of the window but she could still see out the top. The white lawn glistened, an absence of color, of warmth, of life. There were no footprints, and no trees. What caused her body to lurch forward, face pressed close to the slats, were the strange almost primitive scratchings in the frost. The etchings seemed to form the letters *A.N.N.E.*

With a yank, she pulled the blinds tightly shut. Terror gripped her and she raced back into the well–lit living room. Surrounded by radio chatter, the clock, the familiar, she stood shaking, afraid to move, fearful of standing still. A loud, thunderous crash split the air, rocking the house to its foundation, causing the lights to flicker and the radio to sputter. The rumble centered in her body now, shoving terror up from her stomach and ripping a scream from her throat.

Propelled to action, she grabbed the phone, punching in Sue's number. After two dozen rings, she hung up. Her hands trembled so badly she dropped the address book trying to find Dr. Fuchs's number. Finally she called him, too, and a metallic version of his voice invited her to leave a message following the beep.

Embarrassment flooded her. What would he think, being disturbed in the middle of the night? And only last week Dr. Fuchs had asked, "Will you do something for me?"

She felt reluctant to commit herself but he was more than kind and she did trust him. "If I can," she finally agreed.

"Good! The very next time you become afraid there's a monster around, I want you to invite him inside to join with you. I know this sounds frightening, but I'd like you to try. Just let him in. You've got to let him in."

Dr. Fuchs will think I'm completely out of control, she thought, *and really, not much has happened. There's a storm, loud thunder, and I'm not feeling well. I'm here alone, that's all. And*, she reminded herself guiltily, *I haven't even tried what he suggested.*

She was just about to hang up without saying anything when she remembered the letters on the window. "Dr. Fuchs," she blurted into the phone, "it's Anne. Anne Martin. Help me! Please! I'm really frightened. My grandfather's still away and Larry should have been home and—" But the machine cut her off. There was a pause, then nothing.

She depressed the button until she had a dial tone, thinking to call back. But Anne knew the window would have to be checked first. "Calm down," she told herself sternly. "Those scratches, you probably imagined them. In the state you're in, it would be easy to see letters where moisture ate into the frost." She even started to giggle at her silliness as she lowered the receiver. *I really am being ridiculous,* she thought. But the impending relief was cut short when the dial tone died. She returned the receiver to her ear but there was no sound. Quickly she pressed the button several times but couldn't return the phone to life.

Even before this new terror of being completely cut off got a solid grip, the doorbell rang, and she thought she saw the doorknob turn. "No!" she whispered. But something compelled her to cross the room, part the curtains and peer out. The landing, the steps, the lawn, all were a deathly white, as undisturbed as they had been.

As if in a dream, Anne released the curtain and slowly backed across the living room. Her hip bumped the edge of a table. She tripped over a cord and the radio disconnected. The lights flickered before going out completely, but Anne hardly noticed.

She pressed herself against the wall farthest from the door, back into the secret place inside herself where she had always retreated to escape the dead–eyed things that dwelled beneath her bed, inhabited closets, and chased her through the eerily silent mazes of nightmares.

Either time passed slowly or it just seemed to pass that way. Her grandfather's clock clicked/clacked, collecting the seconds that made minutes and then hours, subtracting from the span that was her life. And all the while Anne cringed and huddled, shriveled to the tiniest possible version of herself.

Eventually a sharp sound penetrated. She grew to recognize it, translating the noise into an insistent knocking. Then she heard a deep voice calling what might have been her name again and again. *It's Daddy,* she thought in a child–like way, although her father had been dead many years. Grandad. Larry. Dr. Fuchs. All of them melded, forming a strange mental image that resembled none yet encompassed all.

The image was familiar enough to ignite a spark of hope, and Anne found herself standing, legs shaking. Blindly she groped her way across the dark room towards the window. All the while the knocking reverberated in her head, and the muffled voice softly echoed, "Anne! It's me. Let me in!"

She struggled to will herself to pull the curtain aside. But natural instinct had been snuffed out, replaced by frozen emotion. She watched her hand rise mechanically, as though being lifted to the fabric by an alien force.

"My God!" she screamed, rushing to the door. She snapped the dead bolt and turned the knob. "Please! Come in!"

As Dr. Fuchs stepped through the opening, Anne threw herself into his arms. She buried her face in his chest and, in a flood of choking tears, released the terror.

But the arms surrounding her began to feel suffocating. Wooden. That caused her to look up. The room was dark, and she hoped the shadows were responsible for turning his eyes the chilling grey of a devouring sky.

As the straight line where his lips met expanded, an ebony cavity formed. For the first time in her life, Anne felt clear. Out of his darkness something sharp would emerge. And when it did, finally, everything would be revealed.

Metal Fatigue

Iron talons slid down his spine, slicing skin like a wire cuts cheese.
Marvin screamed. He couldn't figure out why he had a hard on. If the
restraints had allowed it, he'd have twisted to safety. Hell, he would
have been out of here!

It was like this every time he had sex with the aliens. They made it
seem like a great idea, until Marvin was bound, trussed up like a
Thanksgiving turkey.

Face down, his knees had been bent back at a weird, uncomfortable
angle to make his legs stick up and cross over the top of his ass like
drumsticks. The aliens pinned his arms to his sides—bird–wing style.
He rested only on his belly, his lower half off the bed, head pulled up
and far back, mouth forced open, balls and erect cock dangling, ass-
hole exposed for stuffing.

He'd been plucked and basted and knew he was about to be
microwaved.

His body trembled. They never went on past daylight, so it couldn't
last much longer. They had to get back to their home planet and gear
up for the next time they came down here and seduced guys like him.
Regular guys with jobs and wives and kids and mortgage payments.

One of the aliens stood directly over his face. Marvin looked up at
the rigid steel pole of a cock and the silver cunt hole. They were all
hermaphrodites, so he never knew what he was going to get or have to
give. This one told Marvin telepathically it wanted his tongue. One
behind him was about to use his nether mouth for a receptacle. A
third, below, took the whole of his genitals into its liquid metal trap.
Bound the way he was, Marvin could only enter and be entered and
be entered upon. He could only submit.

He slid into the icy cave and opened to the frozen stalactite while
a glacier formed at his groin. Their hot ice seared him from three directions until the crushing cold tore through his body and collided, and
he screamed.

Marvin swallowed coffee and said to Rita's back, "It happened again."

His genitals and rectum were raw, the corners of his mouth split from being stretched to the limit. They had cut the flesh over his backbone to insert the little radio transmitters along his vertebra so they could keep track of him. His back pulsed with pain.

Rita flipped his eggs and said nothing. The terrycloth bathrobe hid most of her shape, which had gotten larger over the years. Strands of fading brown hair clung to the nubby fabric at her shoulders. She was no sex goddess, but she was a good woman. She shouldn't have to put up with a husband who fornicates with aliens, even if it was against his will, or partially so. "They came for me again. Used me all over. Like the other times."

She slid the eggs onto a plate with the toast, already buttered, and placed it before him, then got herself a mug of coffee. "I'm sore," he said.

"There are no aliens." Her voice was even, like she was talking to one of the kids, stating the way things were, the way they would be. She opened the refrigerator and took out a carton of half–and–half.

"They put things in me. In my backbone. So they can track me."

She pulled his collar behind him and looked down his work shirt at his back. "No marks," she said, taking a seat.

"The marks are invisible. You know that."

"You dreamed it. Like the last time."

"It happened."

"You'll be late for your shift," she told him, sipping her coffee.

Down at the factory, Marvin assumed his position on the production line. The continuous–motion silver machines clanked and banged, sending an eternal series of hollow metal tubes with holes drilled through each side along the conveyor belt at his left, and on the other belt at his right, threaded eight–inch poles. A plastic bin to the back of his work station contained wing nuts. With his left hand, he took a tube and with his right a pole. Automatically he impaled the tube with the pole as far as it would go before it got too thick. He slipped a wing nut over the tip of the pole and spun it down the threads, making sure the pole and tube were bound together securely. He inserted the whole thing into a gaping metal hole above his head that mechanically fused the parts. Even that brief second of staring up caused him to be temporarily blinded by the brilliant florescent tubes in the ceiling. Vision blurred, he laid the tool on a third conveyor belt running perpendicular to the other two, at crotch level.

He picked up a new tube and impaled it with a new pole, and repeated the process for the next eight hours. Marvin left his station to another man, who took the next shift, who would leave it to another who would work his shift, then Marvin would return.

It was endless.

When Marvin got home from work that night, Rita was sitting on the couch watching the tail end of Geraldo. "When's dinner?" he asked.

"Fifteen minutes," she said, her eyes never leaving the tv.

Marvin decided on a shower. The hot water beat down on his back, tapping the invisible scar tissue along his spine. He wondered if the aliens were getting static on their receivers. After last night, he felt nervous. They'd never been with him so long before and he was scared. He couldn't tell when they would come again. They never came two nights in a row, but then they'd never implanted transmitters into his body before either.

After fried farmer's sausages, French fries and canned sweet peas, he and Rita watched tv and finished off a tub of Neapolitan ice cream, then went to bed and watched some more tv. Rita fell asleep around eleven facing him, but Marvin lay awake at 2 AM, listening to the white noise of the dead station, not bothering with the converter, staring out the window at the night sky.

If they came for him they would fuck him again, all night long. The way they fucked was mechanical, poles ramming in and out like pistons, metal mouths clamping tight and opening around him with precision timing. It was painful. Damn painful.

Rita snored and the noise irritated him. He nudged her until she turned over and the snoring stopped.

How could you hate something and, at the same time, need it? Marvin wondered. He had no idea why the aliens came here, why they'd picked him. They never talked to him, just screwed him until his brain turned to molten steel, ready to be bent any way they wanted.

Rita farted, a long slow one in her sleep. He wondered what it would be like to enter her behind. It had never happened in all the years of their marriage. Rita wasn't like that. Back when they still used to do it regularly, she liked him on top, face to face, nothing kinky either in the mouth or the butt. And she liked it in the dark too, unlike the aliens. They wanted all the lights blazing. Maybe on their planet, wherever that was, it was light all the time, probably white light, like those damn florescents. That's why they had quicksilver eyes, from absorbing all that light.

Wind blew the curtains into the room and Marvin trembled. This was their sign. That they were coming. Or maybe it was just a breeze. He didn't know anymore. There were signs everywhere. All the time. On the tv tonight there'd been a preview for a show about UFOs and Rita had turned to him and said, "Up your alley." He didn't know what she meant by that remark. Was it some kind of sexual come on? His alley? His anus? Then she'd licked the back of the spoon she ate her ice cream with, her long, fat pink tongue dragging slowly over the smooth silver metal.

Marvin!

The liquid silver voice sliced down his spine. His muscles tensed. The curtains blew wildly and the air chilled.

He wanted to run, to get outside, to find a place in nature where he could hide. He had this idea: if he could just make it into the woods, far from everything mechanical, and root himself to the earth like a tree, if he could just get out of here...

But he couldn't move. His backbone felt glued to the sheet and the sheet to the mattress. The bed under him rocked, the table, lamp, the tv. It was as though he had been caught in an avalanche. Rita, dead to the world, didn't wake when he shook her. He tried to yell, but they'd gotten his voice again. He was mute. Paralyzed. Suddenly all movement stopped. All sound. Silence pierced his eardrums—that was their language, silence, they spoke it on their planet. The language of death.

Marvin watched helplessly as the first silver shadow slid through the half inch opening of the window. Its rod penis stood erect, it was always erect. Quicksilver dripped from the hole between its legs. The alien was otherwise featureless by every standard Marvin knew. It had arms and legs, but they seemed useless. They only used them to tie Marvin up in their invisible wires, then it was all fucking.

Soon the room was crammed with glittering translucent beings. They filled every inch of floor space and then stood on top of the dresser and the tv and the bed. The room shimmered silver. The air grew cold but dense, as if much of it had turned to ice crystals.

Even if he could have moved, there was no way to get past them. And even if he could, and he knew from trying that he could not, there was nowhere to go. The clock had stopped at 3:15. There was nothing to do but assume the position. Reading his mind, they permitted this minimal movement. He turned onto his stomach and bent his knees until they were chest level, butt hanging over the edge of the bed. It would be less painful if he let them enter him, rather than fighting them and losing. Already his cock was hard and he hated that they had this power over him.

He lay there for the longest time on his belly, waiting, but nothing happened. They still clogged the room, a silent forest of metal. But this was unusual. He felt edgy. Whatever they were up to, he guessed he wouldn't like it, at least later on.

Suddenly Rita moaned. Two of the aliens turned her and another lifted her flannelette nightgown over her head.

No! Marvin shouted, unable to move now; they'd frozen him.

He watched, horrified, as the steel beings wrapped his wife in the invisible wires, arms folded at her sides like wings, ankles pulled over her ass and crossed like drumsticks.

When her head was back and her mouth pried open, they woke her. Her eyes darted about as her body struggled to move from a position that left no options. Out of the corner of her eye she saw Marvin; he picked up her silent plea for protection. But Marvin could not help her. He couldn't help himself.

He steeled himself, knowing he would soon witness the violation of his wife in every orifice by these perverted creatures. They had no feelings. They were perpetual–motion machines, pounding in and out, in eight–hour shifts, relentless.

He waited, terrified. Rita waited. Nothing. This was so unlike them to hesitate. They operate automatically, without thought, obeying silent commands. What could they be waiting for?

Suddenly Marvin felt the individual vertebra of his backbone come alive. Each one was tapped in sequence, from his neck to the end of his spine, then back up again. He felt like a xylophone being played, but he didn't recognize the tune, only that the notes went up and down.

His body was free and yet not free. He moved, but not of his own will, and only where they willed him to move. He jerked, a puppet pulled by invisible strings. On his back, the scale was repeated, endlessly, bone by bone. He wondered now if they had planted more than transmitters.

Marvin was on his knees, but they made him stand on the floor. He was crushed by cold silver life forms. Erect metal rods prodded him from all sides. Against his will, his penis swelled. He was jerked and nudged and goaded until his genitals hovered behind Rita. He looked down and saw his cold metal penis, hard as steel, and below Rita's hot inferno waiting to melt it.

Tied the way she was, her orifices exposed, she had no choice but to submit. He slid deep into her furnace. A tear trickled down the side of her face but he soon forgot about it. He thrust in and out like a piston, oblivious to her needs and wants, bent only on getting the job done. It would be a long shift. Five more hours to go. There were so many holes to fill with his steel rod. The job was endless.

About the Stories

"Woodworker"
For a while, I studied what's called cabinet making, which is building fine furniture. There was a woman in my class who was going to be married soon, and was building a huge cannon–ball type bed out of heavy oak. Something about this woman and her intense focus on her woodworking wedding project came to me when George Hatch asked me for a story for his next anthology *Eclipse of the Senses*, which ended up not seeing the light of day. Fortunately Janet Berliner was doing *Desire Burn*, erotic horror by women, and this fit right in.

"Alien Love"
What can I say? I'm an *X Files* fan.

"What Matters"
This is a vampire vignette, a way to spin a standard plot.

"Heartbeat"
Toronto hosts a Caribbean festival each summer, with hundreds of thousands of people dancing in the streets. You get caught up with the intensely erotic rhythms of the steel drums. I wrote "Heartbeat" hoping to catch that hypnotic eroticism.

"Megan's Spirit"
When I was doing non–fiction articles, I interviewed a ghostbuster in Toronto, who went to houses with a psychic and de–haunted dwellings. The ghostbusters in this story are very loosely based on those two. I've always figured most ghosts are up to no good, and the people who interact with them are inviting danger.

"When Shadows Come Back"
The house in this story is a bit like the three–story house I lived in as a child. The dark quality, the feel of the old wallpaper. I tried to capture a borderline sense of reality because I've always loved stories that play with reality.

"Snow Angel"
For a few years I had a fascination with the north. I wanted to go to the Northwest Territories, or to the Yukon, or Alaska. I almost went on a non–fiction assignment to an Inuit settlement near the Arctic Circle, but that trip was cancelled. I grew up loving Jack London stories. Consequently, I wanted to write something about that type of basic, no bullshit environment, the beauty and the inherent danger.

"Brina"
Brina is a Brother's Grimm fairytale gone bad.

"The Children of Gael"
Grosse Ils (Gross Island) in Québec functioned a bit like Ellis Island did in the US—a check–in point for immigrants. In the 1800s tens of thousands of Irish immigrants fleeing the potato famine died of cholera on Grosse Ils. I visited the island and have written about it twice. The Children of Gael is a collaboration with Québec writer Benoit Bisson. I found the huge Celtic cross erected on the island to remember the dead intriguing. The inscriptions in English and French are similar but not even close to the Gaelic inscription, which spells out the anger and resentment directed at the English landlords who drove the Irish from their homes. You can feel the ghosts on the island are just waiting to rise up and haunt someone.

"Animal Rites"
This anti–fur story is one of the first horror stories I wrote, which ended up years later being published.

"Base of a Triangle"
I love the idea of a ghost in the subway system, which torments the living and, in turn, is tormented by the transit system's train schedule.

"Creature Comforts"
Yes, the musician is based on Marilyn Manson!

"Horrorscope"
I wanted to do a story about one of those flaky astro chicks who seems to have no brains whatsoever, and yet when the chips are down, often turns out to be a shrewd and savvy sister.

"An Eye for an Eye"
From time to time I enjoy a rousing game of Devil's Advocate on paper. I wanted to find a way to build an airtight case.

"Generation Why"
So many serial killers seem to be enamoured with the media. The media can be a dangerous catalyst propelling someone prone to major psychological problems into dissociation.

"…And Thou!"
I think I was spending too much time at the photocopy shop when I wrote this!

"Rural Legend"
Urban Legends are the sexy cousins. But at least in the city there's a chance of help reaching you.

"Youth Not Wasted"
Our culture is youth obsessed to the point where I sometimes feel that older people are usurping the rightful place of youth.

"The Power of One"
As a kid I read Salinger's *Franny and Zooey* and one of the passages that struck me was when Franny was sitting on the toilet in a restaurant counting the tiles. Who hasn't counted tiles?

"Truth"
Mothers and daughters have a special relationship, the dark side of which can be hellish.

"Inspiriter"
I am not a very visual person, and consequently I admire people who are, for example, painters and photographers. Also, everyone working in the arts needs inspiration, but it's a common experience that inspiration can not only be a two–edged sword, but can lead in an unanticipated direction, not always a good one.

"Punkins"
The old man in the story is right out of my childhood, a creepy guy in the neighborhood that we kids called Punkinhead, and around whom we wove urban legends.

"Vermiculture"
Like most people, I have a love/hate fascination with yuppies.

"The Middle of Nowhere"
This story involves loss and loneliness, themes that have permeated much of my work

"Cold Comfort"
"Cold Comfort" seemed to come out of nowhere. I think there are a lot of undercurrents here that relate to class, politics (in Canada), language, psychology and spirituality. The underbelly is alienation.

"Whitelight"
I've always liked stories that are more obscure. I know they are not popular today—everything has to be obvious, in–your–face. Endings have to be clear. Still, there's something about leaving a lot to the reader's imagination that appeals to me.

"Projections"
I often try to walk lines. This story has the protagonist teetering between trust and paranoia. With the supernatural mixed in, well, it's fun!

"Metal Fatigue"
My only science fiction story!

Nancy Kilpatrick
March, 2001

About the Author

Award-winning author Nancy Kilpatrick has published fourteen novels, 150 short stories, five collections of stories, and has edited seven anthologies. Her most recent works include: *Bloodlover*, the 4th novel in the *Power of the Blood* series (Baskerville Books, 2000); *The Vampire Stories of Nancy Kilpatrick* (Mosaic Press, 2000); *Graven Images* (co-edited with Thomas Roche, Ace Books, 2000). Visit her website at: http://www.sff.net/people/nancyk

Nancy lives in a lovely gothic apartment in Montreal with her black cat, Bella. Her favorite activity is travelling with her companion, photographer Hugues Leblanc, visiting cemeteries, ossuaries and mummy museums around the world.

Other Works by Nancy Kilpatrick

Novels

Bloodlover from Baskerville Books, 4th volume in the *Power of the Blood* series, October 2000

Reborn from Pumpkin Books, 3rd volume in the *Power of the Blood* series, October 1998.

Dracul from Mainstage Productions/Lucard Publishing, October 1998.

Child of the Night from Raven Books (Robinson Publishing), May 1996. Reprint from Pumpkin Books, October 1998

As One Dead collaboration with Don Bassingwaithe from White Wolf, Vampire: The Masquerade, February 1996.

Near Death (horror) from Pocket Books, October 1994. Reprint from Pumpkin Books, October 1998.

French editions of *Child of the Night, Near Death, Reborn, Bloodlover* from Editions Alire, Quebec, beginning October 2001.**

The Darker Passions: Dracula (erotic horror—pseudonym Amarantha Knight) from Masquerade Books, December 1993.

The Darker Passions: Dr. Jekyll and Mr. Hyde (erotic horror— pseudonym Amarantha Knight) from Masquerade Books, January 1995.

The Darker Passions: Frankenstein (erotic horror—pseudonym Amarantha Knight) from Masquerade Books, February 1995.

The Darker Passions: The Fall of the House of Usher (erotic horror—Amarantha Knight) from Masquerade Books, April 1995.

The Darker Passions: The Portrait of Dorian Gray (erotic horror—Amarantha Knight) from Masquerade Books, September 1996.

The Darker Passions: Carmilla (erotic horror—Amarantha Knight) from Masquerade Books, September 1997.

The Darker Passions: The Pit & the Pendulum (erotic horror—Amarantha Knight) from Masquerade Books, July 1998.

The Darker Passions series (erotic horror—Amarantha Knight) reprinted by Circlet Press, beginning October 2001. **

Collections

Cold Comfort Dark Tales, foreword by Paula Guran, trade pb, Spring 2001. **

The Vampire Stories of Nancy Kilpatrick Mosaic Press, introduction by Chelsea Quinn Yarbro, trade pb, July 2000.

Endorphins Macabre, Inc., August 1997.

The Amarantha Knight Reader Masquerade Books, August 1996.

Sex and the Single Vampire Tal Publications, June 1994. (Part of a 3 book set—*The Vampire Trilogies*, with Brian Hodge and Ron Dee.) Introduction by Nancy Holder.

As Editor

Graven Images (trade pb dark fantasy anthology edited by Nancy Kilpatrick and Thomas Roche) from Penguin Putnam, Ace Books. Contributors: M. Christian; Storm Constantine; Esther Freisner; Nina Hoffman; Jack Ketchum & Edward Lee; Kathe Koja; Tanith Lee; Brian McNaughton; Yvonne Navarro; Katherine Ptacek; Robert J. Silverberg; Lois Tilton; Gene Wolfe; Chelsea Quinn Yarbro; Lawrence Watt-Evans October 2000.

In the Shadow of the Gargoyle (trade pb dark fantasy anthology edited by Nancy Kilpatrick and Thomas Roche) from Berkeley Publishing (ACE Books). Contributors: Jo Clayton; Don D'Ammassa; Charles de Lint; Harlan Ellison; Neil Gaiman; Charles L. Grant; Brian Hodge; Nancy Holder; Caitlin Kiernan & Christa Faust; Katherine Kurtz; Brian Lumley; Alan Rodgers; John Mason Skipp & Marc Levinthal; Lucy Taylor; Melanie Tem; Wendy Webb; Jane Yolen & Robert Harris. October 1998. PB edition October 1999.

Demon Sex (pb erotic demon anthology edited under the pseudonym Amarantha Knight) from Masquerade Books. Contributors: Neil Gaiman; M. Christian; Sheila Cohill; Dawn Dunn; Gemma Files; Lois Gresh; Joe Murphy; Thomas Roche; Edo Van Belkom; Sidney Williams. March 1998.

Seductive Spectres (pb erotic ghost anthology edited under the pseudonym Amarantha Knight) from Masquerade Books. Contributors: Mike Arnzen; Benoit Bisson; Ron Dee & Lois Gresh; Gemma Files; Nancy Kilpatrick; Brian Lumley; Brian McNaughton; Thomas Roche; John Mason Skipp; Caro Soles; Karen E. Taylor; Edo van Belkom. October 1996.

Sex Macabre (pb erotic supernatural anthology edited under the pseudonym Amarantha Knight) from Masquerade Books. Contributors: Poppy Z. Brite; Dawn Dunn; Nancy Etchemendy; Sephera Giron; Nancy Holder & Melanie Tem; Tina Jens; Nancy Kilpatrick; Gregory Nicoll; Robert Partain; S. Mark Rainey; Mandy Slater and Marcelle Perks; Del Stone, Jr. July 1996.

Flesh Fantastic (pb erotic Frankenstein anthology edited under the pseudonym Amarantha Knight) from Masquerade Books. Contributors: Margaret Carter; Don D'Ammassa; Jan Barretta and Dave Smeds; Nancy Holder; Brian McNaughton; Nancy Kilpatrick; Robert Partain; Katherine Ptacek; Michael Rowe and Ron Oliver; Lucy Taylor; Steve Tem and Roma Felible. August 1995.

Love Bites (trade pb erotic vampire anthology edited under the pseudonym Amarantha Knight) from Masquerade Books. Contributors: Scott Ceincin; Dave Clark; Nancy Collins; Ron Dee; David Dvorkin; Nancy Kilpatrick; Jim Moore; Kathy Ptacek; Karen Taylor; Lois Tilton; Dave Wilson. December 1994.

Comic Books

VampErotica, Brainstorm Comics, comic issues #5 and #6, based on story "Dead Shot", June and August 1995. *VampErotica*, *Theater of Cruelty* and *Metadrama*, issue #13, March 1996.

Graphic comic of four issues plus prose stories.

(** forthcoming)

Welcome to the
DarkTales Community...

DarkTales is more than just a publisher of dark fiction, it's also a web-based community of professional writers, editors, publishers, artists, critics, and fans of outré art and vision.

At the heart of the DarkTales community is an active elist hosted by egroups at http://www.topica.com. Sign on and prepare yourself for a barrage of emails on a wide range of subjects. With few rules, the DarkTales elist is recommended for mature subscribers.

Visit the DarkTales website at http://www.darktales.com to learn more about the elist, upcoming titles, and new DarkTales anthologies currently open to submissions.

...we're bringing horror to the world.

www.darktales.com

Support Your Local Independent Bookseller!

One of our West Coast retail outlets slapped us upside the head a while back, complaining we spread a lot of ink about how to purchase DarkTales titles from our website, while ignoring the existence of the independent bookstores that carry and sell DarkTales titles, lending their support to the whole endeavor. The last thing anyone at DarkTales wants to see is a world completely overrun by the monster booksellers so, given the opportunity, please purchase your DarkTales titles through the independent outlets who have shown us such good support. We'll make a little less money per title, but we'll sleep better at night.

For a current list of DarkTales booksellers, stop by our website at www.darktales.com. If you're a retailer and presently not carrying DarkTales titles, get hip and stop by the website for details and contact information. Dave's ready to take care of you.

As always, the website stands ready to serve customers who can't find a local outlet. Stop by for a list of current titles and order on the spot with your credit card.

DarkTales Novels
$17.99—$19.99

DarkTales brings you the finest novels from established writers like Yvonne Navarro and J. Michael Straczynski, as well as new voices on the scene like Steven Lee Climer and Sephera Giron.

Currently Available
A Darkness Inbred by Victor Heck . .$17.99
Clickers by J.F. Gonzalez
& Mark Williams 19.99
DeadTimes by Yvonne Navarro 19.99
Eternal Sunset by Sephera Giron 17.99
Secret Life of Colors by Steve Savile . .17.99
Tribulations by J. Michael Straczynski . .19.99
Soul Temple by Steven Lee Climer 17.99
Demonesque by Steven Lee Climer . . .17.99

Coming in 2001
Faust: the screenplay by David Quinn
The Shaman Cycle Series by Adam Niswander
A Flock of Crows is Called a Murder
by Jim Viscosi
Harlan by David Whitman
and more...

Coming in 2002
Eternal Nightmare by Sephera Giron
Dream Thieves by Steven Lee Climer
The Harmony Society by Tim Waggoner
and more...

**For a Current List of Titles
and Prices visit...**

Order by mail or via the web at:
www.darktales.com

DarkTales Publications
P.O. Box 675
Grandview, MO 64030

Shipping Charges:
$4.95 U.S.; $6.90 Canada; $10.00 overseas
(plus $1.00 per each additional book)

A *personal invitation from Alister James:*

Sinister Element Online is the best dark zine on the web, published the first of the month, every month, free to all that possess the courage to venture within. Merely partake of the folklore, philosophy, esoterica, and fiction,or participate in its creation— the choice is yours to make.

We're waiting for you. So what the hell are *you* waiting for?

http://www.sinisterelement.com

Cold Comfort was initially printed by DarkTales Publications in April, 2001, using Rotation type on 60# offset white. The cover stock is 10 pt. stock with glossy finish. Cover art by Alan Clarke, typesetting and book design by Keith Herber. Editorial, Butch Miller, Keith Herber and Christine I. Speakman.

Printed in the United States
2039